FROMAGE

First published 2021 by
FREMANTLE PRESS

Fremantle Press Inc. trading as Fremantle Press
25 Quarry Street, Fremantle WA 6160
(PO Box 158, North Fremantle WA 6159)
www.fremantlepress.com.au

Cover illustration and design Nada Backovic, www.nadabackovic.com
Printed by McPherson's Printing, Victoria, Australia

 A catalogue record for this
book is available from the
National Library of Australia

ISBN 9781925816778 (paperback)
ISBN 9781925816785 (ebook)

 Department of
**Local Government, Sport
and Cultural Industries**

Fremantle Press is supported by the State Government through the Department of Local
Government, Sport and Cultural Industries.

Publication of this title was assisted by the Commonwealth Government through the
Australia Council, its arts funding and advisory body.

SALLY SCOTT

FROMAGE

FREMANTLE PRESS

Sally Scott was born in the shadow of Mt Roland in Sheffield, Tasmania, and wrote her first novel as an eleven year old. It was a *Famous Five* pastiche and every word was precious. She kept writing crime until an arts degree led to experimentation with short stories – none of them publishable, but joyous to write. Then 'life' happened and creative writing gave way to articles, papers and grant applications needed for her to pretend to be an academic. Having lapsed from teaching, she worked at a weapons systems contractor and then at a gaming machine testing consultancy. After eight years interstate, Sally returned to WA to do a last hurrah at Curtin University before establishing her own business development consultancy in the engineering and construction sector. In August 2018 Sally was diagnosed with cancer and decided to refocus her mind. She has been writing almost every day since then. *Fromage* is the first novel in the Alex Grant series and she is currently working on the second, *Oranges and Lemons*.

**Published with support from the
Fremantle Press Champions of Literature**

In memory of Heather Gordon: dear friend, mentor and reader.

CHAPTER ONE

Before it all began, I'd taken myself off for a holiday in Croatia. In the scorching hot July of 1993, I was savouring the last days of a summer holiday that had started in London and was ending on the pebble beaches of the Dalmatian coast. I had sunned myself during the day and drunk myself to a happy tipsy in the evenings before staggering over cobblestone streets to my B&B where my hostess would shake her head and pour me a bedtime rakia.

Being a freelance journalist meant money was too tight for Italy or France, so I'd opted for Croatia where Turkish coffee cost fifty cents and fabulous antipasto platters filled my stomach for about four dollars. I'd eaten at so many restaurants and bistros that I'd be able to write enough food reviews, with the summer on my tongue, to get me through a bleak southern hemisphere winter. Food and sun were my definition of heaven.

I had laid myself out every day of my holiday, daydreaming and people-watching, fascinated by the Russians who flocked to the coast in vast numbers, wearing tiny bikinis or racing bathers stretched taut over fat pale thighs, with bellies resembling verandas flopping over elastic waistbands threatening to snap. With hairy bikini-lines reaching almost as far as their knees, the women paraded back and forth, slapping recalcitrant children, pouring lavender oil on their skins and lying on their lounges, turning frequently like chickens on a rotisserie.

Daydreaming is the dominant feature of 'me-on-holiday'. This state of mind includes a complete inability to use any part of my brain other than the brain stem, enough for showering, feeding and ambulation. I develop a satisfyingly high tolerance of alcohol and a need to eat six meals a day to supply barely enough energy to stumble between my B&B, the beach and the restaurants. I become an unashamed pleasure-seeker, mostly in a soporific haze, emitting the occasional purr of contentment.

But it was not without its downside. Men, many so young they were barely out of school, sat quietly on beach chairs, sunrays touching the broken bodies ravaged by years of a war with Serbia that was rooted in centuries of cultural and religious resentments. There were men whose limbs had been blown off or amputated. Others had bodies pockmarked with bullets possibly still embedded in the soft tissue of their backs and arms and wasted legs.

These men were a jarring sight, disrupting the usual patterns of holiday nonchalance. Screams of joy once emanating from the floating water slide anchored off the beach had been silenced, the plastic edifice dismantled in deference to the suffering bodies basking in the sun. The adults on the beach were respectful. Some approached the men, shook their hands and thanked them for defending Hrvaska. Others offered cigarettes or fresh fruit. Children were more furtive, glancing fearfully at the hurt men and the scars or the stumps where legs and arms used to be.

I was like the children. Coming from Perth at the bottom of the world, I didn't understand how humans could kill and maim each other for cultural and territorial advantage. It was particularly bewildering because for me, the outsider, there was no difference between Belgrade and Zagreb.

These musings were flashes of consciousness as I lay on my sun lounge like an oily lizard. I'd coated myself in the lavender concoction sold from wicker baskets by women as they wandered among the bodies spread out on the beach. It was probably just olive oil they dressed up with the purple scent. Who cared? My skin was walnut brown – a colour that would elicit envious responses from my winter-pale friends when I returned to the southern hemisphere.

But, as the saying goes, 'the end was nigh' and I had to ready myself for the inevitable return to reality. I was flying back to resume a life dominated by writing restaurant reviews, suburban features and the occasional obituary for a prominent local who had appeared so often in the society pages they were considered a celebrity. Sometimes though, banal reality can explode holiday lassitude to smithereens.

I was enjoying a last sizzle in the sun when one such reality check blasted my holiday haze.

Having a thing for voices, no matter how long it's been since hearing it, I can immediately recognise a speaker. This talent kicked in when Marie Puharich screamed at me across the pebbles.

'Yoo-hoo, Alex! Yoo-hoo!'

In hindsight, I should've kept still, pretending to be asleep. Or maybe, when she stumbled to my sunbed, I could have squinted up at her, put on a roughly Slavic accent and exclaimed about the strangeness of an Australian woman who looked exactly like me. But these methods of escape only came to me later.

'Yoo-hoo! Yoo-hoo!'

I tried to ignore the sound of stamping feet coming in my direction, noisily scattering stones.

We had gone to school together – one of those all-girl institutions that gave us a 'ladies academy' kind of education. Marie was different because she was Croatian – a 'wog' who stood out in a school of WASPs. Marie was unfazed by her difference and the snobbery of the other girls because she had an unshakeable belief in her cultural ascendancy. Sometimes she expressed sympathy for me – as an Australian I didn't have the benefit of a long socio-cultural history symbolised by centuries of castles and cathedrals and yodelling folk dancers. Marie was arrogant: tall, olive-skinned, with a stream of thick black hair that she arranged in elaborate scrolls, or let hang loose, to the chagrin of the school principal. Mrs Smith tut-tutted over the suggestiveness of free-flowing locks, but Marie shrugged her shoulders. The rest of us pony-tailed young ladies loved or hated this audacity. Mostly I felt bossed around, something not native to my temperament.

Now she was coming towards me on a beach in Croatia.

'Alex. Alex Grant,' she bellowed. 'This is unbelievable.'

I had to bend my head right back, tucking it between my shoulder blades, as she bent over me.

'Marie. Well, hello.' I sat up, swung my feet around and got up, forcing her to step back. Our noses were almost touching, yet she didn't back away. Personal space had never been her forte. 'Fancy running into you this far from home.'

'This is totally, totally unbelievable!' She went to give me a hug.

I broadened my smile and held my hands out to ward her off. 'You'd better not touch me. I'm covered in that lavender-scented oil.'

She laughed and lightly touched my arm with a finger. 'You'll burn to a crisp with that stuff. Let's get out of the sun and have a catch-up.'

Various excuses to stay on the beach came to mind: a lack of vitamin D threatened rickets, severe nervous exhaustion, or I'd eaten the equivalent of a small herd of swine in prosciutto and was no longer able to walk. There was no arguing with Marie. She gestured towards a beach café, whose tables spilled out over the pebbles. Grabbing my wrist, she started to pull me into a trot before I could squeak a response.

'It's terrific to see you. Just the person I'd want to meet … under the circumstances.' She steered me through the crowd clogging the boardwalk that split the plaza into two neat halves. Marie plonked me at a table and called over a waiter before I had time to draw breath.

'This is such a difficult time for my family. Seeing you is the best thing to happen for me.'

'It's great to see you too.'

My natural affinity for lying surfaced immediately: it is a primal survival instinct. I was brought up to understand there are no such things as white lies – a porky is a porky. With Marie, however, the only way to suppress my flight instinct was to lie through clenched teeth that hopefully resembled a smile.

She grasped my hand across the table. 'It's been too long since we've seen each other. Caitlin's christening was the last time?'

I nodded, remembering a fat, dark-haired child in a ridiculous silk and lace gown, screaming her head off as the priest tried not to drown her in holy water.

'Yeah, it's been a while. How old is she now?'

'The precious thing, such a sweetie-pie mummy's girl. I've got photos here somewhere. She'll be six in August and is the cleverest little poppet. You wouldn't believe what she gets up to.'

And nor did I care. But I murmured a suitable response as the waiter came to take our order – thick sweet Turkish coffee for me and a herbal infusion stinking like compost for Marie. I let her coerce me into a plate of *krostule* and *fritule* – totally delicious ribbons of light buttery pastry and round balls of fruity cake that looked like the holes from doughnuts. Becoming addicted to both, my derriere had a new plumpness.

'So, how are all your family?' My strategy was to get Marie talking about her favourite subject; she could blather on and I'd nod and daydream and sip my coffee.

No such luck. Her family was big news and its current situation piqued my interest.

'Oh, Alex, I'm here for a funeral.' She didn't try to hide the excitement in her voice.

'What's happened?' She had a vast network of relatives. Thousands could have died.

'It's a terrible, terrible tragedy. My grandfather lives in the hills behind Split and he's been cared for, over the last thirty years, by a lovely couple called Zorka and Jure. They were too wonderful for words and they've been totally loyal and kind to him.' She paused and reached for the pendant around her neck featuring a tortured Jesus in his underwear. 'And now they're dead.'

For a second, I thought she was going to cross herself. But even for Marie that was taking Catholic theatricality a little too far.

'That's awful. How did they die?'

Marie said nothing. I watched her constructing the narrative in her mind, selecting the best bits, editing for effect.

From over my shoulder a hand deposited a coffee cup and a plate of sweets in front of me. The waiter gave my cleavage a brief look of interest and sauntered off. Leering was a common pastime among Croatian men and it was flattering and obnoxious in equal measure. After all, I had engaged in my own fair share of 'appreciative looking' while watching the local men play water polo in teeny-weeny swimmers.

Marie took a long slurp of her tea and jammed a *fritule* into her mouth. 'It's so hard to talk about. The whole thing's such a scandal. Dida, my grandfather, is incredibly upset, as you can imagine.'

Well, no. Trying to imagine without a hint was beyond even my overly dramatic mindset.

She paused to sip her grass clippings and for dramatic effect. 'It was a murder–suicide.'

As a journalist I like to think I'm calm and objective, not easily surprised by the proclivities of humankind. This little titbit made me do a double take and I sensed those at other tables had pricked up their ears when they heard the word 'murder'.

'You're kidding?'

'No, no. It has actually happened. And to *our* family.' Her tone was one of dismay. This was less about the murder of her grandfather's retainers, and more about a threat to the status of her family.

'It seems like the typical story. Jure killed Zorka and then turned the gun on himself. Blood and brains everywhere.' Marie watched me, assessing the impact of her words. 'Dida said he had no idea they weren't happy. They always seemed to have a completely normal marriage to him.'

Having never been there myself, marriage was a mystery. My family 'did' marriage; my father had made a habit of it. But the words 'marriage' and 'normal' hadn't ever coalesced in my circle of relatives and friends.

'Why did he think it was about the state of their marriage?'

'What else could it be? Jure Simich was Dida's groundsman and Zorka was his housekeeper. They all lived on the same property, my grandfather in the big house and they had the cottage my great-grandparents built when they got married. If anyone was going to see that they were unhappy or that Jure was unstable, it'd be my grandfather. There was nothing. No indication at all.'

We were both silent. My previous job as a court reporter had convinced me that there were as many motives for murder as there were ways of doing it. All sorts of other possibilities came to mind: maybe Jure was having an affair and couldn't bear the guilt. Or maybe he'd found out that Zorka was having an affair and killed her in a blind rage, then, realising he'd go to prison, he shot himself. Or maybe one of them had been terminally ill and they decided to die together rather than be parted. I was probably escalating the drama, but my holiday was nearly over, and here was an event that aroused my journalist instinct. A crime of passion may be a satisfying denouement to my European escape. A suitably creative segue into a return to my real life.

'What a dreadful shock for your grandfather. What will he do now?'

'I don't know. He seems so stunned by it all. I don't think he's capable of making a decision.' She gave a melodramatic sigh. 'The poor man is a shadow of himself. He seems to have aged twenty years overnight and he's not a young man.'

My scepticism went up a notch. I had met her grandfather in the early 1980s. He had been visiting his sons in Australia and checking on his business interests. I remembered a man who dominated the spaces around him. Tall, speaking in an emphatic, heavily accented voice, he had commanded attention and took for granted the fear and respect of his sons and their families. Disdainful of an *Engleski* girl, he treated me with mild scorn barely hidden by an exaggerated politeness. He was steely and cold, a hard man whom I could not imagine diminished even under the most horrendous circumstances.

'My father's worried this might kill Dida.'

I was doubtful. 'I'm sure he has a lot of support. What about his children, your parents and aunts and uncles?'

'They're all over here, so he'll be looked after. My grandfather is highly respected and he's helped an enormous amount of people by employing them in the business. They really love him.'

A nice euphemism for 'scared out of their wits'.

'The rellies are scattered everywhere, looking after branches of the family company. We've all gathered to help him get through.'

Marie tucked into the pastries with gusto, even though the topic of conversation was dead bodies. She munched through the pile of *krostule*, small flakes of the delicate pastry sprinkling her bosom. I bit into a *fritule* and nearly wept. The taste of the small round balls of dough, deep-fried to a light crispness, was something else. Plump sultanas, dried locally on racks spread out in the sun, mixed with the flavours of brandy, lemon and vanilla.

I spoke around the taste sensation in my mouth. 'It's great you've travelled all this way to be with him. He must be so pleased to see you here.'

'It's the Croatian way. We believe in family above all other things. Your lot have the old saying about blood being thicker than water and mostly you just say it. We believe it and live it. There was no question that Branko and I would come over.'

At the mention of that name, my stomach did a major U-turn. My face must have registered some of my 'emotion'.

'Do you remember my brother Branko? You know: Brian?' She dipped her head and looked at me slyly from under her plucked-to-death eyebrows.

How could I forget? The years from fifteen to eighteen are very dicey for a girl and the last thing she needs is an unwelcome suitor with a surfeit of testosterone and self-belief. Brian was two years older than Marie. He'd gone to one of the prestige boys schools that spit out their young men with a judicious amount of polite misogyny. Studying law, he became infatuated with me when he found out I was the daughter of Charles Grant, AO, SC, judge and, therefore, an influential man in a curly wig.

Marie adored her brother and assumed I shared her feelings. Brian had asked me to accompany him to the law ball in his first year at university. I spent ages trying to get my mother to ring him and say I was sick with a highly contagious disease. Luckily for me, I broke my leg jumping from the roof of the garage a week before the grand event and was having metal pins inserted in my shin bone while Brian was tripping the light fantastic with the daughter of some other prominent man. It's amazing how after all the years that had passed, I still felt a chill of anxiety at the mention of his name. And to think he was in the vicinity! There needed to be an international law under the Geneva Convention limiting the movement of people with brains the size of amoebas and egos the size of a small moon.

I took a long slug of coffee.

'Yes, I remember Brian. How is he?'

'Absolutely terrific. He was always going to do great things. He's now an associate partner.' She gave a wistful shrug. 'Of course, the long hours mean he hasn't managed to find the right woman. Mum would love him to have a son. Sometime soon.'

'It's great he's been so successful.' Ping! I was racking up the little white lies.

'It's a shame you two didn't get together.'

Hopefully my grimace passed as a smile. I pushed my chair back and stood. 'I really have to go. I'm sorry about the deaths and the terrible time your grandfather is having. I hope all goes well. Say hi to Brian for me.'

She looked past my shoulder and started to wave. 'You can say hello yourself.'

CHAPTER TWO

It was one of those slow-motion dreamlike sequences when you can see the danger, but you can't escape. Brian Puharich was striding towards our table, a clown grin stretched across his face. Everyone in the café turned to watch as he lunged towards me, lips extended in a toilet-plunger pucker. He kissed each side of my head; it felt like the moist, scratchy lick of a lizard.

'Alex Grant!' He held onto my shoulders. 'It's been so long. You're looking really well. Very well indeed.' His mouth-freshener breath puffed across my face.

He took my hand and moved me back to my seat.

'What an amazing coincidence. We can renew our friendship.' He cocked his eyebrow in a 'winning' way.

'I was just leaving, Brian. There are many, many things to do. Huge amounts.'

'Come on, Alex. You're on holiday. Stay for a while. The drinks are on me.'

'No, really. I must be going.'

'I won't take no for an answer. We've a lot of catching up to do.' He gave me a little wink and clicked his tongue. I thought I was going to heave.

He pulled my chair out and tapped me on the shoulder to sit. He waved a finger at the waiter and ordered a bottle of local wine. I felt like asking the waiter to bring a straw and another bottle only for me.

'How's Judge Grant? I read that he's been working on the Fordham Brothers collapse.'

'He was fine the last time I saw him, and I don't really follow the cases he's overseeing.'

'Shame. Has Marie told you about our news?' Brian looked between the two of us with an attempt at gravitas.

'Yeah. I'm really sorry for your grandfather. These people obviously meant a lot to him.'

'That's not the least of it.' His self-importance was noxious.

Although Brian was tall, about six foot five, his frame had remained at a pre-adolescent, skin-and-bone stage. The biggest part of him was his nose, which extended out from his face like a giant shark fin – he'd scare the pants off anyone who saw him floating on his back in the sea. He had the same lustrous black hair as his sister, cut into a trendy style that emphasised the squareness of his head. I'd never been able to tell the colour of his eyes because they were shadowed by his nose and the jutting extension of his monobrow.

To give him credit, he always dressed tastefully and with an innate sense of what good leather and cashmere could do for a man. Sitting across the table from him, I surreptitiously peered at the beautiful soft leather of his deck shoes and the exquisite weave of the sweater draped over his bony shoulders.

'Branko, Alex doesn't want to hear all the gory details.' Marie looked at him indulgently.

Gory details were better than trying to make polite small talk. 'It's perfectly okay, Marie. I'm sure Brian can't tell me anything worse than what's on the police rounds.'

He wet his lips with the tip of his tongue. 'I arrived here before anyone knew something was amiss with Jure and Zorka. I come over every summer to look over my grandfather's legals and catch a few rays to tan up the bod.'

He looked appreciatively at his long skinny arms, while I tried not to imagine his string-bean body in Speedos, slick with lavender oil.

'The first thing wrong was that Jure didn't pick me up from Split airport. No one was there and I had to take a taxi to the creamery. Second thing wrong, no one came to the door when I rang the bell at the big house. I started to get a bit worried. My grandfather is in a wheelchair after a fall, so he's dependent on Zorka and Jure. I went around the back and broke the kitchen window. The alarm sounded and scared me half to death. So that was the other weird thing. No one seemed to be at home, yet they all knew my date and time of arrival.'

Maybe everyone had deliberately made themselves scarce.

'I went up to Dida's room and there he was. Still in his pyjamas. He'd been alone since Jure had left the night before and he hadn't come back in the morning to get my grandfather ready for the day. As you can imagine, he was on the verge of panic.'

This was not a word I'd associate with Grandfather Puharich, who was overbearing and defiant. I didn't see him falling into the degrading state of panic.

'He hadn't been able to get down the stairs or get Jure on the intercom. My grandfather doesn't like to have a phone in his bedroom. He says the ring makes his tinnitus worse.' Brian shrugged and rolled his eyes – such are the peculiar habits of the old.

'What did you do?'

'I made him comfortable, got him fresh water and some bread and cheese. Then I tried to find Jure. He wasn't around the house or in his shed. I called out but didn't expect an answer because Jure and Zorka are as deaf as posts. So, I went to the cottage. Long story short, I found the bodies.'

He was clearly thrilled he'd been the first on the scene. I looked at him in horrified fascination. He began to run his fingers through his dark hair and looked at me from under his veranda eyebrow. He gave me another wink and the pink tip of his tongue appeared briefly between his lips.

'What a dreadful thing to find.' I finished my wine in one gulp and refilled my glass, being careful not to catch his eye.

'He was so brave to go and look for them on his own.' Marie liked the idea of her brother as hero almost as much as he did.

'I had to do something. Dida couldn't take any more upsets.'

'Where did you find them?' Curiosity was starting to usurp my aversion. There was definitely a feature story in that cottage: 'Killing, Croatian Style' would be a catchy headline.

'They were sitting in the kitchen. At the table, like at a normal dinner. Except Zorka was slumped back in her chair with a hole right in the middle of her forehead. Not much blood on her, because it was mostly spattered on the wall behind. It was a different story with Jure. He'd fallen forward on the table and there was blood over his plate and down his fingers and all over the floor. The gun was next to him. It's something I'll never forget.' Brian's voice dropped away. The memory of the bloody scene was enough to subdue even his exuberance.

'I'm glad Dida wasn't able to go and find them,' said Marie. 'It's enough for him to know that they've died, without actually finding the bodies.'

'Did you have to identify them?' I asked Brian.

He nodded. 'I called the police as soon as possible. It was hard to understand what had happened. Let me tell you, Alex, it took a while to sink in. It looked like madness in there.'

I couldn't imagine the scene Brian had discovered, or the smells that must have hit him when he entered the room. 'Who said it was a murder–suicide?'

'That was pretty obvious. Zorka had been shot at close range with an old hunting pistol, one from the war. Jure must have kept it from when he was fighting the communists. Zorka's eyes were open, and she was just staring at me.' He sipped some wine. 'Jure was a real mess. His first shot hadn't done the job, so he managed to pull the trigger a second time. That one had blown his face off.'

I began to wonder. Instead of a love triangle or an expression of tender release, Brian had raised another possibility. If Jure fought against the communists, there was every chance he was in the party of Nazi sympathisers, the Ustaše, who committed crimes only possible under the extreme inhumanity of war. Despite the passing of decades, was it possible that someone sought revenge?

Marie was shaken by Brian's visceral telling. 'It's too much to think about. I'd have nightmares for the rest of my life if it had been me. Lucky for Dida, Branko isn't so squeamish.'

I looked at the siblings. What did I know about these people? I'd spent five years at what was, in essence, an Anglican convent with the sister. I knew the brother primarily through her unreliable narratives describing his wide-ranging virtues. In the years since leaving school, I had learned how little you know about the people with whom you went to school. It is a small, protected world. A glass dome under which girls experiment with various 'selves' that shift alarmingly. Friendships are made, unmade and remade. Groups coalesce and then fragment. Where you belong is contingent upon complex interstices based on unstable relationships which rarely survive the lifting of the dome. In the case of Marie, this 'unknowability' was overlaid with cultural difference.

My first conclusion was that this sort of horrendous bloodletting didn't happen in normal families. That common decencies and ingrained ethical understandings stopped extreme transgressions from shattering familial ties. There had to be something about the Puharich clan that attracted such violence. Marie had always postulated the uniqueness of her family. And this wasn't arbitrary – there was something about them. I didn't care how special the siblings thought their family were, it was very possible Jure and Zorka had been killed by someone within the insular circle who was protecting their grandfather. It beggared belief that Jure had the capability to pull the trigger twice. There had to have been a third person in that room. One who'd given the old people a brutal send-off.

Brian's voice interrupted my thoughts. 'I avoided going back to tell my grandfather until the ambulance and police arrived. They were quick because my family are very important in this area. Cheese is big business.'

'Cheese? Aren't your family into property development?'

'That's a sideline now. Cheese is where the money is. My grandfather started small, taking over from his father after the war, and now we're the biggest manufacturer and exporter of cheese in the Eastern Bloc, including to Australia. We have a facility at Margaret River, which we use as an export hub to the whole of Southeast Asia.'

Brian instantly became more bearable. Cheese was one of my passions. Up there with shoes and wine. I swear I can remember hints of a triple-cream camembert in my mother's milk.

'Once all the emergency services arrived, I left them to it and returned to the big house. Jesus,' he shook his head, 'that was the worst thing I've ever had to do. Walk up the hill to tell my grandfather.'

Marie leaned over and took her brother's hand, tears balanced on her lower eyelids.

'It's okay. I'm okay.' He looked towards me. 'When I told him, he didn't say much. The shock was huge.'

I tried to imagine the old man and his grandson and the words that must have sucked the air out of the room.

'Has there been a post-mortem and a ruling on the circumstances?'

'Yep. They were done the same day I found them, and the bodies were released for burial the next day, when the coroner had written his report.'

Wow, things happened quickly in Croatia! I thought about the months it sometimes took for the coroner to deliver the findings at home. Was it really possible, under the archaic Croatian bureaucratic system I'd witnessed just trying to post a letter, to manage dead bodies so efficiently?

To me, the speed showed a lack of due process and a desire for a hasty conclusion. My journalist's nose twitched and I smelt vermin.

'The coroner found Jure had killed Zorka and then turned the gun on himself. There's little point in a complicated investigation when it's going to reach the same conclusion.' Brian's tone was guarded. 'He respects my grandfather and didn't want to cause him more distress.'

'I see.' Not really. A swift response in a country which prided itself on public service somnambulism seemed far-fetched. 'Have they had the funeral?'

'No, that's tomorrow.' Marie kept her eyes on her brother.

Brian turned to me. 'Hey, why don't you come?'

I was horrified. 'No. No. I didn't know these people and I don't know your grandfather.'

'That's not an excuse. You've known us for such a long time. Marie would appreciate a bit of moral support.'

Marie nodded and smiled. 'It'll be nice to have a friend from home.'

'I'm sorry. It's not really appropriate. I'd feel funny.'

'Oh, please, Alex. Croatian funerals are so intense. The two of us will make you feel more than welcome.'

I looked at Brian, who was now putting on a hangdog face, presumably to tug at my heartstrings.

'I'd like to take you to our family funeral.' He made it sound like we were going on a picnic date.

I was overwhelmed by the strangeness of the invitation. I wanted to laugh: shrill, like a tortured banshee. I managed a pallid grin, which they both took as an affirmative.

'This is so good of you. Now you're coming, I feel much better.' Marie reached across the table and patted my hand.

I would have liked to feel the same. Coming from a family who looked suspiciously upon 'gushing', I was ill-equipped to cope with the emotional effusiveness of a Croatian funeral.

'If you tell me where you're staying, I can come by tomorrow morning and pick you up.' Brian gave me a lopsided smile, sexy in that *Pretty Woman*–pimp kind of way.

'That's okay. There's a taxi stand outside the B&B. Tell me the location and time and I'll be right.'

'Absolutely not. I insist on coming to pick you up.'

'No, please, that's okay. There's no need.'

And, so it continued – he got more insistent and I got more frustrated as we escalated a ridiculous to-and-fro.

Marie cut across our bickering. 'Alex, you must let Brian pick you up. It's the right thing to do. Tell us where you're staying, and he'll be there at ten.'

Brian looked at me with childish triumph. I had to suppress a scowl.

'I'm at the Bijela Kuća on the main road.'

'I know it, up from the plaza.' Brian put his hand on my arm. 'Don't worry, it's no trouble picking you up. You're an old friend.'

I felt like slapping myself. Loathing passivity in women, I was angry for bending to the will of the Puhariches. I needed to grow some balls. Looking across the table at Brian, I didn't think I'd find them in his trousers.

I stood. 'I'll see you tomorrow. The old "people to see, places to be".'

Brian quickly pushed his chair back and raced around to pull out mine.

'Thanks. You always were a bit of a smoothy.' I'd need to rely on the useful skill of charming artifice to get me through the next twenty-four hours.

He lowered his voice, trying for suave, delivering squawk. 'I'm pleased you haven't forgotten me.'

'How could I?'

Marie watched us indulgently, like an old woman overseeing a successful matchmaking. 'We'll see you tomorrow then. It's so great I ran into you. Unbelievable luck.'

'Yeah, unbelievable for me, too.' I felt a tiny pang of guilt at my churlishness. 'It's great to see you looking so well, even under the circumstances. Remember some of the fun times we had back at school?'

At least in this last bit I wasn't lying. There had been some great, girly moments – singing into hairbrushes to 'Bohemian Rhapsody' and 'Devil Woman'. Typical teenage musical eclecticism reflecting our shared devotion to *Countdown*.

Marie nodded. 'It'll be good to see you tomorrow.'

I walked away as quickly as politeness allowed. I felt them watching me and wondered again at their reasons for asking me to the funeral. Once out of sight, I changed direction, reluctant to go back to the B&B where the owner fussed, asking questions about my day and telling me I looked too skinny as she brought large chunks of bread, cheese and smoked ham to fatten me up.

Strolling to the little port area of town, one thought occupied me: was I expected to view the body? I hoped they'd managed to sew Jure's face back on and putty up the bullet hole in Zorka's forehead.

~

There's a deep ghoulish streak in my personality. Like all good daughters of divorced parents, I blame my father. With his background in criminal law, I can remember him coming home and talking about his cases with anthropological detachment, forgetting there were two children with eyes the size of saucers listening. A reason for my popularity in primary school was my business in the retelling of these stories for a modest fee. My father didn't seem to connect his work life with my continual detentions received for scaring the shit out of my audience. He attributed them to my mother's increasing devotion to crystals and batik sarongs.

My interest in violent crime has never abated. Writing court reports for the *West Australian* provided an opportunity to apply this knowledge. Perth was never going to be like America where you might be gunned down just for changing your garbage man. Yet it had enough of its own bloodiness to maintain my interest, even if it was white-collar criminals getting paper cuts. It had been one such Zegna-clad, Canary Island banker who had spelt the end of my mainstream journalism career. Back in those days, I'd worn suits with vast shoulder pads and had my hair scorched by a poodle perm every month. Then I'd poked my nose into the golden trough where I found a high-profile investor, a paper bag full of one hundred-dollar bills and the Minister for Land Development. I was booted into freelancing quicker than you could say 'pollie on the take'.

Wandering through the crowds of exhausted holiday-makers, I considered the scene Brian had discovered in the kitchen. The biggest puzzle was: why? Of the three of us, I appeared to be the only one pondering the possibilities. Brian and Marie seemed uninterested in cause, only effect. There was an odd absence of curiosity about motivation. Reasons were superfluous. It had become a simple matter of cleaning up the mess and putting them in the ground.

I turned into a cobblestone street and headed for the restaurant where I'd eaten most of my dinners. Sitting down, a waiter approached and I pointed to a number on the menu. Each meal was like going down a culinary rabbit hole. So far, I'd consumed freshly caught fish in lemon gin sauce, lusciously braised lamb and huge piles of homemade pasta dripping in garlic and cheese. Cheese! It had been lavishly stirred through every meal and a great pot was always on the table for that little bit extra. Inevitably I had finished this off by licking my finger and swishing it around to collect the very last morsels, giving thanks lactose intolerance was foreign to my constitution. Now I wondered if the cheese had come from the Puharich creamery.

I gazed across the road to the wide promenade on the other side where flowerbeds and a line of huge palms bordered the little bay that formed the arc of the marina. Bulbs flourished in multicoloured masses, merging purples, pinks and reds. During the day, with the dazzle of the blue water, it was almost too much for eyes to bear. The froth and bubble of the flowers was matched by the up-and-down tones of the old men who sat on the marina walls smoking and talking from the time the fishing boats went out at dawn, until they came back at dusk. Their wobbly old men's voices changed pitch to match changes in topic.

Now the masts of the boats jutted up into the twilight. They had strings of small fairy lights attached at the tops, dropping to trail along the decks. I heard the voices of the fishermen as they sat cleaning up after a day at sea. Their cigarettes, dangling loosely from their lips, flared intermittently as they exchanged news. The next day, and the day after that, they would hold the same conversation with all the ebullience of new acquaintances.

On the menu, I had pointed at *Tripice na Dalmatinski*, which turned out to be a tripe and tomato stew. My first impulse was to send it back. The lining of an animal's internal organs was not high on my list of must-have experiences. But, after a tentative sniff of the plate and poke with my knife, I decided to ignore its peculiar bubbly texture. Maybe I could write a review about my conversion from being a believer that stomach linings are best left in the beast, to a tripe aficionado who was quite happy to unite my innards with those of a cow. As I ate, the power of association soon had my mind off the white flesh in red sauce on my plate and back to the blood and guts sprayed around Zorka's kitchen.

What was most interesting was the rarity of the murder–suicide scenario Brian and Marie were so keen to accept. The way Brian described the scene suggested deranged violence, maybe something induced by vast amounts of alcohol. It was impossible to imagine that the old couple, eating their evening meal, would allow someone so addled to enter their home. And there was the Croatian constitution to consider. I'd watched the locals gulp down more beer and spirits than were consumed at a B&S ball, yet they seemed unaltered – no swaying walk, no sliding off chairs, no sleeping on the footpath in their own vomit. Maybe it had been a random druggie, dosed up to a killing mania. Although this seemed even more unlikely. It was difficult to believe there was a frenzied drug culture in a country where urgency was limited to getting home by noon for an enormous lunch and siesta.

Thinking about Jure and Zorka increased my sense of unease about the funeral. After slurping up the last of the tomato sauce, I headed back to my B&B. The only lights to brighten the twilight sky were coming from the windows of the apartments rising up on both sides of the narrow street. I saw TV screens illuminating rooms where families yelled and gesticulated over the astonishingly popular Russian game shows. I wondered what it would be like to be in one of these large, gregarious households where all emotions were expressed with dramatic fervour.

When I got back to my room, my hostess had been in and tidied up, leaving a large plate of cheese and bread on the bedside table. Not wanting to be rude, I sat on the bed and munched through the cheese, rolling each creamy bite around in my mouth as though it was the last piece I'd ever taste. Not for the first time I thought of the wonderfulness of being dipped in a giant cheese fondue. With my stomach bloated by animal products, I changed into a t-shirt and tracksuit pants, turned on the TV and fell asleep to the smooth tones of Tajči warbling about sun and running water.

CHAPTER THREE

I woke to crackling snow on the TV and a cheese hangover. Like every other morning, the wall-to-ceiling floral tiles, copious quantities of knick-knacks and the baroque mirror above the bathroom basin were a shock to my sleepy brain. I leaned forward to look closer at the pale, puffy face that vaguely resembled me.

'One way or another, you'll make an impression today,' the face said.

Oh God! Funeral.

A swirl of day-old tripe hit the back of my throat. Was it possible to get out of it? If it was still early, I could spin a story to my hostess that my flight had been changed and I needed to get to Zagreb *tout de suite*. This left the landlady to break the news to Brian.

I looked at my watch: nine thirty-five.

The entire population of the Dalmatian Coast probably heard every expletive I uttered as I charged around, throwing myself under the shower, slipping on the ubiquitous little black dress (staple attire for travelling women), and pulling my hair back to secure with a scrunchy, hoping everyone would judge its slick oiliness to be deliberate. I stopped to consider shoes. Taking economies with clothes and toiletries is one thing. Limiting space for shoes is another. I pack like a centipede. I have traipsed around Europe for months with five pieces of clothing, two pairs of undies and a bar of soap, so that there was enough space for the acceptable minimum of eight pairs of shoes. This morning I chose a pair of patent black pumps, with a princess heel impossible to get caught in the pavement. The landlady knocked on the door and bustled in.

'Mees. Your man is here.'

'Okay. Won't be long.'

She remained standing just inside the room. 'He's a Puharich.'

'Yes, I know.'

'Why you going to a Puharich?'

'Do you mean, where am I going?'

She nodded.

'To a funeral for his grandfather's minders.'

She crossed herself. 'I only say. You be careful.' Her voice was low, her face uncharacteristically emotionless. It was unsettling.

'Why do I have to be careful? It's just a funeral.'

She gave a hiss and put her hand over her heart. 'It is never "just" with these people. I will pray you come home.'

Turning, she slammed the door and retreated to the kitchen. This meant she had left Brian waiting on the doorstep. During my holiday I'd noticed the inclusive sociability of the average Croat. A lack of hospitality like this would normally have been unconscionable in a Croatian household, especially towards a single male arriving to escort a single female.

I gave myself a final perusal in the mirror, picked up my clutch and headed out to meet Brian, marooned on the threshold.

'Hi Brian.'

He held the door open, his arm extended across my shoulder, lightly touching the side of my head. 'You look lovely.'

'Thanks. I hope it's all right. A funeral wasn't on my agenda.'

'It's perfect.' His eyes moved up and down my body, making me wish I was wearing a hessian sack.

'I'm sorry you were left out here to wait.'

He shrugged. 'It doesn't bother me. She's a Lekich.'

'What does that mean?'

'Her brother is married to a Serb.'

I was baffled. Before I could ask questions, Brian grabbed my arm and tucked it under his, half pulling me down the steps towards the sleek Mercedes parked at the curb.

For someone who drives a Golf Cabriolet with a leaking roof and rusted holes in the floor, a Mercedes is a leather recliner rocker on wheels. I almost purred as I sank deep into the seat.

'Nice car.'

'It's the same model I have at home.'

'Wow, you've done all right for yourself.'

'Naturally.'

I sucked my lips in and resisted the desire to get out. 'Where are you working?'

'At Blyth Sanders. I'm an associate partner.'

This was impressive. Blyth Sanders was a significant law firm in Australia with offices throughout Southeast Asia. Its lawyers had the reputation for stretching the law to its limits. My father had a wary admiration for the ways they used legal 'flexibilities' when they appeared before his court.

'Well done.'

'It helped that I brought all my family interests to the firm, so we now have offices in eastern Europe. One of the first when the wall came down.'

'Is there much work over here?'

'You'd be surprised.'

The trip was taken up with Brian's stories. He featured as the hero of impossible cases he'd resolved to the immense advantage of his clients. Many of them involved his family and international import–export law. The jargon flew over my head and until I heard him say: 'So, the cheese side of things has been huge.'

'Cheese? What cheese?'

He turned his face and looked at me sceptically. 'Have you been listening to me?'

'Yes, yes. I'm not good with all the legal-speak.'

'I assumed you have a thorough understanding of it.'

'Nope. That's Charles's domain.'

'I've done a great job in pulling together all the cheese businesses into one structure administered from Perth.'

'But we're at the bottom of the world.'

'Not quite.' He had accelerated as we left the town limits and the car glided like it was cruising along a silk ribbon.

'The manufacture of the hard cheeses is done here and half of that is distributed across the eastern countries and into Russia. The other half comes to us for our distribution network. We make all our soft cheeses in Margaret River.'

I imagined pillows of creamy brie coated in a puff of mould.

'I love cheese.'

'Real cheese or the stuff where you can't tell the difference between the cheese and the plastic it's wrapped in?'

'Real cheese, Brian. I'm so fussy, your stuff might not meet my standard.'

'You gotta be kidding me. You won't taste better. We have a blue that's been in the top three at the *Salon de Fromage*, the Paris Cheese Fair, for the last five years. You'll have to come down to Margaret River the next time I'm there. A wonderful chance for us to get reacquainted.'

I weighed things up – spending time with Brian versus the bliss of unlimited access to cheese.

Making it a business trip may make it bearable. Some food reviews would cover my expenses and I'd skip through creameries, wineries and every seafood restaurant scattered along the South West. While I thought about possible angles, Brian blathered on about him and me and us. I didn't start to pay attention until we stopped at a T-junction facing the imposing walls of Diocletian's Palace.

'Wow. It always takes my breath away.'

'I know. We have a real ability to design grand spaces.'

I felt like doing a faceplant on the dash. It sounded like the Puharich family was responsible for everything fabulous, everywhere.

'Is the funeral here?'

'No, we can't get the cathedral, so we're making do with Sveti Frane.'

It was impossible to imagine the brave person who'd had the task of telling them the Catholic centrepiece of the palace was not available to Brian's grandfather. We turned right and followed the wall, going left at the end.

'The church is a good size, but not everyone who wants to attend will fit in.'

'Zorka and Jure had a big family?'

'I don't know, but that's beside the point. People will be here for my grandfather.'

Brian manoeuvred the Mercedes along the marina and parked underneath the shade of an enormous palm, a line of which formed a towering border between the plaza and the sea. He put an embossed sign on the dashboard that said 'Puharich Vehicle' and got out. Clearly, there was no such thing as illegal parking for this family.

We joined the stream of people heading to the church. The women were in their very best, which included a surfeit of black taffeta and enormous gold earrings, stretching lobes to the point of breaking. Laid-back 1990s fashion had not usurped the 1980s gridiron look and helmet-hair for the well-dressed Croatian woman. The men resembled extras from *The Godfather*: dark glasses, double-breasted suits and cigarettes stuck to bottom lips.

The crowd narrowed to funnel through the arched front door and into the church that was beautiful in its uncharacteristic austerity. Most of the pews were already filled with people squashed together in an enforced intimacy, something that made me claustrophobic. Yet everyone there appeared to accept the tight proximity as a matter of course. To my embarrassment, Brian put his arm around my shoulders and steered me to one of the front pews with the rest of the Puharich clan.

A big hat with a felt doodad on the brim turned to me and waved. Guessing Marie was somewhere underneath, I waved back. No one looked at us as Brian and I shuffled along the pew to take our seats. I couldn't see the grandfather. Maybe he really was too upset to appear.

From an invisible corner someone started to groan out notes on an organ and everyone stood. It gave me a chance to look around at the congregation, many of whom sported the square head and jutting brow of Brian. Everyone leaned forward to watch the procession. At least a dozen men in black pin-striped suits were weighed down by two ornate coffins exploding with flowers. Immediately following the priests, escorting these final receptacles of Jure and Zorka, was Grandfather Puharich.

The single difference to the man I had once met was the addition of a thick black cane that he swung with military precision. He was clearly over the wheelchair stage of recuperation. Still tall and upright, it wasn't immediately clear why he needed even a cane. It lightly touched the ground before he flourished it back and forth. With a heavy gold handle in the figure of a lion, it looked more like a weapon than a walking aid. His face was a cipher. There was no expression reflecting the occasion or the sanctity of the location. Without acknowledging the crowd, he walked to the front and sat on a seat directly under the pulpit. Here was a man with the supreme confidence of someone unafraid of putting their back to a congregation that, I had no doubt, contained more enemies than friends.

With the coffins side by side at the altar, a man in a fancy dress and cape spoke for two hours. Periodically we had to stand; on one or two occasions we had to kneel. Mostly, we sat. My bum went numb, my feet turned purple with cold and my hip sockets felt welded into the sitting position. I ceased to care about the old people or the Puhariches or the presence of Brian whose thigh pressed hard against mine.

The organ came to life with a tune close to a foxtrot. Everyone stood. The men at the altar in dresses and fancy hats lined up to parade back down the aisle. We all watched in silence as Grandfather Puharich rose, turned, and, with a sweep of his cane, led the priests out the door. Only when they were standing at the bottom of the steps did we begin to move. People pushed forward, desperate to get into fresh air and sunlight.

Brian pulled me into line behind Marie. The fluffy bits on her hat tickled my nose as she stretched her arm behind her back to grab my hand. Brian clutched my other one. I found myself forming a three-link chain with the siblings as we moved out of the church.

Our eyes had barely readjusted to the summer sun when the kerfuffle started.

What I took to be close family had gathered in a loose proximity to the grandfather. He was on his feet, standing with a rigid back making small nods to acknowledge the crowd as if he was making a careful tally of who was in attendance.

Suddenly the multitudes were jostled apart. Pushing through was a heavy-set man, his broad face fixed with an expression of hatred. It was not the type of loathing you might have for lamb's fry or someone else's football team, but a deep implacable hostility that made his eyes gleam like jet. He was in front of Grandfather Puharich before anyone fully registered he was there. With his fists clenched in front of the old man's face, strings of venomous words erupted from the stranger.

Although I didn't know a word of Croatian, I understood the tone. The crowd stood mute as statues, witnessing something so unexpected we were incapable of intervening.

Grandfather Puharich kept his senses. He looked directly as his assailant, his eyes narrowing, the increased grip of his hand on the lion's head an almost imperceptible hint of his feelings. Then, in a single impulse, those in the immediate vicinity broke their paralysis and lunged at the man. Before they captured him, he placed his index finger on the old man's jacket and pushed. Grandfather Puharich jerked back slightly as the man shouted something that made those around me gasp. He turned and ran back through the crowd, which parted to let him through as though his fury made him too hot to touch.

Then everyone moved forward, the family forming a circle around the grandfather, while the priests mixed with the jumble of mourners trying to calm and disperse them.

'What was that about?' I leaned towards Marie.

'Nothing,' she whispered, and looked in the direction of her grandfather.

'Nothing? I don't think so.'

'It's a family thing.' Marie pulled her hat further over her eyes and pushed into the family circle.

'Brian!' I poked my finger into his shoulder. 'What was that about?'

He looked down as though astonished to see me there. 'Family business.'

I moved closer to make him look me in the eye. 'Listen, I have a sore bum, cold feet and I'm hungry enough to eat a cow. I want to know what just happened.'

His voice was subdued. 'That was Jure's brother. He just accused my grandfather of murdering Jure and Zorka.'

CHAPTER FOUR

My shock was twofold. Firstly, none of my friends or family have ever been accused of murder, so this was a new experience. And, secondly, it was hard to believe that someone was brave enough to front up and accuse that imperious man. I was both impressed and frightened for Jure's brother. Brian's grandfather didn't seem shocked at all. Instead, there was a vibration of formidable rage spreading out from his body like a force field.

He held his cane up in the air and said something that made four men scuttle away in the direction taken by the brother. Then he lowered the heavy stick. The family took this as the sign for them to move. No one touched him. It was clear questions were being asked about his wellbeing. This infuriated him further. He gestured to a man dressed as a chauffeur who rushed to his side and waved to the circle of family to move aside. Like a group of obedient schoolchildren they parted and watched as the patriarch made his way through the crowd to the limousine parked near the front of the church. It wasn't until the car door shut that the spell broke and everyone started to talk.

'Jesus. That was intense.' I heard the fear in my own voice.

Brian looked at me with an expression I couldn't read. 'Yes, it was unexpected.'

'That's a bit of an understatement.'

'These types of things can happen.'

'I don't think it's all that common, Brian.'

'Nonsense. Bad behaviour and rudeness are everywhere. It's a pity it had to happen here.'

Now, I have been accused of bad behaviour, often by my father after reading one of my exposés about his friends who 'may' have been caught-up in the 'alleged' illegal shenanigans of the 1980s Wild West corporate world. This, however, was an entirely different category of badness.

'I don't share your definition of rude. The guy was furious.'

'He wasn't serious. It was only a heat-of-the-moment type of thing.'

'You've got to be kidding.'

Brian held up his hand, his palm almost touching my face. 'Don't get carried away, Alex. This is none of your business.' Then his voice changed. 'It's probably an old argument that's been going on forever. I don't even understand how all this stuff works, so I don't think you should waste your time on it either.'

I was being put in my place. Silence was probably politic. It was a topic that could be stored away for future discussion with Marie. The crowd was dispersing, heading for cars to carry them up into the hills above Split for the interment and wake.

I hadn't been looking forward to another car ride with Brian. But this one proved to be far more interesting.

~

My weakness for shoes is matched only by an appreciation of tall, dark, handsome men. I barely suppressed a squeal of delight when I saw one leaning against Brian's car with the kind of arrogant 'bad boy' demeanour I find irresistible. Dressed in a stunningly cut black suit with a discreet maroon shirt and tie, his slim, broad-shouldered physique sent sparks to all points of my body. He was perfectly still, head bent, watching a thin trail of cigarette smoke waft up the arm hanging loosely at his side.

Brian looked sideways at me. The slight slump of his shoulders suggested my response was both unwelcome and not surprising. He raised his hand.

'Hey, Marco.'

In one languid movement, Mr Dark-and-Gorgeous dropped his cigarette and repositioned his body to face us.

Front-on, he was even more delectable. As we approached, I took in the smooth olive skin, big brown eyes and full red lips. Shining black hair was matched by thick, curling eyelashes so long they looked false.

'This is Alex Grant. Alex, this is my cousin Marco Puharich.' Brian's introduction was restrained.

I squeezed Marco's hand. 'Pleased to meet you. It's a shame about the circumstances.'

'Nice to meet you.' With his eyes looking deeply into mine, he lit another cigarette. I wanted to ask for one – as a prop to get closer to the luscious pecs that stretched the buttons of his shirt.

'I'd like a lift, if that's okay?' Marco continued to look at me as he posed the question to Brian.

'Aren't you going up in one of the official cars?'

'I've done my duty by the old man. He's got people all around him and I've had enough.'

'Not a problem,' Brian scowled. 'You can't smoke in the car.'

Marco looked with amusement at the freshly lit tip of his cigarette before throwing it to the ground and stepping on it with one well-shod foot. 'Whatever you want. It's your car.'

'You got that right.' Brian was belligerent.

'You shouldn't be so sensitive, cousin. Not in front of your friend.'

'She's not my friend. Marie knew Alex at school.'

'Then it should be okay for me to be her friend too.' He winked at me.

The brinkmanship was cut short by the arrival of Marie.

'Have you got room for me? I can't stand the thought of going up to the house with Dida and those hideous hangers-on.'

'Sure.' Brian opened the front passenger door and looked in my direction. Marie stepped forward and plonked herself down before he had a chance to offer it to me.

She pulled the seatbelt across her lap. 'Come on. The sooner we get this over, the sooner I can have a drink.'

I decided to make the most of the situation by sliding into the passenger seat behind Brian. That way I could enjoy the company of Marco without the scrutiny of his cousin. I wobbled my bottom deep into the seat and angled my body to face Marco, who had settled himself next to me.

Ah yes, I thought, assessing his perfect profile, this trip won't be so bad after all.

'Have you been in Croatia for long?' He turned and smiled, his voice a cigarette growl.

'Just two weeks. Leaving tomorrow afternoon.' Like wanton women everywhere, I hoped my smile was coquettish.

'Going to a funeral is a funny thing to do on your last day. How'd you get roped in?'

Marie's face was hidden by the ridiculous hat. A dipping of the head towards the back seat indicated she was listening.

'I ran into Marie at the beach yesterday. She asked if I'd come and I was happy to oblige.' To my ears the lie sounded sincere. 'Do you live here in Split?'

'Most of the time. Occasionally I go to Margaret River to check on the business for my grandfather. I'm like his eyes over there.'

Looking in the rear-view mirror, I saw Brian grimace, barely containing himself from making a riposte.

'It's good to see that Marie has such loyal friends,' continued Marco. 'And such good-looking ones. That helps, hey, Brian?'

I blushed, not exactly comfortable in being used as a stick with which to poke his cousin but pleased at the compliment. Brian's hands gripped the wheel as though he was strangling the life out of Marco.

'It's nice for Marie to have someone here for support.' Brian's response was one of restrained politeness. 'I don't really notice what my little sister's acquaintances look like.'

Marco roared with laughter; I squirmed, and Marie pulled tissues and make-up from her bag in a 'nothing to see here' kind of way. Brian shot off a look of satisfaction at Marco, as though he had scored points.

If testosterone had substance, it would have completely fogged up the car. I looked out the window, thinking a judicious silence was the best retreat. After fifteen minutes I felt a light touch on my arm. I turned towards Marco, who had dropped his hand to rest on the seat next to my thigh. I felt the heat of his fingers through the fabric of my dress.

'Your grandfather appears to be holding up well.'

'You have met him before?'

'I did see him a few times when he visited Perth. That was a long time ago.'

'He hasn't changed.'

'No, he's still very commanding.' I wondered if Marco was open to questions. 'Jure's brother certainly caused a stir. What do you think that was all about?'

Marco didn't look at me, but I felt the twitch of his fingers against my thigh.

'I have no idea.'

'It wasn't appropriate.'

'No one will care about the ravings of a half-bred idiot. Certainly not my grandfather.' Marco's handsome face was impassive, but there was an edge to his tone. 'He wouldn't waste energy on such a man.'

'Is he that far removed from these people?'

'Of course he is. Dida has the kind of power that no one questions. It's part of the Puharich mystique.'

Sitting in the back seat with Marco, I experienced some of this magnetism. Although dark and brooding, I was happy for this magic to be 'an art lawful as eating'. And there were so many ways to imagine sinking teeth into Marco. A not-unpleasant shiver ran down my spine. 'There's the old saying that power corrupts.'

'My grandfather makes the rules that are best for everyone.'

'There were men like that in Australia during the eighties and they all came a cropper.'

'Some men can't hold their nerve. And they take stupid risks. My grandfather has never done either.' Marco tipped his chin up, proud and audacious.

'You obviously revere your grandfather.'

'He's been a great mentor for me. He believes the talent for leadership runs in families.' He looked towards his cousin. 'Though it skips some. What do you think, Brian?'

'I think you're like any other hanger-on of Dida's. Reflected glory, isn't it?'

I watched muscles ripple along Marco's jaw as he clenched his teeth.

The ill will between the men was becoming tiresome. I leaned forward to get Marie's attention. 'Did you get the photos of Caitlin that you wanted to show me?'

Marie gave me a look of gratitude. 'Yeah, I did.' She rummaged around in her bag and handed me a thin A5 folio of prints. 'She's the best thing that's ever happened to me.'

I took the album and leaned back into my seat. A rotund baby turned into a toddler with chubby thighs and sparkly brown eyes. Glossy black curls sprung out at all angles. In picture after picture, her cheeks were cherry red, and her smile suggested she was laughing to burst.

'She looks very sweet.'

'More than sweet. Caitlin is clever, well up on the average. She'll be able to take over the business by the time she's ten.'

We laughed. Neither Brian or Marco found it amusing. I sensed Marie, under her hat, was working up to *the* question.

'Do you think you'll have children?'

I gave my standard response. 'I can't even keep a boyfriend at the moment.'

Brian caught my eye in the rear-view mirror and gave me a wink. I thought about opening the car door and leaping out. But I was inexperienced in diving from moving cars: it would mean scratches, torn stockings and ruined shoes. And abandoning the delectable Marco.

From the front seat, Marie gave the predictable reply: 'You had better hurry up. Being a mother is such a gift.'

Despite having the great, albeit daffy example of my own mother, I wasn't convinced my uterus was suitable for habitation. 'I dunno. It's a big responsibility.'

Marie altered her voice: gone was cheery, replaced with something more ambiguous. 'It's not until you become a mother that you realise how great is the urge to protect another human being. They don't even have to be your own. In my culture, the old babas are the most ferocious type of mother.'

'What's a baba?' I had a picture of lemon sponges dripping with rum.

'They're the old women who take care of children as though they are their own. Those women are much more possessive than the real grandmothers.'

'How do you get a baba?'

'They hitch themselves onto powerful families from their villages. It's a way to get a better life.'

Brian took a hand off the wheel and slapped his sister's arm. 'Don't be cynical. Our baba was wonderful.'

'She was your baba, not mine. Always making it very clear that you were her first love.' Marie turned slightly in my direction. 'Possessive old bitches if you ask me. Particularly of their boys.'

Marco shifted in his seat. 'You're bitter and twisted. Afraid that babas are better at mothering than you are?'

Whoa! The air in the car was getting so frosty, I expected icicles to start forming on Brian's prodigious nose.

Before she could reply, Brian spoke. 'Stop it.' I wasn't sure who he was addressing. 'Our babas sacrifice so much. Leaving their own families to take care of us.'

'And there he says something with which I can agree.' Marco tapped the back of Brian's seat. 'They are exceptional women.' He looked at me. 'You might learn a thing or two.'

Maria turned and sat back in her seat before I could ask further questions about these uber-mums. It left me to flick through the photo album and to wonder if I'd ever develop that tiger-like maternal instinct. Given that I'd once killed a cactus by under-watering, I doubted my ovaries would ever do the fandango with a fertilising fish.

~

We reached the overflow of mourners' cars parked along the road about a kilometre before we got to the house. Instead of looking for a space among the vehicles crammed on both sides of the road, Brian continued to drive until we were halted by enormous wrought iron gates flanked by two men in dark suits, both wired with earphones, their eyes hidden by black wrap-around sunglasses. The guy on the left-hand side of the gate walked forward to talk to Brian. They had a quick exchange in Croatian before the guard looked down a list on a clipboard. He stopped at a line and gave a large tick with a slowness suggesting he was new to the ticking business.

Brian looked towards the other Dark Glasses to open the gate. This one spoke into a microphone hanging loosely on his lapel and the gates swung inward. As we moved forward, I noticed the bulge of a gun and holster underneath the jacket of the ticker.

'Are firearms a normal thing for a Croatian wake?' It was an attempt at levity.

Marie turned around and poked her head through the gap in the seats, her hat squashing inward to form a feathered beak. 'My grandfather is very security conscious.'

The grandfather needed to be a much more powerful man than the average cheesemaker to warrant this type of security, even in Croatia. Though where were the security 'personnel' when Jure was supposedly shooting a bullet into Zorka's head?

Another tap on my arm from Marco diverted my attention.

'Don't clog up your brain cells trying to work it all out.' His look was one of well-practised smoulder. 'Croatians do a number of things differently to Australians.'

'So I've noticed.'

'For example, there are a whole array of talents Croatian men have that you probably haven't had time to discover.'

'I can imagine.' I lowered my voice in what I hoped were alluring tones.

His fingers played a little rat-ta-tat-tat on the back of my hand. 'This could well turn into a long and pleasant evening.'

Unabashed at this less-than-original line, I nodded. 'Maybe.'

A hormone-fuelled silence settled heavily in the back seat while Brian manoeuvred the Mercedes into a parking spot. He'd barely stopped the car before jumping out and opening my door.

We were on an expansive paved area at the back of a very substantial house. Its two storeys seemed to tower over the concourse where dozens of cars were lined up. The house had a flat façade with rows of windows and a huge wooden door, slightly off-centre. Drapes drawn tightly meant there was no view into the ground-floor rooms. The building was covered in white stucco with terracotta roof tiles, the high pitch finishing at the edge of the walls, leaving no room for eaves. A wide path to the right led to a small cottage about three hundred metres from the big house. This little house was much more to my liking. It was covered in a profuse bougainvillea that almost obliterated the leadlight windows. A single storey, it had a low slate roof with a slightly open dormer window, its net curtain sucked in and out by a gentle breeze. It was very cute and romantic.

'That's where I found them.' Brian's breath was hot against my cheek.

'Jesus, you scared me. Don't creep around.'

'Sorry. That's where Jure and Zorka lived.'

'Yeah. Thanks.' Thoughts of cuteness and romance evaporated. 'It looks much older than the big house.'

'It's the original cottage where our fathers were born and raised.'

'It's lovely. I would have been sorry to move.'

'My grandmother was dead by then, so Dida was unencumbered.' Marco's voice suggested she had become surplus to needs.

Brian shifted his body to stand in front of me, blocking his cousin. 'A new house, with all the mod cons is critical to maintaining the status quo. It's important to show the community that times are good. My grandfather's big new house made everyone feel like a success.'

Conspicuous consumption as a community service? This was a take on ostentation I'd not heard before.

Marco went behind me and lightly touched the small of my back. 'Come on, Alex. Let's get the burial out of the way. Then we can share a glass of wine.'

'Wine sounds good.' I imagined an extra piquant bouquet when sipped with such a divine creature.

Brian took my arm. 'I'll make sure you get a glass of the best when we come back.'

Marco looked at him with amusement, then turned his gaze on me. 'I'll come and find you later. Then I'll show you some real Croatian culture.'

With a suggestive raising of one eyebrow, he turned and walked away, leaving me in a flutter of anticipation.

I unhitched my arm from Brian's and swivelled towards Marie, who had been leaning against the car watching our three-way drama. 'I'll be fine. Marie will take care of me. You go ahead and be with your grandfather.'

Couched in those terms, he wasn't going to refuse. 'Fine.' He gave his sister a significant look. 'I'll see you both later.'

Marie and I watched him stride around the corner of the building. We dawdled at the rear, sharing an unspoken reluctance to participate in the last funereal rituals. Then Marie stopped altogether, putting her hand on the rough render of the house as if she would go no further.

'What's up?' I said. 'If we don't get a move on, the whole thing'll be over. Then your grandfather will be pissed off with you.'

'Yeah, probably. I'm tired of the lot of it.' She bent over to pull a weed out of the pavers. 'I've got a confession.'

'I'm not a Catholic,' I said.

'Neither am I anymore.'

We stopped and stood face-to-face, or rather, face-to-hat. A babble of voices and snatches of sonorous music came from a distance. There was no one else in sight.

'I feel frightened here.'

'Well, people are dead. And there's nothing natural about the way they died. Your fear is understandable.'

'I don't understand what happened.'

'Brian seems to think it was all cut and dried.'

'Brian has a blind spot where our grandfather is concerned. Even from Croatia, Dida has watched and supported my brother's progress since he was at high school, so Brian is loyal and protective to a fault. It's the same for all of his grandchildren, particularly the boys. To them, he's almost a deity.'

'So, what do you think?'

'I don't know. I've never heard of Croatians being this organised and moving this fast.'

'Why do you reckon things have gone so quickly?'

'Who knows? That's the point.' She tipped her head, making her hat tilt to reveal a fuller view of her troubled face. 'Jure and Zorka get their brains blown all over the kitchen. Then the coroner passes a verdict immediately and now they're putting them in the ground. All within a few days. You know about these things. Surely that can't be right.'

I shook my head. 'I'm not an expert, even at home. Doing the police rounds isn't much of a qualification. But to hazard a guess, I'd say it's pretty speedy.'

'Yeah.' Marie was subdued. 'Why stick them in the ground this quickly?'

'I don't know the system or the old people. Had you met them before?'

'Of course, heaps. Every time I came over here, and then they'd stay with us when they came to Australia. They loved Margaret River. Could hardly wait to get there from the minute they touched down.'

Was it possible that Jure and Zorka were dedicated foodies like me? Surely, they didn't go for the surfing.

'My grandfather organised the trips,' Marie continued 'They seemed to be part of their wages and most of the time they'd come with a truckload of baggage. Dida loaded them up with paperwork, instructions and goodness knows what else to take down south. I suppose it was their reward for being so loyal.' She lowered her voice to a whisper. 'What if it's some kind of cover-up?'

'Who by?'

'The coroner. The police. Maybe someone bribed the officials.'

'For what purpose?'

'So someone can now get at my grandfather.'

'I have to admit, the man who rocked up to the church was a bit strange. It all got a little out of control for a moment. Though, from what I've seen, your grandfather is pretty much untouchable.'

Marie sighed, 'Yeah. The police are probably investigating Jure's brother as we speak.'

'I'm sure it's as straightforward as it seems.'

If a liar's pants really were combustible, I was about to get third degree burns on my arse. The police weren't going to look further into the deaths of Zorka and Jure. Why should they? Grandfather Puharich had wanted it dealt with quickly. They complied. If there was a cover-up, it was at his behest. I had no doubt the file had been buried in the archives, if they'd bothered to open a file in the first place.

At that moment one of the security men appeared. He pointed towards the left of the building and yelled. Using international sign language, I flipped him the bird as Marie pulled me away.

No one noticed us merge into the back of the crowd. They were all too busy leaning forward to watch the coffins being lowered into the ground. Up on tippy-toe, I tried to see the proceedings. This is my favourite part of a funeral. Every hair on my body stands on end with the tension of watching a coffin clunk against the sides of the hole. In my mind's eye, I can see the lid coming loose and sliding right off, revealing the dead body: bluey-white with eye shadow, rouge and lippy applied by undertakers in an effort to make it look 'alive'.

Both coffins were put into the same grave: a husband and wife together for eternity, whether they liked it or not. The crowd was dispersed among the large, ostentatious headstones of the Puharich dead. A heavily decorated fence, about six-foot tall with spear-shaped tips, surrounded the area, much of it still grassed, waiting for future generations.

I wondered why Zorka and Jure, who were not family, were being buried in the Puharich plot. The appearance of the brother at the church proved they had family of their own. I assumed there was a little plot somewhere in the mountains where the bodies of generations of the Simich family lay under the gaze of a sad porcelain Madonna whose outstretched arms protected and gave solace. Yet, here they were, in the corner of another family's cemetery, a space impossible to visit, where flowers could not be left. For the Puharich family, this was probably the safest option. The local constabulary was never going to ask the Puhariches if they might dig up the bodies of Jure and Zorka, on the remote chance the angry brother was able to get another investigation. The burial of the old retainers in a cemetery, far away from seething siblings, was extremely convenient.

Once everyone had wandered up and thrown a handful of dirt into the pit and crossed themselves to give thanks it wasn't them in the box, there was a rush to get out. It was clear I wasn't the only one who was hungry and in need of a beverage.

Marie turned to me. 'Let's go back up to the house and grab something before the hoards descend. We can go out the back gate.' She headed in the opposite direction to everyone else. 'Please don't mention what I said to Brian or Marco. I'm probably overly tired and they'll tease me for being hysterical.'

'It's okay. I won't say a thing. But I want you to know, I agree with you.'

CHAPTER FIVE

The walk back from the little cemetery gave me the first view of the mansion from the front. It had an enormous portico rising the full two storeys, which sheltered three sets of windows on each side of elaborately carved front doors. Mechanically operated shutters were closed over all the windows, making the house look like a highly decorated giant bunker. Having gasped my way up the hill, I stopped under the portico and turned to take in the view. I had to hand it to Marie's grandfather, he'd picked a sensational site to put his palace. A formal Italianate garden spread in terraces. Closely mown lawns, small neat hedges, shaped conifers and an array of garden ornaments were arranged along precise steps. On the other side of the furthest hedge, wild grass and native bushes took over, giving a peasant frill to the formal regularity. Beyond this fringe, the cattle pastures began; bovine clusters speckled the slope and spread into the valley. I could see for miles, right to the Biokovo Range that rose magnificently on the other side of the valley. Without the music, which had started up on a hi-fi somewhere in the house, the silence would have been absolute. No wonder Grandfather Puharich had such a sense of self-importance. He was the king of a sensational domain.

'Beautiful, isn't it?' Marie whispered.

'Completely wonderful. I can see why Jure and Zorka didn't mind looking after your grandfather all this time. I'd be happy to babysit for this.'

She laughed. 'This view doesn't compensate for the isolation.'

'I dunno. It might be easy to get used to.'

'Alex, apart from the fact it's a long way to the nearest café, you couldn't live so far away from the sea. Think about it. A two-hour round trip to the nearest beach, and that's in summer traffic. You can forget winter. Most of the roads are closed to everything except the heaviest snow vehicles.'

'What's snow if it isn't cold water?' Of course, Marie was right. I was carried away with visions of me churning butter and singing Julie Andrews tunes. I knew the reality was not my scene. 'Come on, where's the wine?'

She looked at me slyly. 'I think Marco was the first one to offer you wine.'

'And I have delivered.' A hand holding two glasses appeared at my side. 'At the mere mention of my name, you have conjured me up.'

'Like an evil spirit.' Marie didn't take the proffered glass.

I wasn't deterred. 'Thanks. I've been gagging for this.'

'Better be careful, Alex. My dear cousin might be right. Maybe you should call me Bacchus from now on.' He winked, and Marie groaned.

'Salute.' We clicked glasses and looked towards the mountains.

'Let me guess what you're thinking.' Marco had positioned his body to block Marie. 'The house, you think, is a complete horror. A monstrous blot on the landscape. The view, however, has you absolutely captivated.'

'Maybe.'

'No "maybe" about it. You Aussie girls are all the same. Sentimental. Romantic. You think people like us, Croatian peasants, should be happy to live in thatched roofed cottages, tending vegetable gardens and killing our own meat.'

There was an unexpected edge to his voice. I bristled at the implied criticism.

'That's not an accurate assessment at all.' I took a sip of wine. 'It's true that this isn't the kind of architecture I like. That's not to say your grandfather doesn't have a right to it. You're being defensive. Had an unhappy love affair with an Aussie girl?'

'Didn't take you long to get around to my love life.'

'Oh, please!' Marie pulled a face. 'I'm out of here. Alex, I'll look for you later. After Marco has finished with his shit. I should go and see Dida.'

She turned and disappeared through one of the doors, leaving me with her dangerously sexy cousin.

But the flirty conversation, underpinned with a certain 'come-hitherness', was not to eventuate. After a pause in which he looked moodily to the mountains, I asked, 'Have you had the opportunity to speak with your grandfather?'

'Briefly. Everyone wants to have a word with him at the moment.'

'They feel concern. He'll have to find a new caretaker and housekeeper.'

'That's not it – they're doing it to prove they were here. None of these gutless bastards want my grandfather to think they didn't come.' He finished his glass in one gulp. 'Australia pretends to be a democracy. People like you don't get to see who really runs the place. Over here it's different. Everything's transparent. People know my grandfather is boss and he'll look after them if they do the right thing. Just like they know the consequences if they do the wrong thing.'

'What are the consequences?' An image of a blasted skull sprang to mind.

Marco's face was inscrutable. 'They're more clear-cut than where you come from. Sometimes people need a reminder of how the system works.'

'You'll need to explain this system to me.'

Marco looked at me in surprise, as though he'd just realised how the tone had changed. 'Jure was a strange old coot. Been living in the hills for too long. And he was a Serb, not good genes.'

'Serbs probably say the same thing about Croatians.'

He laughed. 'No doubt. The difference is that we're right. How about you stay here and I'll go and find us another drink?'

'What say you go and find us a whole bottle.' There was little point in holding back. It was the last night of my summer holiday and I was going to make the most of it.

As he walked away, I scanned the crowd, watching the mourners as they eagerly entered the house. Marco wasn't gone for long before I had to use the loo. It's one of the mysteries of the universe that, when you need to stay put, your bladder decides its reached maximum capacity. I needed to find the bathroom before my Bacchus returned with the bottle of bubbles. I followed the crowds into the house.

~

The interior was hardly a revelation. I expected a certain rich 'ethnic' style and it was there in truckloads. The entry hall had the proportions of a small ballroom. The ceiling rose the full two stories, its height exaggerated by a deep, wide dome whose surface was covered in a mural depicting a quaint scene. Merry-looking shepherds tended to frothy white sheep and goats while lovely maidens in aprons and stiff caps carried bouquets of flowers. Around the rim of the mural, bumptious cupids were chasing each other trailing daisy chains.

The foot of the staircase was at least three metres wide, each step a single slab of marble, climbing steeply before curving to the left. I leaned forward to catch a glimpse of the second floor, but there was only more marble and walls covered in garish interpretations of Tintoretto masterpieces. The same subjects featured in the tapestries hanging on heavy gold chains around the walls of the entrance hall. Everything was big and gloomy and cold. The huge chandelier hanging low from the middle of the dome did little to brighten the scene.

It was obvious Marie's grandfather didn't want people wandering into other parts of the house. Four sets of double doors on each side of the entry were closed and guarded by the impassive forms of the black-clad men who had greeted us at the gate. The only toing-and-froing was going on around the back of the staircase. This, I guessed, was where the kitchen and toilets were to be found.

Unable to see a sign to the bathroom, I jiggled on one foot and then the other until I fell in with a giggling clutch of women who walked past with bulging cosmetic bags.

Sitting on the loo was a bizarre experience in itself. The ceramic cistern was covered in cupids whose little bows had arrows pointed straight at my bare bum. Inside the bowl, ivy twisted in circles, its bright green leaves obviously thriving on wee.

I pushed the belly of a jolly sprite and joined the chattering masses at the dual vanity which was topped with gold fixtures in the shape of flying swans. On the wall above the sinks was a mirror partly decorated with the same puffy-cheeked cherubs that cavorted in the stalls. With the cracks of their arses framing my face, I patched up my mascara, blotted my make-up and applied an extra thick coat of lipstick. Having renewed myself, I returned to the hall.

The smell of cooking food made me register my hunger. From the other side of the stairway, waiters were emerging with heaped trays. They were immediately pounced upon by mourners whose gnashing teeth could be heard above the cacophony of voices.

Fighting through the crowd might see me miss my rendezvous with Marco. I surmised that going through the kitchen and around the outside was the quicker route. By following one of the waiters, I found myself amidst a staggering amount of food. Platters were piled high with pickled vegetables, great chunks of cheese and kilos of sliced ham. Other platters were covered in bite-sized fish, scrolls of beef, and lamb meatballs. The smell, the noise, the whole freakish commotion of it, was overwhelming.

I walked among the benches looking for an exit to get me back outdoors. Grabbing balls of cheese and pieces of bread, I made my way past a long row of tables covered with food like a feast in a fairy tale. Only the thought of the luscious lips of Marco stopped me from throwing myself among the chocolate *madarica* and *kremšnita*.

At the far end of the room was a heavy door. Pushing it open, I found myself in an enormous garden. Beds of every imaginable vegetable spread out in straight lines. Tomatoes and beans twisted up frames, and down one side a trellis of grapevines formed a border between the garden and a road going at right angles halfway down its length. I wandered towards the road, popping cherry tomatoes and grapes into my mouth.

On the opposite side of the house to the cemetery, the road curved away towards another building whose modernity was out of place. High white walls and a pitched roof dotted with air conditioning and refrigeration ducts were a contradiction to the bucolic surroundings. Was this where the cheese was made? Not for the first time in my life, curiosity got the better of me. Marco could wait while I took a quick peek. I broke into a trot, conscious that at any moment one of the guards might discover me.

Arriving at the building, I was astonished to find the door unlocked. This was a thrilling turn of events. I pushed it open and found myself in a room dominated by stainless-steel benches. The whirr of enormous refrigerators along the back wall blocked out all other sounds. On the counters were wooden racks holding glass test tubes, and piles of shallow ceramic dishes were stacked neatly at intervals along the shining silver surfaces. Gas burners periodically jutted up through the benches and deep sinks were positioned at the ends. Everything was meticulously clean. The air was cool and smelt faintly of antiseptic. I knew nothing about the manufacturing of fromage, yet even with my scant understanding, the room wasn't very cheesy. The space had the look and feel of a laboratory rather than the artisanal cheese-making which Brian had described.

Distracted, I didn't notice Marco until his hand gripped my shoulder.

'You're a long way from the wine.'

It was not so much a jump as a whole-body spasm that responded to his touch. I choked on an intake of breath.

'Oh my god! What is it about you Puhariches and sneaking?'

He kept his hand on my shoulder as I twisted around to face him. 'Do you always wander around other peoples' property?'

'No.' My voice was a dry croak. 'I had to go to the ladies.'

'Does this look like a bathroom?'

'No. Of course not. I thought I was taking a short cut to get back to our meeting place.'

'So, on the way you decided to poke around our property?'

'I'm not poking. I found myself in the vegie garden and saw this building. My curiosity was piqued.'

'My grandfather doesn't take kindly to people wandering about.'

'Your grandfather likes to exercise his power. He's an interesting man. Great interview subject.'

He put a finger on my lips. 'Interview Dida? There are better ways to occupy our time.'

With that, he stepped forward, slid his hands around my waist and pulled me towards his chest. I tipped my head back and felt his breath across my cheek before his lips pressed against mine. The smooch would have been perfect for the cover of a bodice ripper. It was hot and soft and slurpy in exactly the right way.

CHAPTER SIX

On the plane the next day, I was still having hot flushes and tingling lips every time I thought of that kiss. It had completely distracted me and like every experienced Lothario I had thus far known, he left me wanting more. But it was not to be.

Any aspirations for more advanced exchanges of bodily fluids were blown apart when Brian exploded into the room.

'What are you doing in here?'

'I guess I got lost,' I said.

'I'm not talking to you.' My whole body blushed. 'What are you doing Marco?'

'It's none of your business.'

'You shouldn't be here. The lab is out of bounds, particularly for non-family.' Brian, then Marco, looked accusingly at me.

What the hell? Moments ago we'd almost been giving each other a tonsillectomy. I opened my mouth to defend myself. Marco immediately held up his hand.

'I was in the carpark and saw Alex walk down here. What idiot left the door unlocked?'

'Not me. I haven't been in here this trip. You're meant to be in charge of security. It's your fuck-up.'

Marco moved towards Brian. Both men clenched their fists. For the first time I saw how the hard planes of their faces revealed a family resemblance.

I stepped forward. 'Boys! Come on. This is no way to behave at a funeral.'

They ignored me.

'You're an inconsequential legal clerk to my grandfather,' said Marco.

'*Our* grandfather.' Brian pushed him away.

'What is this place?' I said. 'It looks like a science lab. How can you experiment on a chunk of edam?'

'Leave it, Alex.'

Here was a Brian I didn't recognise. His whole body was rigid with bitter fury.

'Go away, Brian. You can't throw your weight around over here. You're pathetic.'

'And you're a prick.'

An electric silence buzzed around them as they stared each other down.

'That's enough!' My voice had enough force to make them look at me. 'This is my fault, Brian. I went to the ladies, got distracted and ended up down here. Marco came to find me.'

Marco sneered. 'I don't need a woman to make excuses for me.'

I turned my body towards Brian, trying not to show my hurt. 'I'm sorry. I didn't intend to cause trouble.'

Marco leaned in towards Brian. 'What's *your* excuse for wandering around?'

'I've been watching you.'

'Spying or jealous?'

'Get lost! This is our intellectual property in here and you left it unlocked. You let a stranger come in. You're as useless as your father.'

This hit a nerve. Marco's anger stiffened every fibre in his body. When he spoke, his voice was low and strained with rage. 'Let's leave our fathers out of it. They are both useless. The choice is you or me to take over. And Dida won't look to you.'

'Says who?'

'Me. The whole lot will pass from him to me. And you'll be the first out the door.'

'I think we should wait and see. I know where all the skeletons are buried.'

Some dark emotion crossed the surface of Marco's handsome face. But it was fleeting.

'Can I interrupt?' I waved my hand between them. 'Let's go back to the house and act like normal people.'

'Not possible. You're in Croatia now, Dorothy. Normal doesn't live here.'

Marco shifted his tone to one resembling his former flirtatious self. 'Let's meet up once you get bored with Brian. Say, five minutes?' He laughed and pushed his cousin to one side. Then he strode to the door and disappeared.

The refrigerators hummed and somewhere a tap was dripping, the water making a cracking sound as it hit the stainless steel.

'You shouldn't be in here.' Brian didn't look at me, instead he focused on a point over my right shoulder.

'I wasn't expecting the door to be unlocked,' I said. 'Too curious for my own good sometimes. It comes with being a journalist.' I surveyed the room. 'What is this place?'

'It's where our food technologists experiment with different forms of mould and new ways to preserve the product without affecting the taste.'

'Sounds interesting. Worth a story because I'm sure most people have no idea how complicated cheese can be.'

'Progress in production is about experimentation. What we do here is our intellectual property. You can't write about that.'

'Of course.'

'This is meant to be secure. The fucking door should have been locked.'

It was the first time I'd heard Brian swear. He seemed as surprised as I was.

'My apologies for my language. Don't write anything without passing it by me first. Terrible shame if we had to take you to court.'

I wasn't sure if he was joking; his face revealed nothing.

'And now we go.'

Brian didn't so much as lead me from the room, as frogmarch me out. He turned to lock the door and punched in a code before taking my hand and dragging me back up the hill, through the vegie garden and into the main hall where the air was heavy with cigarette smoke and the belches of three hundred tipsy Croatians.

The old man was seated on an enormous chair, positioned in front of double doors like an ancient Rottweiler guarding who knows what. His chauffeur was to his right. Every so often, a person broke away from the main group and approached the old man. They stood stiffly, periodically bending forward to listen to him speak. After a short exchange, they'd bow their heads and hurry back into the boisterous crowd.

~

Brian didn't leave my side for the rest of the afternoon and into the night. My sole opportunity for freedom were visits to the ladies, which increased in frequency as I sipped my way through glasses of white, red and bubbles. By ten o'clock I'd reached my tipping point. One more glass would lead to bare feet, dancing on tables and a lousy hangover.

'I need to go, Brian.'

'Really?'

'I'm at my limit and I have to get up early.'

'You're lacking in sticking power?'

'I can't do this Croatian thing. Where do you all put it?'

'Takes practice. We start with wine and water when we're little kids.' He shrugged. 'I'll get them to bring my car to the front.'

'No need to take me. You'd be driving over the limit.'

'You don't seriously believe there is such a thing as over the limit here?'

After too many hours with the Puhariches, I was beginning to understand that rules and regulations were a matter of personal choice rather than governmental authority. 'I'm sure someone is leaving to go back to Split and I can taxi from there.'

Brian looked at me sceptically. 'What taxi do you think you'll get at this time of night?'

'I don't want you to leave on my account. Surely your grandfather expects you to hang around until the bitter end?'

'Don't worry. I'll go and say goodbye and we'll head off.' He waved at someone across the room. Marie appeared at my side. 'I'm taking Alex home. Can you keep her company while I see Dida?'

'Sure.'

Marie had ditched the hat, leaving her hair fused to her head. Black tufts stuck out at right angles over her ears. With bright cheeks and lips red-wine stained, it was clear Marie had gone beyond her own tipping point. Her eyes wandered over my face, unable to focus.

'Brian loves you, and you should love him.'

'That's the wine talking, Marie.'

'No, no. You make the cutest couple.' She gave a winey burp. ''Scuse me. We could hang out like old times.'

'I don't think you can get back old times.'

'Course you can.' She swayed in front of me. 'Please come down to Margaret River.'

'I would like to.'

'You must!' Her voice was, at the same time, wobbly and emphatic. 'Come and write about us.'

'Absolutely. I'd love to see your business. Brian says it's very successful.'

'It is. My dad and uncle don't understand how things have changed. It's all about branding these days. And we have to listen to our consumers. They're our bread and cheese.' A gurgle was the closest she got to a laugh.

'I promise to sample as much as I can. I can write a review on your best cheese.'

Brian reappeared and put his hand on Marie's shoulder. 'My sister is always talking about marketing as though we make mass-produced curdled milk masquerading as cheese. She forgets we make finely crafted fromage. It's partly why she's not involved in the business.'

'What are the other reasons?' I asked.

'Dida doesn't believe women belong in the workforce. We have a very multi-faceted organisation that's hard enough for me to get my head around, let alone a woman.'

Marie rolled her eyes. 'Yes, women are too unsophisticated to understand cheese.'

'Just a joke.' His smile seemed slightly cruel. 'Don't worry, Marie, Alex has already agreed to come down with me at the end of the month.'

'Good! That's fabulous. I can't wait.' She gave me a booze-clumsy hug.

Brian turned his sister around and gave her a little push in the direction of the front door. She staggered off.

'The end of the month?' I had no intention of visiting Margaret River in two weeks! His arrogance was mind-boggling.

'You agreed to come down with me the next time I went. And that's at the end of the month.'

He took my hand and bustled me out the front door. One of the mafia-types was doubling as a valet and Brian's Mercedes was parked, its engine idling, at the side of the portico. Brian opened my door and grinned at me.

'You don't actually have to travel down south with me.' He walked to the driver's side and got in. 'You can bring your own car and have the freedom to go around and see a bit. I'll be too busy to act as your tour guide every day, so I'll make sure there are plenty of samples. We do a very popular high tea every Friday, Saturday and Sunday afternoon from two.'

'I'll see, Brian. I'm not making any promises.'

'Great! I'll organise your accommodation.'

Jesus. What was wrong with these people?

I was too tired to argue. We'd only just driven through the gates when I fell asleep. I woke up aware that Brian's hand was on my knee and dribble had saturated the collar of my dress. My tongue felt like it was stuck between the gap in my front teeth and my eyes were glued together with mascara. I looked towards Brian, my lashes forming a gluggy grille.

'How long to go?'

'About ten minutes.' He tapped my knee. 'You snore.'

'Well, that's embarrassing.'

'I thought it was cute.'

Good grief. Asleep and snoring was a level of intimacy I was not prepared to share with Brian. I shuffled about in my seat, pulling my dress down, making him drop his hand. I obstinately looked out the window, refusing to converse, until we pulled up at the B&B.

'Here we are.' He got out and walked around the car to help me. I had no choice but to accept; my legs were rubber and my head felt like it was on a spring. He walked me to the door.

It was *that* moment. He was opening his mouth like the back of a garbage truck, so I knew he was going in for the whole enchilada. With a swiftness I didn't think possible in my current state, I stood on tiptoes and dabbed a clumsy kiss on each cheek.

'Thanks for taking me and bringing me home. It's been quite a day.'

He didn't hide his disappointment. 'I'm glad you came. Shall I see you to your room?'

'No need. I'll be fine from here.'

He had to move away. Persisting was too demoralising, even for Brian. I went inside, turning to give him a wave before shutting the door. Leaning my back against it, I closed my eyes and tried to gather my scattered senses.

'You are back.'

The voice of my hostess made me drop my clutch.

I bent to pick it up. 'Why wouldn't I be back?'

'You went with that man. I have rosary all day for you.'

With that, she returned to her TV, leaving me to stumble up the stairs wondering why I needed the rosary.

CHAPTER SEVEN

Thirty-six hours after grilling myself under the Croatian sun, I disembarked to be hit with a brisk south-westerly and a five-degree winter morning in Perth. After an hour in the immigration line, then another hour at the baggage claim, I pushed my cart through the final door and into the arrival area, where a sea of faces looked at me expectantly. Shoulders drooped when they saw I was not their nearest and dearest. Walking past a long line of crestfallen faces, I sought out one who might be glad to see me home. Clearing the main throng, I recognised the beaming smile that was only for me.

'Darling, darling! Welcome home.' I was enveloped in my mother's floral-scented embrace and felt the hard pressure of the crystals she tucked into pockets sewn into her clothes. Jessica was the Earth goddess who had discovered New Age before it became fashionable. While other mothers in the 1980s were building cathedral-like shoulder pads into their tennis dresses, my mother adopted flowing cheesecloth and hand-made sandals. During school pick-ups, the other mums were polite – after all Jessica was married to Judge Grant – but she was never invited to their afternoon champagne teas or to be on their charity committees. I'd never asked her if she minded the snubs. She was probably too busy traversing other spirit dimensions to bother about them, although Jess was always very happy to fix their auras if they had asked.

It took us quite some time wandering around the carpark to find her little Mini Minor. Jessica moved vaguely down each row telling me she had parked next to a red convertible. When we found her car next to a black four-wheel drive, she put herself and her crystals behind the wheel and we put-putted out of the airport and onto the road home.

My mother's conversation was a mix of happenings during my absence and questions about my holiday. Although she didn't fly (her vacations were taken in the landscapes of her inner consciousness), she was fascinated by other places and the people who inhabited them. Our conversation bubbled along in a pattern that always gave me comfort and a quiet joy.

'Did you see anyone from home you know? I saw in the cards that your path intersected with familiar people.'

'Actually, I did. Do you remember the Puharich family?'

'No, I don't think so.'

'Marie was at school with me. The girl with big hair. She wore the huge purple taffeta dress to the year twelve ball.'

'Of course. She had that brother. The one with the unfortunate nose.'

I laughed. 'The very one. I bumped into them a couple of days ago.'

'I seem to remember a mother who spent her entire time cooking and indulging her son.'

'That's them. They asked me to their grandfather's funeral.'

'Their grandfather died?'

'Not exactly. He was at the centre of the whole thing, though it was his housekeeper and groundsman who died.'

'Let me guess,' said Jessica, 'the second one died of a broken heart.'

'They didn't die peacefully, Mum.' I was not keen on disrupting my mother's sweet cheerfulness. 'It seems the old man shot his wife and then himself. It was all rather grim.'

'How dreadful.'

'Pretty unsettling for everyone. But Marie's grandfather took it all in his stride.'

'I imagine he would.'

'Did you know him? I was introduced to him once.'

'We saw him quite a few times back then. It was in the days when there seemed to be dinner parties all the time and when we didn't have to sit around someone else's table, your father and I had to have them sit around ours. I'm sure the Puhariches were among them. The grandfather is surely too old to travel now?'

'His grandchildren seem to think so. I think he could rustle up the energy if he needed to.'

'He was a big man back then with a huge presence. Your father said he had the cunning of a rat.' She shook her head. 'Charles wasn't too keen on any of that family. They were heavily involved with a businessman who invested money for people, and then ran away to Poland.'

'So, they were dodgy?' I liked the idea. Crooks making cheese was an interesting angle. More appealing than straight-up reviews of their products. An exposé of the Puhariches might be more salacious.

'Oh, darling. Please don't jump to conclusions. They gave huge amounts of money to charity. They were probably among the most generous.'

'They're called tax minimisation schemes, Jess.'

'You sound like your father. How was Marie? And what has happened to that peculiar-looking brother?'

'They were both well, and Brian is still misshapen.'

'I remember him as an ambitious young man who wanted to take you out. He asked your father.'

'You're kidding! Charles never told me that.'

'He seemed to be quite smitten. He thought it was polite to ask. You were only sixteen.'

'What did Dad say?' I pictured an obsequious Brian sitting in 'my father's study.

'No idea. The boy did hang around for a while, even after you left home. I think he was actually more attracted to Charles than to you.'

'He still is.'

We both laughed. My father loathed sycophants. Charles' old-school politeness was probably too subtle a deterrent for Brian. At the time I wasn't offended by his transparent use of me to get close to my father. He wasn't to know my decision not to follow Charles into the law had irreversibly damaged our father–daughter relationship and that my father judged all my associates with a jaundiced eye.

The rest of the journey to my apartment was spent in descriptions of the food I had eaten and the beauty of the Dalmatian coast.

When driving, my mother knows two speeds: full-on or stopped. So, when my fence came into view, she didn't alter her speed until seconds before contact.

'Here we are. I think your apartment has probably missed you,' she trilled, as the smell of burnt tyres filled the car. 'And look, Benjamin is out to meet you.'

I looked up from the brace position and raised a hand at the best human being in the world who was, at that moment, walking around the corner of my apartment building.

The word 'apartment' is probably too posh to describe the place where I lay my head. Like a cheap toupée, it sits atop a mid-century house in spitting distance to one of the glorious beaches stretching along the length of Western Australian. Every morning, propping myself up in bed, I look through the triangular shapes of Norfolk Island Pines to see the blue of an ocean that went all the way to Africa. The entire house is owned by my father: the bigger ground-floor apartment is rented to Benjamin Arthur Reginald Murchison-Burrows. Ben Burrows and I were kids in primary school when we first met. His family seemed to own most of the scorching interior of Western Australia, so Ben was packed off to a private boys school in Perth where he could learn how to become appropriately condescending. The same age as my older brother James, Ben had rapidly become a pseudo-sibling, who treated me with more thoughtful affection than my real brother. He had a pathological need to do good and to be on the side of the righteous. He was an oddity in a household dominated by people with varying degrees of self-absorption. This innate sense of public service had led him to the police force where he'd become a senior detective in the Major Crime Squad.

Ben was waving back at me. He'd kept well clear of the fence where Jessica may or may not have stopped. After she turned the engine off, he walked over and opened my door.

'Hello, traveller. It's good to have you home.'

Ben pulled me in and gave me a tight hug, his wide shoulders curving around in a protective arc, squishing my nose against his chest.

'I'm so glad to see you.' My voice was muffled by muscles, body heat and the crisp cotton of his t-shirt.

He held me at arm's length and looked me up and down. 'Nice tan. And is that the beginnings of a double chin? Been eating your way around Dalmatia?'

'I'd hate to let you down.'

He laughed and tucked me under an armpit while he stooped to kiss my mother.

'We're glad you're back. Jess has been worried because your cards have been diabolical. She's kept me informed every day.'

'Oh, Jess. I was having a holiday. No need to stress.'

'I know, darling, it's just that I drew The Tower on three consecutive days.' She took my hand. 'You attract trouble. I don't want to see you hurt, or worse.'

I sighed. 'Why don't you go home, Mum? I'll come and see you when I'm back into my routine.'

She brushed her soft cheek against mine. 'I'm sure Benjamin will be much more useful than me.' With that, she floated back to the car, got in, reversed and accelerated away before I had a chance to get my bags from the boot.

I waved furiously at the rapidly disappearing Mini. 'Bloody hell. Seriously?'

Ben was laughing. 'You can get your stuff later.'

With arms around each other's waists, we went down the path to his front door. 'Come in with me. I've just made you breakfast with all your favourite things.'

'Thank god. Plane food is still ugly and the coffee tastes like paint stripper. You make me glad to be home.'

That was the thing about Ben – he was a carer. When he first came to live with us, his single-minded focus was on going to Duntroon and becoming an army officer. Then he realised he was gay and it politicised his world view. Sensibly, he recognised the army was probably not going to be kind to a 'poofter', so, still fixed on joining a service, he signed-up to the police force. I wasn't sure it'd be much better, but he became a one-man crusade trying to create change from within, rather than pushing shit uphill from the outside. The degree to which his colleagues liked and listened to him suggested he may have succeeded – either that, or everyone accepted he was a great bloke irrespective of his, or their, orientation.

It helped that Ben was a spunk. A six-foot four, tanned, muscular Mr Universe crossed with Hugh Grant at his most dapper. Women swoon, and guys get territorial the minute he walks into a room. I take great delight in watching the penny slowly drop: women stop pushing their bosoms against his chest and the blokes head back to the bar, knowing they have nothing to worry about. Some women don't get the vibe and they chirp and whisper in his ear, dropping notes with their phone numbers into his jacket pocket. I had lost count of the number of women under arrest who'd tried to seduce him in an effort to be let off. He tells me these stories with a sense of exasperation, while I roll around laughing. I find the entire concept of Ben as a handcuff-wielding, gun-toting Casanova absolutely hysterical.

We stepped into his bright, open-plan lounge-dining room and he pushed me into a chair at the table.

'Sit. I'll put everything together. You can pour us a coffee.' He moved to the kitchen while I filled two large mugs with a dark stream of caramel-perfumed black gold from a coffee pot.

The smell of frying eggs and the popping of bacon soon filled the air. Over the rim of my coffee cup, I watched as Ben whisked pancake batter, toasted bread and created some sort of juice extravaganza in the blender. Those who can cook, should definitely cook. Those of us who can't, should eat. That is my essential recipe for a good life. I have never used an oven or a slow cooker or even a mixer. However, I can set a beautiful table, match wines to food and eat a twelve-course degustation dinner without drawing breath. Between his culinary mastery and my palate, we made a dream dinner-party couple.

'Anything else interesting happen while I've been away?' I was salivating at all the delicious aromas.

'Not that I know of.'

'Work okay?'

'Yep. It's always quiet in winter. Too cold for criminals.'

'Then I got more action than you.'

He came to the table and set down a plate of eggs, one of bacon, and another stacked with pancakes dripping with butter and lemon juice.

'Really? Please tell me you didn't do something stupid like fall in love with a bloke who has a wife and six kids hidden away. Again!' He sat down.

'No. I had a wonderful, relaxing time on my own.' I put a bit of everything on my plate and began to eat. 'Ran into the Puhariches on the penultimate day.'

Ben stopped mid-chew and looked at me. 'Puharich? Isn't that the skinny lawyer with the expensive car and big nose?'

'That's him.'

'You went all the way to Croatia only to run into your one true love?'

'Oh, shut up. There were no dates. No nothing.'

'From what I remember, he was quite taken with you, braces and all.'

'I was merely the conduit to Charles.'

'How did you manage to unearth him in Croatia?'

'Seems he goes over every year to do something or other in the family business. They're all in the cheese-making caper.'

'Sounds like your perfect man.'

I stuffed another piece of pancake into my mouth. 'Being a Puharich is a big deal over there. I went to a family funeral that made my head explode.'

Ben looked startled. 'Why would you do that?'

Polishing off the rest of the breakfast, I related the story of blood and scattered brain matter dominating the last twenty-four hours of my holiday.

'Let me get this right,' said Ben, sitting back in his chair. 'You're lying on the beach. Proboscis Puharich bails you up and asks you to the funeral of people you do not know, and who have been murdered and/or committed suicide?'

'That about sums it up.'

'Only you could get caught up in something that bizarre, Alex.'

'I pride myself on doing the unexpected.'

'You've outdone yourself with this one.'

I picked a pancake crumb off my lap and popped it into my mouth. 'Do you know anything about the family?'

'Not much. I know that the Fraud boys looked into some of their business dealings at the time Goldberg was doing his creative accounting. I believe they were one of the first big investors in Margaret River. Other than that, I know nothing. They certainly haven't crossed into my patch.'

'No dead bodies over here?'

'Not that the police have found.'

'Not even skeletons? A few of those might be interesting.'

Ben shook his head.

'Shame.' Something scandalous added some colour and interest to Brian's beige personality. 'Brian's invited me down to Margaret River to see the creamery.'

'Well, that will be the end of their profits for the next decade.'

I giggled, burped and sneezed.

'You're all class, Alex.' Ben moved to my side, bent over and kissed the top of my head. 'If you go and get cleaned up, I'll make more coffee and give John in Fraud a call to see if he knows anything about them.'

'Thanks.'

Leaving the table, I gave him a hug then climbed the external staircase to my little unit. I was in a self-satisfied torpor thanks to a full stomach and the presence of Ben. For a moment the strangeness of the last few days left me, replaced by the reassuring comfort of home.

CHAPTER EIGHT

The tang of lemon antiseptic mixed with the saltiness of the sea greeted me when I opened my door. Ben must have been in and wiped down benchtops and dusted furniture. When I opened the refrigerator, it would contain fresh milk, bread, butter and an array of fruit. Vegetables were a waste of money: they had never been seen in my apartment in the eight years I'd lived there. I was proud that pots and pans bought by misguided friends as house-warming presents were safely tucked away in their boxes, never to be opened.

I adored my little home. Sparsely furnished with bits 'volunteered' by Jessica, it had a couch with sunken flock cushions, a smelly grandfather chair and a television big enough to be seen from space. It was a thirty-two inch Sony Trinitron monster my father had imported from Japan. But his trophy wife considered it dangerous to the intellectual development of their nine-month-old twins, so he had relinquished it to me. Now and then, on the pretext to his wife of playing golf, Charles arrived at my door with red wine, chocolates and the TV guide. Watching programs in vibrant colour on a bold piece of ultra-new technology was the only time I enjoyed my father's company and the feeling was probably mutual.

I headed for my tiny bathroom where there are more cleaners on the shelf above the vanity than age-defying potions. A couple of times a week, I wipe down the tiles on walls and floor with the satisfaction of knowing a trillion microbes have been annihilated.

Taking off travel clothes after thirty-two hours is like shedding a crusty skin smelling of stale plane air, sweat and the mystery detritus on seats occupied by thousands of bodies.

I thought about the Puhariches as I stood under the rejuvenating water of my shower. I hoped 'John-from-Fraud' came back with something scurrilous about the family. Needing money, they might provide enough material to keep me fed for a few weeks, if not months. I'd visit Pop the first chance I got.

Pop was the editor of a number of local papers in Perth. They were owned by a guy in the western suburbs who wasn't really interested in newspapers. It was the potential notoriety attached to them that was so attractive. He gave Pop free range over editorial decisions. This meant that most of the mastheads had better journalism than the state paper.

How he came to be called 'Pop' is anyone's guess. He wasn't married and didn't have children – he was a rude, obese cigar smoker heading for an early grave. Those who wrote for his papers respected him, but loathed being in the same room. Personal hygiene was not high on his agenda. He'd been an important mentor for me, guiding me through the process of researching, then writing the kind of reports that put the frighteners on half the businessmen in Perth. He was also responsible for paying above award rates, which meant I kept a roof over my head and my bum on restaurant chairs.

It took a while for me to register that my body was cooking under the blazing hot water. After drying off quickly in the steamy bathroom, I ran naked to my bedroom, and donned grandma knickers and my favourite yellow leopard-print tracksuit before turning to a mirror to brush my hair. It was an out-of-control frizz-fest at the best of times and when it was wet, my head became a fierce nest of dark blonde knots – with chocolate highlights – taking at least twenty minutes to get under control. I attacked the tangle with an afro comb, unsnarling as much as my patience allowed, before clumping it together with a scrunchie. After smacking some moisturiser on my face, I opened my wardrobe to find some shoes. With five pairs of LA Gear sneakers, assessing the appropriate match to my sportswear was likely to take more time than my entire bathroom ritual. I tried them all on with much toe pointing in front of the mirror before donning a red pair with white stripes and blue piping. It was a happy colour and lifted the fug of tiredness numbing my brain. My bed, covered by a multicoloured 'positive aura' quilt made by Jessica, was a huge temptation. Before succumbing, I ran back down the stairs to Ben's front door.

He opened it before I put my key in the lock.

'What took you so long?' He looked at my feet. 'Stupid question.'

I plopped down on the pristine white sofa dominating his living room.

'Don't put your feet on the couch,' he said automatically as I stretched my feet to his glass-topped coffee table.

'And not on that either!'

He fussed about, getting a black leather ottoman, lifting my feet and dropping them down. 'How many times do I have to tell you?'

'You're such an old woman.' It was our habitual exchange.

'I rang my mate. Interesting people, your new boyfriend's family.'

I rolled my eyes. 'What did he say?'

'The business is run by the two sons of the old man. He came over here after the Second World War and bought all the land and then returned to Croatia. He's made short visits since then.'

'He seemed more controlling than that.'

'I'd say he does quite a bit from there. One of the sons lives in Perth and the other one is full-time in Margaret River. They've got quite a large compound.'

'The one in Perth must be Marie and Brian's dad.'

'That's one of the weird things. Their dad is down south. Apparently, he's never lived in Perth.'

'I saw him at their house.'

'According to John, the mother lived up here with the kids so they could go to school. Their dad is the boss at the creamery. He's seen the business grow from a small shed to quite a large holding. The other son lives up here and is in charge of marketing. Marie's dad manages all the manufacturing and distribution from Margaret River. John doesn't know him. His dealings have been with her uncle.'

I watched Ben pour coffee into a mug. 'Chuck in some sugar for a pep up. What's the uncle like?'

'Difficult. Very arrogant and a bit dim. When the Fraud guys had to deal with the family, there was a phalanx of lawyers even before the investigation really got underway. John reckons he barely heard Ivo Puharich speak for the six months the case was active. And when he did say something, it was mindless bumf about their fantastic business. One day, he even set up a cheese tasting. No idea about the seriousness of the situation.'

'What were they investigating?'

'It was tangential to the main accusation against Goldberg. Apparently, it involved money laundering via the buying and selling of art.'

'Art?' I remembered back to the wall hangings in the style of Tintoretto and the gambolling cupids. 'I can't imagine the Puhariches have much interest in art.'

'They had quite a collection in the eighties. It was clear to John that the uncle had no idea about the art, hence the cops' suspicions.'

'Were any charges laid?'

'Nope. There was no shit they could stick to that blanket.'

I groaned at an analogy I'd heard a thousand times before and one representing Ben's vast number of ludicrous aphorisms.

'So, what happened?'

'That's the thing. During the investigation, the team found a paper trail of sorts, but it came to nothing because all roads led to Croatia. John's people didn't get any cooperation from their police. It was a totally closed shop, right from the first request for information. With nothing to work on, the team had to pack it in.'

I sipped my eye-wateringly saccharine coffee. 'Brian's in charge of the legal whatsits and I can't see him as a big-time criminal.'

'Be careful, Alex. Ugly doesn't mean dumb. Just as handsome doesn't mean clever. That's a trap you've fallen into before.'

'At least they were beautiful disasters,' I said. 'Is the business big? According to Brian, they are the cheese leaders of the free world.'

'Massive. A huge operation.'

'Are they making money? It must be capital intensive. Distribution from Australia can't be cheap and refrigerated shipping must cost a bomb.'

'I don't know. John says they've got the best equipment available. The Puhariches are serious and canny businessmen, or at least the old man is. According to John, they're ruthless in the way they get rid of their competition.'

I raised my eyebrows.

Ben shook his head. 'Not like that. They buy them out or drive them to the wall through price gouging. Trust me, there are no squads of Croatian hit men killing all the cheesemakers so they can pick up a bargain dairy.'

This was disappointing. Most of me wanted to think the very worst of the Puhariches, because it helped with my theory that Jure and Zorka had been murdered. Maybe by someone they knew. Marie and I had been close, but it was in the past. Now, I smelt a story: one that had an imperious old man in it commanding an empire from the top of a pile of delicious cheese.

'I'm looking forward to my trip down there now.'

'Brian will be thrilled to see you.'

'He has such a big ego, he won't notice I don't find him anywhere near as fascinating as his family. It's interesting the old man has put Brian's father down south. He must be good at logistics. Managing the imports from Croatia and then shifting the cheese around Australia and Asia must be complicated. Yet the sons are unimpressed with their fathers as businessmen. They see themselves as the deserving heirs to their grandfather.'

'Not surprising if the grandfather plays favourites.'

'I didn't think much about their family dynamics when we were at school.'

I had mostly hung out with Marie because she had a serious record collection, an amazing sound system and a lock on her bedroom door. Something my own parents refused to do; for Charles, who thought in extremes, girls' locked doors meant climbing out of windows, drunken boys and pregnancy. To us, the lock represented uninterrupted freedom to experiment with hair-curling wands, frosted eyeshadows and to practise the latest bump dance moves. Marie and I took hours to get ready for concerts and when we got there, we were too busy screaming and tossing our hair about to be able to hear the music.

'You really are going to Margs?' Ben was wary.

'Yep. Brian aside, it might be what I need.'

'What do you mean? You've just got back from a holiday.'

'Exactly! My finances are dire. If I go to Pop, I'll pitch some ideas for articles. It's been a while since I've done something with a bit of punch. An opportunity hasn't presented itself, but the Puhariches might fit the bill. It certainly gives me an excuse to do a bit of poking around.'

'This family isn't going to take kindly to poking.'

'If I go this week, I can get there before Brian and ask the locals some questions. Maybe even hunt down one of their workers for an insider's perspective.'

Ben busied himself, taking away my mug and swishing a cloth across the coffee table. 'Your sticky beak will get you into trouble again. As they say, "You're as subtle as a train wreck. On a boat".'

I shook my head. 'I have no idea what that means. I'll use research for food reviews as a cover for going a bit deeper.'

'The local police won't be sympathetic when you get caught doing something stupid.'

'I won't get caught because I have no intention of doing anything naughty.'

Ben looked at me sceptically. 'If only that were true. How do you intend to get down there anyway? Your pile of junk won't make the distance.'

'Nothing wrong with the Golf.'

'You drive the only car I know where you have to use an umbrella when it rains!'

He had a point. 'I'll swap it for Jess's Jeep.'

This sent him into peals of laughter. My mother's rusty old farm vehicle was barely more roadworthy than mine. But it was dry inside and big enough to hold all the cheese and wine I intended to bring home.

'When will you go?'

'Overlapping with Brian is a bad idea. He's got to get romance out of his head. These lips won't lead him to Charles.'

Ben dropped onto the couch next to me. 'You'd make a cute couple.'

'You're worried I'll stay single for the rest of my life and you'll miss the opportunity to be my bridesmaid.'

He got me in a headlock and we spent the next ten minutes in a ridiculous Hulk Hogan wrestling match before I tapped out and collapsed on the floor.

'I've gotta go and have a sleep. You can make me dinner.'

He pulled me to my feet, hooked his arm across my shoulders and walked me to the door. 'Sleep well. I'll make sure there's a pile of cauliflower cheese and a slab of steak when you wake up.'

My last muddled thoughts as I sank into sleep were about Brian, Marco, the grandfather and blood from a slab of meat splattered across a kitchen wall.

CHAPTER NINE

I spent the next week in a jet-lag stupor. Everything took twice as long to do: two days to unpack and wash clothes. Another day to pay bills.

There's nothing like writing cheques to make you understand the diabolical state of your finances. Despite all the fifty-cent coffees in Croatia, I was seriously skint. A visit to Pop and the promise of publications was top of my 'To Do' list. If I couldn't get some of my expenses covered down south, the Jeep was to be my transport *and* accommodation.

On the day I went to Pop's office, the deadline for the next edition had passed and the atmosphere was jovial, at least as much as Pop's taciturn personality allowed. When I opened the door a thick cloud of bonhomie and cigarette smoke wafted over me.

'Shut the fucking door. It's fucking freezing.' Pop's voice was a deep rat-a-tat coming from somewhere in the stinking mist.

I stepped in and the door shut behind me.

The building was an old railway ticket office and its high tin ceiling echoed every sound. The room was divided by laminated desks and steel filing cabinets. There were stacks of paper everywhere: stuff was spat out by the printer, typewriters, a fax and every other possible piece of machinery capable of ejecting paper. In the corner was a glassed-in office from which Pop bellowed instructions and insults.

Most people had got the memo about smoking and cancer and all the other diseases that could be sucked into lungs. Newspaper offices were one of the last places where cigarettes, booze and photocopying bums was still *de rigueur*. And Pop was a traditionalist, hence his female journalists looked like Barbie and the males wore nylon body shirts that were at least ten years out of date. He tolerated me because I had familial links with the old-money elites, and his inner snob thought this gave his papers ties to 'important' people. Over the years, I like to think he valued me mostly for my articles: stories that sometimes made life uncomfortable for those in the purple circle. Pop loved to have a go at me about my dedication to hyperbole but he appreciated my 'dog with a bone' approach to researching for my articles.

'Hi, Pop.' I leaned against his door and squinted through the fog. 'You in there?'

'Don't be a smartarse.'

I waved my hand around, clearing the air. 'I'm back.'

'Yeah.' He sat like a deflated Michelin Man behind a desk once belonging to a mining magnate who owed him a favour – there were many such men. 'You got anything for me?'

'It's only been a few days.'

'So?'

'Jet lag has crippled me!'

'I don't give a rat's.'

I sat in a chair positioned as close to the open door as possible, turning my head every so often to take in a gasp of the slightly cleaner air of the outer office.

'I'm looking to go down to Margaret River. Maybe get something on the wine and food industry.'

'What angle? I need something with an edge, not just reviews.'

'The food thing is my excuse to be there. I think I can do something sharp about the doctors that are propping up the vineyards. Maybe a bit about tax dodges?'

'Might be something there. What else?'

'My invitation to visit came from Brian Puharich.'

He leaned forward. 'Really?'

'I caught up with him and his sister in Croatia. We were at school together.'

'That'd be about right.' His face was cunning. 'Do you know the sons?'

'I met one of them, years ago. I don't know if it was Marie's dad or her uncle.'

'Wouldn't mind a profile on the Puhariches. No one gets as rich as they are by doing the right thing.'

'My thoughts exactly. Marie is nice enough. Brian is an egomaniac. I met the patriarch in Croatia and a cousin, who Brian hates, and who I found rather tasty.'

'I don't give a fuck what they look like. Is there a story?'

'Money and power, and a business that may be a tax dodge or maybe ...' I shrugged. 'As you say, they're a wealthy family.'

'Okay. Where that lot is concerned, you might have something to work with. What do you need?'

'A Think Pad is always useful and some discs. The local library will have a fax and printer if the need arises.'

'Recording?'

'Ben will have something more subtle than your stuff. Charles is giving me a new phone, which, knowing him, will be the latest and greatest.'

'You in the good books?'

'It's become surplus to his needs because Trophy Wife won't use it: causes the brain to explode apparently.'

'Good on Charlie. What a fine chap.'

'Careful, Pop. He's been supportive of your favourite causes. Don't bite the hand that feeds you.'

He gave one of his characteristic humourless laughs. 'You can get one of the boys to fix you up with the computer. And get Carly to give you something from petty cash. Keep your receipts and stay out of trouble.'

'Thanks. Don't worry, I won't cause any waves.'

'That's not what I want to hear. Go down there and stir up as much trouble as you can to get me a decent story. If you get caught doing something wrong, I'll deny any knowledge of your existence.'

'Of course you will.'

I coughed my way back through the room, stopping at the desk of the office tech nerd.

'What?' he didn't look up.

'Think Pad.'

'When.'

'Now?'

He grunted. 'You think I got one stuck up my arse?'

'I hope not.'

'This afternoon.'

Experience had taught me not to push my luck. 'Okay.'

'After two.'

I left the office and took huge gulps of fresh air. My hair and clothes smelled like an ashtray for the rest of the day.

~

With a few hours to fill, I decided to visit my father to pick up the mobile phone. Charles had moved to posh offices when he was appointed to the District Court. Trophy Wife had taken it upon herself to 'style' them, hence they looked like a filmset from a 1950s courtroom drama, saturated with her ambition. I called his office from the nearest payphone. His secretary answered.

'Hi, Lynette, it's Alex.'

'Well, hello. Back from holiday?'

'Yep. Tanned and happy.'

'Good. Any trouble?'

I wasn't sure why everyone felt the need to ask me about trouble.

'No. It was a relaxing time spent with good food.'

'What can I do for you?'

'Is the great man,' a faint chuckle came down the line, 'available to have lunch with me today? It's short notice, but he has a phone that I forgot to pick up before my holiday.'

There was a tapping of computer keys as she pulled up his calendar.

'He's available in fifteen minutes if you can get here. Otherwise, you'll have to wait until Thursday.'

'I can be there now. Can you get him to meet me at Mrs Oliphant's?'

'Oh dear, must you?'

'It's cheap.'

Another chuckle. 'All right, I'll let him know. And be kind. They're having a bad time with the twins. They're teething.'

'I won't make any promises.'

I sped through traffic and parked in a loading zone outside the café. Illegal parking is another of my talents and it drives Charles to distraction. I had calculated it was cheaper for me to risk a parking fine than it was for me to pay the exorbitant hourly fee. My father arrived a few minutes after I settled into a booth.

'Hello Alexandra.'

We pecked each other on the cheek.

'Hi Dad. How's the family?'

'Teething.'

'Oh, well. It won't be for long,' I noted helpfully.

'Churlishness is unbecoming.' He pulled a box out of his suit pocket. 'I have no idea why you want to eat in this place. It's hideous.'

He was right. The café was trying to be an 'olde English tea shoppe', with its cabbage-rose fabric, long ruffled tablecloths and net curtains. It was relentlessly kitsch, but their chocolate cake, filled with fresh cream and strawberries, was an unrivalled delight.

A waitress appeared at our table.

To my father's obvious annoyance, I ordered the cake with a side of homemade ice cream. He studied the menu slowly.

'I'll have the open ham sandwich without the bread.'

The waitress stopped scribbling. 'That's not a sandwich. I can do a ham and salad plate.'

'That's fine. Extra cheese and no dressing, unless it's olive oil.'

The waitress bustled away.

'Good grief, Dad. Fussy eating these days?'

'Melanie and I are on the Atkins diet. We also jog every morning.'

Picturing my post-middle-age father in running shorts and t-shirt puffing around the affluent streets of Peppermint Grove was hilarious. I couldn't help tittering.

'There's no need for that, Alexandra. Your stepmother has my best interests at heart.'

Oh please! 'Cut the stepmother bit. She's younger than me.'

He pushed the box across the table. 'You disappoint me. Here's the phone.'

Disappointing my father was symptomatic of our relationship. Over time I had become immune to the sting.

I took the phone out of the box and sat the shiny miracle in the palm of my hand – it was black and grey with a little antennae ear sticking up on the top. 'Nokia C15. Nice.'

'I bought it when I was in Japan in March. Beautiful thing. The charger is in the box and your number is on the back.'

'I appreciate this. I'll return it when I get back from Margaret River.'

'Don't bother. It's yours. Although I don't see the point in taking it down south. Connection will be hit-and-miss. But then that's rather like your career.'

My father's cheap shots were very familiar. 'You never know, I might get lucky and on more than one front.'

'Now you're being crass.'

Like a thousand times before, we fell into a silence that crackled with an antipathy typical of father–daughter relationships where common ground and understanding was never sought by either party. We were too busy blaming each other.

Our food arrived. My father looked across at my enormous piece of cake. The smell of chocolate rose up. I closed my eyes and breathed deeply. He looked at his lump of ham sitting on iceberg lettuce, wedges of tomato and grated cheese.

'Here, cover it with pepper and salt.' I moved the condiments in his direction. He didn't look any happier.

'Why are you going to Margaret River?'

'Guest of Brian Puharich.'

'And I ask again: why?' His tone was supercilious.

'Just curious.' I wasn't going to tell him about the deaths. 'Pop thinks it's a good idea.'

'That makes me feel better.' Deadly sarcasm was my father's forte.

'Do you have to be so negative? It's an opportunity to go down south, meet some new people, and maybe get some interesting material.'

'I don't like that family. People from Eastern Bloc countries cannot be trusted.'

'Are you serious?'

'Absolutely. Unscrupulous, all of them.'

I shook my head. My father disconsolately poked at his food. I enjoyed every mouthful of my chocolate and cream extravaganza. As always, we rapidly exhausted our goodwill. His scowl got deeper, I ignored him, and we ate hurriedly, racing to end the outing.

With a last stab at his plate, Charles got up. 'Keep your phone on you at all times and don't forget to charge it every night.'

'I'm not stupid, Dad.'

'Keep your wits about you when driving that bucket of rust you call a car.'

'I'm taking Jess's Jeep.'

He rolled his eyes, saying nothing.

'You don't have to worry.'

'It's not worry. I don't want to deal with the consequences of you doing something ridiculous or illegal.'

There was no point in defending myself. Charles was a man of his class and times. I had learned to tolerate his narrow world view because he provided a cheap and beautiful place for me to rent and an abundance of new technology. We did the obligatory cheek peck and he left the café. As he strode down the street, people turned as he passed, impressed by his magisterial bearing.

I bought a lemon choc-chip cupcake for the road and walked to my car, the phone pressed to my ear in the pretence of listening to someone while blokes went past with giant bricks against the sides of their faces giving me surly looks of envy. In a further triumph, there was no ticket on my windscreen.

On returning to the newspaper, Tech Nerd had my computer ready, with a pile of freshly formatted discs, a dozen or so batteries for the mouse, and a black nylon bag. 'Because you're bound to wreck it if I don't give you something to put it in.'

Carly gave me a wad of money and a long discourse on receipts and the difference between necessary and discretionary spending. I'd heard it all before. Carly liked to feel relevant in an office where words and stories were valued above all else.

I yelled towards the cigar box on my way out, 'See you when I get back, Pop.'

'Fuckin' bring something we can use.'

Smiling, I left the building.

At home, I plugged in the computer and the phone to charge the batteries and put new double AAs in the mouse. Timing my trip was important. The end of the month was five days away and I wanted to be there before Brian. Finding my own accommodation was a priority. Close to the beach where I sleep to the sound of waves.

I let myself into Ben's apartment and found a copy of the country telephone directory. He'd given me a key to his house when I first moved in upstairs. Ben didn't mind my intrusions, even when he had a boyfriend sleep over. On far too many occasions I'd provided him with great amusement when I charged through his door looking to escape my own amorous misadventures.

I made myself an iced tea and sat down on his sofa, my feet resting on the coffee table. I looked happily at my patent leather shoes whose fuchsia pink was nicely highlighted against the crisp white of the furniture. There was a limited choice of places to stay according to the phone book. A cabin at the holiday park in the hamlet of Gracetown was my best bet. I rang and booked and felt so elated I had to raid Ben's refrigerator to celebrate. He always had a stock of excellent cheese because he knew I was an emotional eater. Sad, happy, angry: the type of emotion didn't matter.

I finished my tea, washed the cup and let myself out. I had time to whip across to Jessica's house, swap cars and be back in time for dinner. Once again, I'd schlep downstairs and be fed by Ben in exchange for doing the dishes and providing the wine.

~

Jessica opened the door before the final trilling of the doorbell.

'Thank goodness you're here.' She was agitated. 'This is a disaster.'

I'd seen it all before. Stoically, I stumped after her through rooms crowded with sparkling rocks and crystals and a vast array of candles and smelly sticks. She directed me to sit on a wicker chair at a table in the conservatory. This is a misnomer. It was more like a large cat cage where tall rope-covered scratching posts, fluffy beds and jingly, feathered toys held sway. I loathe cats. They shed tons of hair, spew fur balls and lick their own bums.

'It's terrible.'

'Calm down, Jess. What's happened?'

'Your cards. They're getting worse.' She waved her arms at the coffee table on which lay cards featuring images of medieval death and torture. As the furry fiends wove through her legs and looked at me with smug cunning, Jessica told the frightful story of my life over the forthcoming two weeks.

'You need to go home and lock yourself away, for your own safety.'

'Not happening, Jess. I'm off to Margaret River where I'm going to eat my body weight in cheese.'

'That is not wise, my darling.'

'There's nothing to worry about, except a spike in my cholesterol.'

She sat down in the seat opposite. Immediately a squad of furies leaped onto her lap and curled around her throat. Her hands automatically started to massage their bodies, eliciting loud rumblings. I looked at them with distaste.

'You've got to get rid of some of these creatures. If you were to have a fall and knock yourself out, they'd eat you and all I would find are cats with full bellies picking their teeth with your bones.'

'Ridiculous. The cat is my totem, connected to my previous life as an Egyptian priestess.'

Years ago, this would have made me furious. Getting into my thirties had taught me greater patience. I shook my head and looked at her with affection. 'Don't get yourself in a tizz. Pop has agreed to take some stories, so I've an expense account of sorts and a legitimate reason for being there.'

She was unconvinced. 'Then you must take the farm car. It has positive energy and healing crystals in it for safe travelling.'

'That's why I'm here. I'll leave the Golf and take the Jeep.'

She stood, dislodging furry bodies. 'You'll need the keys.'

When she left the room, it was me and them. A small battalion lined up in front of me and another lot were behind my chair in a classic pincer manoeuvre. We watched each other with mutual suspicion. Thankfully Jessica returned almost immediately and dropped a huge bundle in my lap.

'I don't need all of these. Just the one for the Jeep.'

'It is the car key.'

One little key was obscured by an array of crystals, cat statues and a rabbit's foot, which looked suspiciously like that of my high school pet.

'I'll take all this stuff off and have the key.'

'No!' Jess' screech was uncharacteristic. 'These are part of the layers of protection. They all have a role and you must take it as it is, or you cannot take the car at all.'

'Okay. That's fine.'

'I'll worry. Things are not good for you.'

Wanting to change the grim topic of my immediate future, I got Jess onto her favourite themes of friends' spiritual health and her successful attainment of the Goddess of Astrology status through the Academy of Enlightenment and Self-Actualisation. Despite our different approaches to life, I always enjoyed being with my mother. She was, mostly, serene and gave me unconditional love, something often tested by my chaos. Jess was one of the great believers in 'Life'. She embraced it with a quiet joy that I envied.

After a few hours in her soothing company, I climbed into the Jeep, feeling fully armed: ready to see Brian and face the diabolical misfortunes Jess had foreseen.

The Jeep was a sturdy machine my mother had bought for going to the Denmark farm of some friends. Incongruously called 'The Farm', the place was a cooperative, more commune than a property growing marketable commodities. Self-sustaining, the 'farmers' grew fruit and vegetables, spun wool from their sheep, made cheese from goat's milk and harvested enough mung beans to power all of Australia from the resulting flatulence. Jessica used it as a type of retreat where she was able to meditate and reconnect with 'the living soul of plants'.

'Thanks for this, Mum. My car isn't suited to country driving.'

'The Golf is a disaster, Alexandra. I have no idea why you bought it.'

'It was my dream car. One day I'll get around to fixing it up. If something happens to the Mini, you can use mine as a back-up. Don't forget the passenger door won't open. If you're taking a friend, they'll have to climb in when the roof is down or through the driver's side.'

Getting into the Jeep, Jess pressed two small rocks into my hand. 'Here is an amethyst to dispel negative energy and a black tourmaline to draw positive energy. You'll need them both.'

I looked at her worried face and gave a half-hearted laugh. 'Everything will be fine. I firmly believe only good things can come out of a creamery.'

She gave me a kiss. I reversed out of her driveway and accelerated down the street. Looking into the rear-view mirror, I saw her clutching the crystal she wore around her neck and saw the movement of her lips reciting an incantation I guessed was to keep me safe. For a split second, I felt a spasm of foreboding.

I gave myself one more day to languish around the house and fill plastic crates full of clothes, technology and some food. Eating out is my default position. Breakfast and snacks were the only basics I was happy to 'cook'.

Preparing for my trip, a little shadow of doubt teased my mind. I didn't believe any of my mother's psychomancy but her sincerity was so authentic. My apprehension wasn't enough to stop me: it crouched like one of Jessica's beasts in a back corner of my brain.

CHAPTER TEN

Ben and I had breakfast on the morning of my departure. He'd got out of bed early to make the Classic Canadian: a stack of pancakes, topped with bacon and smothered in maple syrup. When it was ready, Ben banged on his ceiling with a broom handle. I put on my bathrobe, pulled on a pair of ugg boots and went downstairs. Sitting on my usual chair, Ben put a loaded plate in front of me and pushed a fiercely hot coffee into my hand.

'You're looking well this morning.'

'Shut up.'

I am not fit to be seen by other living things before ten o'clock in the morning: white and puffy, resembling a beluga whale with an afro, I have a soaring headache and am incapable of speech before my first swallow of coffee. Ben, on the other hand, looks his usual gorgeous self. It was one of the injustices of nature that it was him – a man – and not me who awoke clear-eyed and with a smile on his face.

I gulped the coffee and filled my mouth with the sweet, salty flavours of Canada.

Ben waited.

'Okay. I'm ready.'

'Have you got all you need?'

'Maybe you could give me the little listening whatsit you have tucked away.'

He tilted his head to one side and looked sceptical. 'Why?'

'It might be useful.'

'You're going down there to do a cheese and wine swim-through.'

'I might need to listen carefully to things. You know, for my real stories.'

'The last time you listened to someone's conversation, you didn't like what they had to say.'

'How was I to know Trophy Wife was going to visit Charles in chambers? I already knew she didn't like me.'

'But not how much. It's bad for me to give you this stuff.'

'I know. You own it, though. It's not as if you nicked it from work.'

Ben had completed a master's degree in surveillance technology and he had a huge array of doo-dads perfect for sticking one's nose into other people's business.

'I'd feel safer. I could set it up in my cabin and if anyone breaks in, I might hear something useful. Maybe get a line on a possible story.'

'You can't be serious? The chances are miniscule.' Our eyes met. 'Although, knowing you, it goes from impossible to probable. I'm assuming you intend to look in places you shouldn't.'

'Yes.' There was no point in obfuscation.

'All right, it's not the latest spyware, very simple to use – probably a bit Maxwell Smart so it'll suit you to a tee.'

'And loving it.'

'Don't get caught setting it up.' He went to his study: a room full of books on vicious true crime and Art Deco interior design.

'Here you go.' He returned to the dining room and put a black case in front of me. 'It has to come back in one piece and if you use this on a Puharich and you get caught, they won't be kind.'

'Come on. Brian will love to think I need to listen to his every word.'

Ben's face was serious. 'Do your food stories and leave well enough alone. You think those old people in Croatia were murdered. How do you know the same thing hasn't happened here? That family were very smelly in the eighties, yet the Fraud boys had nothing.'

'Don't worry. I'm the daughter of Judge Grant and on that basis alone Brian adores me.'

I changed the subject and we spent the next hour finishing off breakfast and another pot of coffee before Ben put on his suit jacket and picked up his keys.

'I'm assuming your father gave you the promised new phone?'

I nodded.

'Leave the number on the bench and please keep it charged.'

'That's what Charles said. Everything will be fine.'

I stood and toddled over to where he leaned against the front door. Reaching up I planted a maple syrup kiss on his lips and wrapped my arms around his shoulders. He returned my hug with an extra squeeze.

'When will you be home?'

'I've booked the cabin for a week. But my options are open.'

'Be careful and don't take any risks. That includes falling in love with Brian.'

'No chance of that happening. I'd prefer to kiss one of mum's cats!'

We laughed and gave each other another hug before he left. I heard the growl of his 1968 Fastback Mustang as he reversed out of the drive and accelerated away.

I did the right thing and cleaned up the breakfast things before returning to my own flat to shower and pack.

Not knowing exactly the length of my holiday, I selected ten pairs of shoes, each in their own see-through plastic box. Some were practical, but, as an adherent to the 'form over function' mantra, most were chosen for their aesthetic appeal. The most wonderful – a pair of purple suede peep-toes with a five-inch stiletto.

It didn't take long to load the Jeep so within a couple of hours, I was on the road.

~

The trip south was up there with the most boring stretches of road in the history of infrastructure. A clogged bit of freeway narrows down to a two-lane disaster where cars are often forced to a crawl when tractors appear from one of the market gardens spreading out on each side. Then there are the factories sending smoke up into the atmosphere, punching a whopping hole in the ozone. Once past this industrial 'heartland', a straggling urban corridor begins. Rockingham, desperately trying to look civilised, spreads to the right before merging into the outer fringes of Mandurah.

Great chunks of land were bought up by 1980s high-flyers. These men made multimillion dollar deals over notorious long lunches that, inevitably, led to salacious gossip of the slap-and-tickle kind. They filled the land with 'exclusive' communities suited to the upwardly mobile. Most of the pseudo-mansions have weird gables, are painted in pale blues, with an overabundance of nautical features like porthole windows and fences made of thick rope. The slow trawl through Mandurah comes to an end with a bridge across the marshy estuary, much loved by mosquitoes and crabs, where tinnies belonging to hopeful fishers bob up and down.

The Jeep didn't have a CD player, just a contraption for cassettes that dangled under the dash, held in place with wire. I took some from the glove box and spent the rest of the trip singing at the top of my lungs to Dolly Parton and Linda Ronstadt. Jess probably had no idea this music was still in the car. Her country and western phase had long been replaced with Celtic flutes and Buddhist chants. To the tune of funky ukuleles, the tedious kilometres eventually passed.

I hit the outskirts of the port city of Bunbury. Like so much of Western Australia, the city clung to the ocean's edge as though the inhabitants feared the relentless heat of the desert that lay behind them.

After the turn-off leading to the urban cluster of Busselton, I got trapped behind a long line of station wagons and four-wheel drives with surfboards strapped to the roofs and back windows obscured with wetsuits. This meant the tedious journey got slower and more infuriating. By the time I stopped at the Gracetown turn-off, I'd had enough of Glen Campbell's twelve-string guitar and John Denver's country roads.

On the verge of hysterics and low on fuel, I turned into the holiday park. Chip packets and sticky Coke cans tumbled out when I opened the door. Twisting my body like a corkscrew, I looked around at my home for the coming week. It was underwhelming. Sleepy even in the summer high season, in winter the park was lifeless. Caravan sites were marked by electric poles with boxes attached where campers could plug themselves in to have the lights and stoves they needed to get back to nature. Cabins in the distance were surrounded by straggly grass, with the sharp rise of sand dunes behind them. To my immediate left was one such cabin. Random chips of paint suggested that it had once been a bright sky-blue. Now its weatherboards had been stripped by the wind and its windows were obscured with a thick crust of sea salt. I had climbed the stairs and rung the bell before I saw the large sign stuck to the wall next to the door.

'Outside of office hours. Use phone. Dial eight eight four.'

Personally, I didn't consider two pm on a weekday to be outside of office hours. Park management obviously worked to a different clock. I picked up the handset of the telephone attached to the wall and pushed in the numbers. It was answered by a male voice sounding like it was coming from the other side of the universe.

'Yeah.'

'Hi. I'm Alex Grant and I have a booking.'

'Hold on.'

There was a shuffling of paper and much grunting before the voice spoke again. 'You're in cabin number five. Straight down and to the right. You got cash?'

'No. Why, do I need to pay now?'

'We need a deposit in case you scarper.'

'How much? I may stay longer than the days I've reserved.'

'Dunno 'bout that. Bookin's are pretty fixed cos other people are comin' in.'

I looked out at the desolated camping ground. 'I've got a cheque book.'

Silence.

'Hello. Are you still there?'

'That'll have to do I s'pose. It's one hundred bucks. Make it out to cash and stick it under the door.'

It was almost the total sum. 'You can't be serious?'

'Yep. You want to stay, you have to put down a deposit.'

I didn't have the energy to argue. 'Fine. How do I get into the cabin?'

'Key's in the lock. How else you gunna do it?'

Good grief. 'Okay. The cheque will be under the door. Is there anything else I need to know?'

'Nope. The Missus went in this mornin' to make up the bed and turn everythink on. She's put an extra blanket on the bed and a hot water bottle on the sink. I dunno why you need that, but. Not cold at the mo.'

'That's great. Thank your wife for me.'

The sound of the handset being dropped into the cradle signalled our conversation was at an end.

'And goodbye to you.'

I got back into the car and looked through the windscreen. A wonky bit of bitumen split the camping ground down the middle. At the far end it stopped at a squat fence made of treated pine logs. On both sides of the road sat three little cabins, their flat faces looking bleakly out across the empty site. I put the Jeep into gear and drove slowly forward. Number five was next to number seven. God knows what had happened to number six. There was no designated car park, so I pulled up close to the door and got out. True to the manager's word, the key was in the lock, a sizeable replica of a surfboard attached to it by a small chain. I turned the key with difficulty and walked in to find that I was at the back of the cabin, a lean-to where wood was neatly stacked against a wall and an array of plastic buckets, spades and beach umbrellas were piled in a corner. I pushed through another door and found myself in the cabin proper.

The interior was rustic with overtones of 1970s caravan. The main room was entirely lined with wood. It felt like I'd stepped into a coffin. There was a clumsy wooden table in the little kitchen area. Blond wood-veneer cupboards had obviously been recycled from a caravan, with the open shelves still bound by the little metal railings that stopped stuff from falling off in transit. Three lounge chairs, whose orange and brown tapestry cushions screamed fondue party, were arranged in a semi-circle in the sitting room. A narrow set of french doors, covered with net curtains, was set in the middle of the wall at the front of the cabin.

I headed for the door to the right of the television, which sat on top of a chugging bar fridge. In the bedroom another set of skinny french doors allowed blurred light into the room. It was taken up by a queen size bed so high off the ground, I might get a nose bleed if I looked over the edge. The surprise was the stunning quilt covering its surface. Stitched on top of fine white cotton, interlocking circles made of small, floral fabric squares were meticulously arranged, each with a delicate flower embroidered in the middle. It was edged with a strip of yellow material and covered with hand-sewn swirls, quilting the spread to create tiny puffy pillows. I assumed it was the work of the Missus. A small bathroom opening from the bedroom completed the cabin facilities. It was with a glad heart I noted the cleanliness of the place; no doubt, courtesy of the Missus.

I lugged in all the crates from the Jeep, arranging them around the cabin according to their function. Wire hangers on the back of the bedroom door designated the wardrobe. I hung clothes, put away food and filled the bar fridge with a couple of bottles of wine I'd brought to tide me over until I could get to a winery. Just because I was going to exist on packet soup didn't mean I wasn't going to have something decent to drink.

By five o'clock all domestic responsibilities had been completed. Flopping onto one of the lounge chairs, I wondered if it was too early to open one of the bottles.

'Maybe a pre-dinner beverage.' Getting a chardonnay from the fridge, I went in search of a corkscrew. The kitchen was scrupulously clean.

'Thank god for the Missus.'

While I was pulling the cork, the mobile phone rang. The bottle dropped and the phone stopped ringing.

'For shit's sake!' I dropped to my knees, picked up the foaming bottle and stuck my tongue in the top to arrest further spillage.

The buzz-buzz of the phone started again. With my tongue stuck in the neck of the bottle, I charged around, hunting for the tech marvel. It was in the sink.

I pulled my tongue out of the bottle with a pop.

'Hello.' My voice sounded foreign even to my own ears.

'Is that Alex Grant?' Male tones crackled and popped.

'Yeth.' My tongue felt pointy and numb at the tip.

'It's Brian. You sound strange.'

'No, no, I'm okay. How did you get this number? It's a new phone.'

'I telephoned Judge Grant on another matter and mentioned that I'd invited you to Margaret River.'

'My father gave you my number?' I found this very hard to believe, given Charles' opinion of the inhabitants of Eastern Bloc countries.

'Not exactly.' The intermittent signal punctuated his sentences, causing an odd staccato. 'I asked his secretary to schedule a meeting. Then I mentioned you and she said you'd headed south. She was happy to give your number to an old friend. I'd like to invite you to the creamery.'

I cursed inwardly the friendly helpfulness of Lynette.

'Asking for my number was a bit presumptuous.'

I wondered if he'd heard me because after a few seconds of whistles and pops, he pressed on.

'Where are you at the moment?' He was trying to sound casual.

'I've just arrived. How about you?' I crossed my fingers and looked to heaven.

'I'm already here.'

I may have flipped the bird. 'Weren't you coming down at the end of the month?'

'Things have happened …' crackle, crackle. 'It's all got a bit complicated since Jure and Zorka's funeral. The police got an anonymous tip-off suggesting there were inconsistencies in the coroner's investigation.

Detectives from Zagreb have decided to review the coroner's report. My father and uncle won't be coming back and there's a business to run here. The investigation is all very inconvenient.'

'You're kidding? Do you know who tipped them off?'

'No idea. We're assuming it was Jure's brother. He's a complete lunatic but certain police have taken it seriously.'

'Wow! That does complicate things.'

'I suppose. Though we do have it under control. My father and uncle are pulling together a team of lawyers.'

'What about you? You're a lawyer.' Best in the universe, according to Marie.

'The situation is sensitive. It needs men who know Croatian criminal law and my grandfather wants to make sure we're well prepared.'

I imagined a room full of men with big noses pushing paper through a shredder.

'So, the police don't like the coroner's findings?'

'At the moment they're looking at the paperwork.'

I'd love to be in the room if they were going to interview Brian's grandfather. 'How long will it all take?'

'We don't know. Our lawyers will fight any exhumation.'

I remembered the look of furious contempt the old man had given Jure's brother. It would take more than a police investigation to disturb his sense of mastery.

Brian's voice was now coming with a two-second delay. 'Have you settled in? Obviously, you didn't need me to book you somewhere.'

'No … managed it all on my own.'

'Where are you?'

Pursing my lips, I wondered if I really had to tell him.

'In Gracetown.' I puffed rather than spoke the words.

'The only place there is the camping ground. Surely, you're not in a tent?'

'No, in one of the cabins.'

'That's marginally better. But the manager is a crook.'

'It suits me. Near the sea and very comfy.'

'Not as close as you can be to us. I can organise something a bit nearer if you like?' His voice was hopeful. 'We're at the estate. East of Caves Road and south of Gracetown. You can meet me for dinner.'

Even over the bad line, this was more a command than a question.

I thought of all the rude ways of saying no. 'I don't think so. I'm exhausted from the trip and I've already opened a bottle of wine.'

'Drinking alone?'

'For relaxation. It's been a long day.'

'What about tomorrow?'

'I was thinking of doing some sightseeing. Getting a feel for the place and the people. There might be an interesting story out there.'

'We can do lunch. You can come here, meet my cousins and I'll show you around.' He took my silence over the crackling line as assent. 'Great. If you've got a pen, take down the address and number and I'll see you at eleven. Okay?

'That might not suit my plans. I don't want to lock myself in.'

'You'll need to eat at some point. May as well be here.'

That was an irrefutable fact: I was not equipped to live on crackers and rehydrated laksa. I jotted down the location and phone number of the creamery. I was making a habit of falling in with Puharich plans. Part of me wanted to tell him I'd come down with diphtheria, but truth to tell, most of me was dying with curiosity to hear more about the investigation in Croatia.

'All right then. It might be fun.'

'You know me, Alex.' He dropped his voice. 'I'm very happy to provide you with some fun.'

'It won't be a date, Brian. More of a family lunch.'

'Let's see where it leads, shall we?'

He rang off before I could reply.

~

The next hour was spent 'cooking' my dinner and drinking the last of the wine, all the while coming up with scintillating ripostes to put Brian back in his box. I plonked myself in front of the TV with my dinner tray and a piccolo of champagne. The menu on my first night in the emerging fine-dining region of Margaret River was tinned tuna mixed with creamed corn on Sao biscuits. Thankfully, the TV had a remote control, albeit the size of a brick, so I didn't have to get up again until bedtime. Channel surfing was limited to two channels. I tried my best to flick the buttons quickly enough to avoid the advertisements. With *Miss Marple* on one channel and a documentary about sheep trials on the other, the stories merged to the point where sheep were killing curates in thatched cottages. I wondered idly if the South West had similarly rustic murders which I might embellish for my city readers.

It was eight thirty when I decided enough was enough. Switching off the TV and the lights, I checked the locks, changed into my sleeping tracksuit and jumped into the middle of the bed, sinking so low into the mattress, the sides rose up: I was the saveloy in a hotdog.

~

The next day, my body was where I had left it. In ten hours of sleep I hadn't moved but had become one with the mattress. Maybe I could stay like that all day: enveloped in my quilted bun. The plan was wrecked almost immediately by the need to wee. With much grunting I rolled out of bed.

There is a saying, 'no good can come of a day that begins with getting up', and that was a neat summation of how I felt. I shuffled to the kitchen, turned on the radio and put the kettle on the hob. I found a toaster and rummaged around in the crates for breakfast. It was to be thick toast with peanut butter and baked beans. I made a water jug full of coffee and sat down at the table. Sipping straight from the jug, I listened to the news and considered my day.

The meal with the Puhariches was uppermost. Through a patina of peanut butter and baked beans, the thought had a strange appeal. There was the problem of Brian. I was hopeful 'alone time' was limited: he'd mentioned cousins. Rather than thinking about all the things wrong with being in Brian's company, I focused on the nature of the samples – maybe some soft cheeses to start, working through to end with a roquefort paired with dates and dried figs. My stomach gurgled in anticipation.

After sticking my nose out the door to test the weather, I decided on layering from a vest all the way up to a denim jacket and scarf. Matching shoes to boot leg jeans is always risky. White sneakers were the most fashionable choice, but with a forecast of rain, they lacked practicality. My black R.M. Williams boots had the required weather-proofing and looked damned good with my dark acid-wash jeans. I puffed up my hair and smeared my lips with my favourite bronze lippy. The look was Brian-proof self-confidence.

I had a backpack, perfect for putting in all the stuff needed to hunt down anything newsworthy. This included Ben's listening device: I was dying for the opportunity to use it. Before leaving, I unfolded the map of the South West which I presumed the Missus had left on the table. To my astonishment, the Puharich creamery was marked as a destination of interest: down Caves Road, south for about thirty minutes and then a left turn directly into the driveway. Although having a problematic relationship with directions, I felt this was comfortably within my skill set.

It didn't take long before it became clear I had overestimated myself. I'd barely left the camping ground when it became obvious the Jeep was not heading south. Instead, I was on a narrow lane weaving between the scattering of houses making up the hamlet of Gracetown. Most were made of concrete sheeting with corrugated iron roofs and wide verandas pushing out over the dunes. They looked as though they were trying to sink into the sand, protecting themselves from the wind blowing in ferocious paint-stripping whorls. The place was redolent of beachy school holidays where families mixed in ways unacceptable in the real world: where children were allowed free rein, sneaking sausages from anybody's barbecue when they were hungry. And where adults could drink too much, laugh too loud and look too salaciously at other men's wives without giving offence.

I had heard about these holidays second-hand. Charles didn't do the beach and Jessica felt the sea belonged to whales, sharks, jellyfish and mermaids. My holidays were always 'learning experiences': art galleries, churches and cemeteries on the other side of the world. Dressed in our Sunday best we ate at restaurants where children should never be seen, but which made Charles feel cultured and wealthy and gave my brother and I a precocious understanding of fine food. Now, looking at the houses, I remembered my feelings of envy and loss, and my hope to one day run around in swimmers getting walnut brown under the summer sun.

Instead, I found myself in a tiny village which seemed to be built in a pattern of small circles. I stopped in front of the Gracetown general store, to the left of a rusted bowser whose petrol had long evaporated. The shop was small and set high off the road. A second-floor addition made it look top-heavy. The façade was covered in ads for soft drinks and ice creams. A steep set of stairs led to an open door screened by a curtain made of long trails of shells. Stepping into the dim interior, I nearly tripped over a sandwich board listing a variety of deep-fried foods suited for breakfast, lunch and a heart attack for dinner. A young man with long bleached hair that had never seen a brush was standing just inside the door, balancing a surfboard on its tip.

'Hi,' I said, slightly intimidated by his aloof cool. 'Can you show me the way out? I need to get back onto Caves Road.'

'You're kiddin'. You're lost?'

'I've come from the caravan park and went south too soon.'

Surfer Dude leaned forward, using the board as a prop. 'Follow this road, turn right at the end and go straight. Then you come to the T-junction. Where you goin'?'

'The Puharich cheese factory.'

He looked at me with interest. 'You a rellie?'

'No.'

'Well it ain't tourist season.'

'I'm not a tourist.'

'What are you then?'

'I'm a journalist.'

He gave a little chuckle. 'Plenty to write about.'

'What do you mean?'

'Nothin'. They're a big family. Pretty tight. I can't see them talking to you.'

'Maybe my journalism skills will bring them out of themselves.'

'If you poke your nose in, its likely to get cut off.' Suddenly, he seemed less like a benign surfer.

'Have you got something to say that I can quote?'

'Nothin' to say to a fucking journo. I know enough to stay on the right side of that lot. You'd be better off doin' the same.'

'It's not just about them. I'd like to talk to the community for background.'

'Good luck with that. Everyone will say the same thing. They're arseholes. But some people choose to suck the teat.'

Before I could ask him what opportunities arose from teat-sucking, he had tucked his surfboard under his arm and walked away. I watched as he disappeared over sand dunes, wondering how many times I might waylay him at the general store before it was called stalking.

~

Following Surfer Dude's directions, I found Caves Road and was on the right track with enough time to make my eleven o'clock appointment, with renewed determination that everything was going to be businesslike with a clear signposting of my intentions.

'Don't get trapped. You cannot offend this man. Be brutal.' I talked to myself as the Jeep rattled along the road.

The turn-off into the Puharich estate was evident from five hundred metres away. An enormous white archway with roaring lions atop the side columns marked the spot. A sign dangling from wrought iron spears heralded the family name and had a crest that looked suspiciously like something adapted from a castle in Transylvania. Unlike in Croatia, there was no gate or men with dark glasses ticking off lists. I turned in and bumped along a driveway so long, I wondered if I'd made another mistake. There was pasture on both sides and black cows huddled together, chewing and occasionally raising their tails to release shit fountains that barely missed the heads of their nearest and dearest.

The road eventually merged into a bitumen driveway running up to a large barn. Or, rather, the structure was barn-like. A carpark stretched along its length and I pulled into one bay, stopping right before the Jeep sucked up the last drops of fuel.

Bugger.

The building towered above me. Walls of beautiful oiled wood surrounded giant arched windows reaching to the eaves. Every so often, the windows were supplanted with graceful french doors. At each side of the entrances were tubs of roses, and sitting at four spots along the structure were Art Deco–inspired statues representing the four seasons. The effect was grand without being pretentious – something completely unexpected.

And that wasn't the only surprise.

As I looked along the building wondering how to get in, I saw the enticing form of Marco Puharich sauntering towards me, a broad smile lighting up his handsome face.

CHAPTER ELEVEN

My heart did a pitter-pat and I wished I'd worn something more beguiling than jeans and layers of winter woollies. At least I was wearing some classic country boots, which, I was pleased to see, matched those on Marco's feet.

'Well, hello, hello. Welcome to Puharich Land.' His tone was breezy. 'Can't keep away from us?'

Marco stopped in front of me and bent down to put a light kiss on each cheek. I returned the pecks with enthusiasm, renewing my private commitment to get to know him better.

'Brian's invited me for lunch. I'm rather taken aback to see you here.'

'I've come over at my grandfather's behest. Things have taken an unexpected turn, so we're needing to make some changes.'

'Oh?'

He laughed. 'No doubt your lover will fill you in as we eat.'

'Brian is no such thing and you know it.' Despite his aesthetic appeal, this niggling was annoying. 'You really have to leave that alone. It's becoming tedious.'

'Heaven forbid the delightful Alex Grant think me a bore. That is strictly the domain of my cousin.' He laughed at my expression. 'It's all right. I won't keep it up. Just checking the lay of the land. I'm glad there's nothing to you and him.'

I hoped my smile was encouraging without being too 'I want to see your underpants'.

'Will you be at lunch?'

'Yep. We'll all be there in fact. Sadly, no cosy twosome. For now.'

I continued to bare my smiling teeth, happy in the knowledge that fifteen thousand of Charles' dollars had been spent on making my mouth a shiny white, dental marvel.

'I've got some work to finish. You don't mind waiting on your own? I saw Brian in the office on the phone, so he won't be long.' This time Marco took my hand, turned it over and put a light kiss on my pulse point. 'See you at lunch later?'

As he sauntered off, I saw his bum had a shapeliness that made my fingers tingle to give it a pat or a pinch – or a great big lustful grab.

'Sorry to keep you waiting.' Brian was suddenly in front of me.

'Oh, that's okay. I haven't been here long, and Marco came up to say hi.'

He grimaced. 'Yeah, he shocked us by arriving two days ago, which is why I came down earlier too. Did you find us all right?'

'It was easy once I found my way out of Gracetown.'

'You got lost in Gracetown?'

'The difference between left and right isn't automatic for me. Road maps look like someone has vomited up red string and stuck it to paper.'

Brian laughed in a pleasantly melodious way. Maybe he shared some of Marco's charm gene. Then I remembered the cut of his cousin's jib.

'It was good that I was able to get a hold of you. Mobile phone connection is a bit dodgy down here. There are towers in Bunbury, Busselton and Margaret River, but it's still hit-and-miss most of the time.' He reached out and took my hand. 'Let's go in.'

He steered me towards the house. 'We have a baba who does all the cooking and she has a very strict schedule. We're terrified of her, so we're never late.'

'I thought babas were only a thing in Croatia.' I imagined a Croatian supermarket where babas lined the shelves and shoppers squeezed them before dropping their ancient bodies into trollies.

'No. Most families bring one out to act as a housekeeper. My uncle sponsored this one to come and take care of the family here. In Croatia she looked after my uncle and then Marco, so she was happy to come and look after *her boy* in Australia, although she constantly bleats about missing her *baby* Marco. She spends time here and in Perth depending on what's happening.'

'You mentioned cousins, so I'm assuming you have other family in the business.'

'Of course. Outsiders always bring complications, so two of my cousins partly manage the place. They're Marco's brothers, a bit thick, but they're family.'

Oh my god! There were two more of Marco! Lunch was going to be delicious in more ways than one.

'Were they at the funeral?'

'No. Stephen and Matthew rarely go back. My father and uncle keep a close eye on them and I make sure they don't have anything to do with the finances.' Brian readjusted his grip on my arm in such a way it was impossible to remove without a skirmish. 'Come into the house. We can have an aperitif while we wait.'

It was pleasant to meander along the building, then onto a cobbled path covered by a trellis, which, in summer, would be weighed down with the bright green leaves of grapevines and cascading bunches of fruit. Now, in the winter, thick canes gave scant cover. On both sides, expanses of lawn spread out, each with large rose gardens arranged in squares and circles interspersed with gravel walkways. In the warmer months they'd make a stunning display with heady perfumes. The end of the path opened out to a broad terrace flanked on the opposite side by a beautiful house. Like the creamery, its windows and french doors stretched from the ground to the eaves, geometric leadlighting patterning the edges.

'What a beautiful place.'

'Yes, it is. A very small part was already here. Apparently, the owner was a cousin of Lloyd Wright, hence the architecture.'

'How odd that it's in Margaret River.'

'Black sheep of the family, apparently. Before being exiled, he was one of his cousin's first apprentices. It was a lucky accident that we got it. My grandfather bought all the titles in the area without looking if there were any buildings. This was a pleasant surprise.'

'Your grandfather didn't come and see what he was buying?'

'He was interested in the land, not buildings. He employed agents, surveyors, and soil specialists. With vineyards already in the area, he knew it was probably the right soil and the lots included small diaries. Those first herds were part of the package. We've consolidated all the titles to create the estate. My grandfather was one of the pioneers of large-scale food production.'

He spoke with pride and I could see why. The impression was one of great success: a business run with unsentimental ambition by a family happy to be outsiders.

'The house is absolutely wonderful.' It was easy to be impressed.

'Wait until you get inside.'

Brian pushed open one of the doors and we walked into a room of majestic proportions. High white ceilings were divided into grids by flat wooden beams, oiled to a smoky black. The floor was made of large flagstones on which were scattered beautiful rugs in native American patterns. Down one end was a table surrounded by a dozen chairs with high wooden backs crafted in geometric veneer. At the other end, the entire wall was stone and at its centre, an enormous fireplace had a hearth that jutted out, creating a space to sit and admire the perfect proportions of the room. The effect was one of calm sophistication so at odds with the temperament of its occupants.

Brian led me towards the fire and pulled a low armchair closer to the flames.

'What can I get for you?'

I held my hands out to the warmth. 'What have you got?'

'We can do something classic and have a sherry, or I have a very good prosecco.'

'I think I'll go with the prosecco.'

'That works for me.' He went to a large sideboard built into the wall and opened a door revealing a bar fridge, no doubt containing more expensive wines than my little cooler back at the cabin. He generously filled two tall glasses and returned, passing one glass to me before easing himself into a chair opposite.

'Why is Marco here?' I wanted to get 'on-topic' right away.

He looked at me warily. 'You know he comes with a reputation?'

'I'm not interested in him,' I lied.

'Women are sucked in by his looks. He always dumps them and moves on pretty quickly.'

'Sounds like a good old-fashioned philanderer.'

'I think he's more dangerous than that.'

'Seriously, Brian?' Nothing he said was going to spoil my speculations.

'Like I told you,' Brian sipped his drink and changed his tone, 'we weren't expecting him. Apparently it was at my grandfather's command. With the mess of Jure and Zorka, my father and uncle have stayed over there, and Marco has come out here. The idea is for all the cousins to work together to restructure the business.'

'I don't understand. Why doesn't your grandfather get another groundsman and housekeeper? I can imagine there are dozens of people who'd want that gig.'

'We've decided that it's best if we bring everything into the family. My mother and aunt will eventually go back to Croatia as well. They'll take care of the house and Dida, while my father and uncle take care of the manufacturing over there. Apparently that means Marco will move here to deal with logistics. Marie and I will manage the marketing and business side.'

'I thought having a vagina interfered with brain function.'

By the look on his face, the 'v' word was outside his conversational lexicon. He chose to ignore me.

'We have to pull everything in more tightly. There will be no outside consultants, other than lawyers and even then, we intend to use a different vetting system.'

I imagined thumbscrews, lie detectors and water boarding as part of the Puharich interview process.

'What will Marie do? Make coffee and cake?'

'She did manage to get a degree in marketing, you know, and that's what she'll do. Her bit is part-time. We're getting a baba out from Croatia to help her with my niece and the house.'

Which seemed like a good chance for a segue. 'What about Jure and Zorka?'

Brian looked at me, in what looked like mock bewilderment. 'What do you mean? They're dead and buried.'

'You've not heard a peep from the Zagreb police?'

'No.'

An indescribable vibe passed between us. We both knew it was a lie: he was probably wondering if Marco had mentioned the investigation, telling me something that Brian didn't know. And I was wondering why he was telling fibs. I did not have the same gaping nostrils as Brian, but I can smell a big smelly porky when it fluffs under my nose.

'Ultimately, Jure and Zorka were not family. It's up to the police to deal with it through the Simiches. We are involved tangentially as their employers.'

The Puharich family law was clear: live according to their laws and you were an insider. Do something to bring scrutiny on them and you were disowned, expunged from the family narrative. All the pseudo-family inclusiveness at the funeral had clearly been dropped in favour of re-establishing fortress Puharich.

We sat in silence, watching the fire and sipping prosecco.

'Branko, *što radiš*?'

The raspy voice, with the timbre of the aged, was startling, and we both turned like guilty children. A three-dimensional rendering of a crone off one of Jess's tarot cards was striding towards me. Bandy legs made her short, and large dangling bosoms made her wide. She was dressed entirely in black, including thick stockings, and with incongruous running shoes on her feet. Her grey hair was pulled tightly off her face and wound into a bun at the nape of her neck.

Photographers are constantly seeking interesting subjects, yet it would be beyond the ability of any photographer to capture the force of that visage. The ancient wrinkles were like the bark on a tree. The nose was strong with flared nostrils above a sour-looking mouth. But it was the hooded black eyes which were capable of scaring people into soiled underpants. They were hard crystals, like jet, small and arrow-like in their penetration. And they were looking straight at me.

'Baba Tete. Come and meet my friend Alex.' Brian stood.

I followed his lead, hiding my glass behind my back, frightened she might think me a lush. I held out my hand as she approached. She ignored it, instead waiting for Brian to step forward and kiss her cheeks. Looking in my direction, she spoke to him in Croatian.

He gave an awkward smile and replied in English. 'No, she's not my girlfriend. Alex was at school with Marie. We caught up in Croatia and she asked to come and see the creamery.'

Well, that was one version of events. I was too scared to correct him. The baba and Brian had another exchange in Croatian. There was much nodding on his part and ferocious finger-pointing on hers. When she turned to leave, she looked in my direction and pierced me with her laser eyes one more time, before she returned to what I imagined was a dark cavern, smelling of sulphur, where cauldrons sent out fiery sparks and the dried hearts of virgins hung from the ceiling.

Brian sat back down, and I did the same. 'Baba Tete has been a godsend to our family,' he said fondly. 'The way she looks after my cousins and this house means they've been able to focus on building the business.'

'Aren't there any wives around the place?'

'No. My cousins have been down here on their own ever since they came over. They're in their early thirties now, so sometime soon they'll go back to Croatia and find wives to bring back here.'

'Australia has women.'

'Alex, there are women a man dates and then there is the woman he marries. Two different things.'

The impulse to punch his nose was enormous, but its sturdy structure was likely to break every bone in my hand and I was conscious of the fact I'd need both in good working order if I was to cut cheese and hold a wine glass.

'Which one am I?'

He looked at me indulgently. 'You're in your own category. The woman who has the power of a great family at her disposal and who needs the kind of man who can show her the best ways to use it.'

I opened my mouth to respond at the same time as the doors at the end of the room were flung wide, putting an end to our *tête à tête*.

'Come on.' Brian held out his hand. 'Time for lunch.'

Ignoring him, I strode in the direction of the new arrivals. Brian was forced into a trot to catch up with me. We arrived at the table together, Brian stepping next to me to face the two men who had entered through the glass doors. At five foot nine, I'm tall for a woman but the brothers were man mountains, at least five inches taller than me. They were handsome in a lumberjack kind of way: both dark with wide foreheads, they had light hazel eyes and the same full lips of their brother. Their mouths looked as though they were ready to smile at any moment, something lacking in Marco's intensity and in the absence of humour in their cousin. They were the type who were easy and funny in the company of men; now, in the company of a woman, they were taciturn.

'Stephen, Matthew, this is a friend from the old days, Alex Grant. Alex, these are my cousins.'

'Pleased to meet you.' I said, holding out my hand.

They each gripped it in turn, pumping it up and down as though expecting water or oil. I think each said hello and that they too were pleased, but they spoke through closed lips, exhaling the words rather than speaking them. Their heavy accents added to their linguistic constipation. It was going to be a very long meal.

Like so many other occasions, I was wrong. Lunch was a short, fascinating whirlwind.

CHAPTER TWELVE

We all sat exactly when a giant pedestal clock chimed twelve. Instantly, a door to the right opened and a stainless-steel trolley, pushed by the witch, came to a standstill at the end of the table. Speaking in Croatian, she began to hand out platters of food to the nearest boy, who'd then put it on the table. At the end of this process, the surface in front of us was covered in food. 'Lunch' is a pathetic word to describe the feast before me. Three plates of meat (lamb and pork chops and grilled venison), a platter of baked potatoes, a bowl of something vegetable mixed with tomato sauce, and a mountain of iceberg lettuce dripping in olive oil and vinegar were plonked on the table in a lackadaisical way, suggesting the commonplace nature of the meal. A vegetarian would die of hunger in this household. A carnivore, however? I could barely keep the saliva from leaking between my lips.

'Alex, please help yourself. Guests first.' Brian dipped his head in my direction.

Too late. Stephen and Matthew waited for no one. Passing the food to each other, they tipped the platters and scraped servings onto their plates: picking up individual pieces of meat with a serving fork clearly took too much time. Once their plates were full, they used both knives and forks as shovels to push food through gnashing teeth.

The old witch came back into the room with a pile of bread cut into chunks and gave it to Matthew. He reached up with one hand, still shovelling food without missing a beat. While I was waiting for my own slab of bread, one of the french doors opened and Marco walked in. The black crone swung around with her hands on her hips and jutted her chin up. She said something in Croatian that made him smile and he returned fire. Astonishingly, she smiled back; he bent down, and she gave him a playful slap on the cheek. Her face was transformed into soft brown folds and she squinted her eyes into tiny slits of good humour.

'*Moja draga*.'

He murmured something and kissed her forehead gently. She turned, and with another spearing dark look in my direction, disappeared through the kitchen door. I turned to Brian. He was staring straight ahead as Marco sat opposite. His tensile stillness made me slightly fearful. Here was a man convulsed by a hatred, deep and long-standing – it infused every atom of his being.

Marco ignored Brian's gaze, instead looking indulgently at his brothers and then at me.

'Aren't you eating?'

'Yes, yes. I hadn't got around to filling my plate.'

'Stephen and Matthew don't bother with niceties when there's food around. Let me help you.'

I gave my plate to him and he served up a bit of everything, handing it back piled high with well-cooked bits of Bambi.

'Thank you.'

'Can I pour you some wine?'

'Don't bother,' said Brian sharply. 'I've had a shiraz breathing on the sideboard.' He looked towards the two eating machines. 'Can one of you go and get the wine over there,' he pointed across the room, 'and ask Baba for some butter?'

The brothers looked at each other as though they didn't know what to think of this interruption. After a few moments, and after stuffing his mouth with more meat for the journey, Stephen went to the sideboard and then to the door where he yelled in Croatian before returning to the table. He put the wine in front of Brian and resumed swallowing his meal.

Brian poured wine into our glasses. 'Salute.'

'Cheers.' I clinked the tip of my glass against his.

'Am I allowed to share?' Marco's voice was silky.

I thought Brian was going to refuse. But his sense of propriety, at least in front of me, was ascendant. 'Get a glass.'

Marco rose and walked to a cocktail cabinet where a variety of stemware was arranged according to usage. Choosing a large wine balloon, he returned, stopping at Brian's shoulder. Leaning forward, he placed the glass close to the bottle.

Brian picked it up and filled Marco's glass.

'I hope you choke on it,' he said.

Marco winked and raised his glass to me. For a few minutes the only sound was the enthusiastic chomping of the brothers. I put my head down and joined in.

The old witch cooked like an angel. The meat was tender and seasoned with enough salt to bring out the individual qualities of each cut. Even the banal lettuce was crisp and juicy with just enough vinegar and freshly pressed olive oil. I wanted to eat slowly, savouring every morsel. This was impossible with the frantic mastication going on around me. The serving platters had been demolished by second and third helpings before I'd cleared my first. Stephen and Matthew ate so quickly, I wondered if they had digestive systems or a series of bovine stomachs. Every second mouthful was washed down with a gulp of wine and they seemed oblivious to the taste and quality of the food.

As they finished, the pair collapsed back in their chairs.

'This is a good drop.' Stephen sucked the berry-infused wine through his teeth. 'Where's it from?'

'Leeuwin. I thought Alex might like to sample one of the best local products,' said Brian.

'So, we have Alex to thank for this.' Stephen raised his glass in my direction.

'Brian wants us to put on our best show,' Marco told his brothers. 'He has ulterior motives.'

Stephen laughed, and Matthew looked out from under his brow as though he was seeing the animosity of his cousin and brother for the first time.

'I hope you liked the food.' Stephen's voice suggested conversation was a tiring business.

'It was sensational. Your baba knows how to bring out the most amazing flavours in everything.'

'Wait until you taste her cheesecake. It's made from our ricotta, our lemons, with a hint of our limoncello.' Stephen smacked his lips in anticipation.

I wondered if she had been listening behind the door, because at that moment, Baba emerged carrying a cheesecake in one hand and a knife in the other. She placed them both in front of Brian. Her eyes flicked between him and me and she muttered something in Croatian that made Brian blush and his cousins laugh. Then she withdrew to the kitchen.

'You could stab someone to death with that thing,' said Marco as his cousin took up the knife.

'That's the first good idea you've ever had.'

'Now, now be polite.' Marco winked again at me.

Brian cut the cake into large triangles and passed the plates around.

From the bowl in front of me, the aroma of sweet cheese titillated my nostrils. The men tucked in and I was quick to follow, shutting my eyes and barely suppressing a groan of delight. A light citrus cheesiness burst on my tongue. Even my companions ate slowly, savouring every bite. The dessert was demolished in minutes. I'd wanted to ask for seconds, but that meant sacrificing further stomach space and there was cheese to be sampled.

'That was absolutely fantastic.' I briefly entertained the thought of licking the plate, or maybe rubbing my face over it.

'Babe Tete is a cook and housekeeper *par excellence.*' Marco was proud.

The brothers nodded.

'Yeah, she's great.' It was the first time I'd heard Matthew speak clearly and his voice was oddly high pitched under its heavy accent. 'Best thing our fathers did, bringing her out here.'

'They've got to be useful for something.' Brian was only half joking.

Stephen was swishing his finger around his plate and sucking up the crumbs. 'Thank god Dida has kept them over there.'

As they all sniggered in agreement I wondered why they judged their fathers so harshly. It seemed thankless and insensitive. I loathed Charles at times, yet it never occurred to me to rid him from my life.

'Didn't your parents help to set up the business?'

'Yes,' said Marco. 'At some stage, everyone passes their use-by date and they were stuck in the old ways. My uncle fought diversification all the way, and my father wasn't much better. They listened to each other. We've had to fight to introduce technology. If it was up to them, we'd have farmers milking cows by hand and maidens churning cheese.'

'I wouldn't mind a maiden to churn my cheese,' Stephen said, and Matthew tittered.

'Okay you two. We have a lady in our presence.' Marco shot me a challenge across the table. 'Are you a lady?'

'Probably not.' I met his gaze.

'Didn't think so.' His lips parted slightly, transporting me back to a laboratory in Croatia.

'Marco, haven't you got things to do?' Brian's voice ended my reminiscences.

'Yes, we all have. I need to go through our agreed changes with these morons.'

Marco's brothers didn't seem to mind the barb. They had obviously heard it all before and their bovine faces were sanguine as they pushed back their chairs and headed for the door, giving me a nonchalant wave before exiting.

'Complete imbeciles. They share a brain cell.' Marco looked after them, contempt on his face. 'My grandfather should take them back, but he has limits to the number of incompetents he can absorb into the business over there.'

'That seems a bit harsh.'

'You're right. It's an accident of birth that makes them family. I'd better be going.' Marco came to my side and bent down to kiss my cheek. 'I'm glad you're here. Nice to have a beautiful, intelligent woman in our midst.'

Brian's face was furious, but he remained silent.

'I'm looking forward to Brian showing me around. You seem to have something really special here.'

Marco stood up straight, showing to good effect his height and beautifully proportioned physique. 'I might see you later, Alex.'

'And there goes the Puharich Adonis,' said Brian.

'Why don't you like each other?'

'In our family mythology, he's Mr Wonderful even though I'm the one with the brains. His good looks have made him a favourite with my grandfather, in fact, he gets away with things that I don't even dare to try. He's always coming up with brilliant ideas and I'm the one who has to make them work. Some are impossible and I'm blamed when they don't come off. I'm sick of all three of them.'

'The other two seem harmless enough.'

Brian shook his head. 'That's one thing Marco is right about. Stephen and Matthew are stupid. It's easy enough to give them instructions, wind them up, and set them going. That's something my grandfather has drilled into us. You can get dumb people to do almost anything you want as long as they get paid with what they value most. In Stephen and Matthew's case, that's plentiful food and an easy life. Part of Matthew's problem is he didn't come over until he was in his teens, and he's thick. Poor bastard was never going to make a go of it on his own, so the family business has to look after him. They make this place feel like a kindergarten. They drive Marie crazy. One day she left them in charge of my niece, they took her to the park and after a while went to the pub, leaving her at the park because they forgot they were babysitting.'

I smiled. 'Didn't they know why they were at the park?'

'They're morons. Enough of them – let me take you on a tour.'

~

I spent the rest of the afternoon like a delirious Miss Muffet smelling and tasting my way through hard and soft versions of curdled milk.

Brian led me back to the building I had admired on arriving. Going in through a side door, we stepped into an enormous vaulted room divided by a glass wall. Behind this wall, gleaming stainless-steel churning machines whirred, and people in lab coats, hairnets and booties purposefully strode about.

Going up to a window, Brian pointed in various directions. 'We make four types of soft cheese: ricotta, mozzarella, brie and a blue based on roquefort. The brie is both double and triple cream and everything is full fat. Without the fat, there's no taste and you may as well be eating slops.'

'I agree, I agree.' At that moment anything was possible: the moon was really made of cheese, Dracula was misunderstood, and Snoop Doggy Dogg could actually sing.

'The people at the steel baths are stirring heated whey. They'll start forming the strings which eventually are stretched and then cut into balls. Care to sample some more?'

'Yes!' I almost clapped. 'Please. I've been looking forward to it.'

'All right. Come along to the tasting bench.'

A long wooden bar was at the far end of the room. I had a desire to take Brian's hand and skip.

'We put this café and retail element in last year and it's exceeded all our sales modelling. People are ready to have another reason, other than wine or surfing, to visit Margaret River.'

'Are there any competitors?'

'Sometimes a person might arrive and set up a creamery. They don't last long. We have contracts with all the dairies in the region, so a newbie's costs to buy and cart milk are crippling. Apart from rich Perth lawyers and doctors looking for tax dodges on loss-making businesses, people can't make a go of it. When they hit the wall, we buy them out.'

'Sounds a bit brutal.'

'That's business, Alex.'

As we approached the tasting area, the smell of cheese filled my nostrils and I breathed in deeply.

Brian was amused. 'I take it you enjoy your fromage?'

'In a previous life I was a French mouse.'

'What would you like to try first?' Brian pulled out a high stool for me, then moved around the bar to open a glass-fronted refrigerator packed with different types of cheese.

'Don't mind. After that huge lunch, probably something light.'

He arranged some crackers on a plate and gave me a glass of water. 'You need to clear your palate between the varieties otherwise you won't appreciate the individual tastes and textures.' He cut off a thin wedge of brie, put it on a plate and pushed it towards me. 'Take a piece. Not so big that you can't roll it over your tongue. And smell it first. Aroma is as important in cheese as it is in wine.'

I had a little sniff – it smelled all right to me. Then I popped it in my mouth. As I let it roll across my palate, Brian rabbited on about salt and sweet and pH levels. He trotted out statistics and the technicalities of starter yeasts as I munched my way through cheeses that were silky, creamy or had a mysterious piquancy. I sat for two hours in a bubble of bliss. As time passed, Brian became more animated and the negative sentiments of lunch were replaced with a buoyancy I hadn't associated with him. Through my cheese-coloured glasses it made him vaguely more attractive.

It was towards the end of the second hour that I had to call a stop.

'I'll explode with another bite.'

'I wondered when you were going to reach your limit.' Through senses dulled with lactose, his smile was soft and rather pleasant.

'I need the ladies.'

'Of course.' He pointed behind him and to the left. 'Go down that corridor, the bathroom is the second door. I'll clean up here.'

I did a half-roll off the stool, my knees creaking as I straightened up, then followed his directions.

In the bathroom mirror my flushed face looked a tiny bit fuller, and maybe the jowls were a bit droopier. It was as though the fat from the cheese had immediately melted into my cheeks.

'It's just bloating. Bound to drain out overnight.'

I reapplied my lipstick, tugged at my clothes and tried to suck in my stomach, which had started to flop over the waistband of my jeans. Thoughts of a starvation diet starting tomorrow began forming in my mind. Distracted, I left the bathroom and turned left, pushing open a door that I could have sworn wasn't there before.

I was right. The door opened to the outside. A cool southerly was blowing. The wind hit my face like a slap. I looked around me. From the back, the creamery looked purely functional: large concrete blocks made up the wall and several solid doors broke up the façade. Not far away, across a grassed block, was another large brick building. As I stood there, invisible hands from inside were slowly sliding the doors open.

Then there came the sound of a car engine approaching from behind me and to the right, where a road ran from the front of the creamery to the bigger shed. I watched as a Ford utility came around the corner. As it passed me, I saw at least half a dozen surfer-types sitting in the tray. Chief among them, Surfer Dude from the Gracetown general store.

CHAPTER THIRTEEN

Without thinking, I moved back and pressed myself against the wall. Seeing him was both surprising and revealing. Clearly self-interest was greater than Surfer Dude's cynicism about sucking at the Puharich teat. I was conflicted, wanting to see what he was up to, but reluctant for him to catch me doing it.

Caution won out. Keeping hidden against the creamery, I watched the surfers, who were sitting with their backs resting against the sides of the open tray facing each other, their legs stretched out in front of them, feet almost touching. Despite the cold weather, they wore thongs, and their tanned legs poked out of sun-bleached shorts. Their torsos were bulky with flannelette jackets lined with faux sheepskin and woollen beanies covered heads whose matted hair and dreadlocks poked out at all angles. Surfer Dude was balancing on his haunches with his back to the cabin. He was the only one talking, gesturing to each of his companions in turn. They were nodding, their faces with the look of resignation common among workers who don't like being told what to do, but who need the cash. Surfboards, uggs, petrol and flannies all cost money. I waited as the doors of the shed opened wide enough to let them drive through. Then they slowly shut.

Cheese-making surfers? Here was a group being led by Surfer Dude – the guy who told me everyone thought that the Puhariches were arseholes. What work was he possibly doing for them? He and his sandy mates were a long way from being milk maidens. And why did he hate the Croatians so much?

A few minutes passed before I realised I'd been gone for longer than the standard wee time. I returned to the passage and quickly returned to Brian.

'Well, hello stranger.'

'Sorry. After all the wonderful food, I was a bit slow putting on my lippy.'

He gave me a smile that made him look a tiny bit like Marco, if only around the mouth.

'Care to have a port to finish off the day?'

'Sounds good.'

He took a bottle from underneath the bar. 'We'll sit over in the lounge area. Let me find some figs and grapes.'

I wandered through a small space reserved for tables stacked with a range of local produce. Fancy glass refrigeration units displayed the Puharich cheeses arranged in triangular stacks, with cut wedges of different sizes wrapped in waxed paper emblazoned with the family crest. I leaned in to read the labels and almost fainted at the prices: this was not the stuff to chuck in the school lunchbox. Doing a quick calculation, I estimated I'd chewed my way through almost two hundred dollars' worth of coagulated milk and mould. My stomach gurgled with satisfaction as I sat down on the studded cushions of a maroon chesterfield.

'This is a nineteen seventy Fonseca Vintage Port.' Brian gave me a tiny glass filled with a deep crimson liquid. 'Small sips, deep breaths.'

I followed his directions and tasted a flavour of cherries and bergamot that I rolled around in my mouth. 'Yummy.'

'A technical term from a true believer.' Brian settled back into the chesterfield and I did the same.

'This is an incredible place. I can understand why you love it so much.'

'Yep, we make the best cheese currently available on the Australian market.'

For a moment I could have hit Brian with a humility stick. But I'd probably have to beat him unconscious before it had any effect.

'Does Marie come down often?'

'No. With the restructure, however, she'll have to soon.'

I picked up a dried fig and popped it in my mouth. 'If I were Marie, I'd be here every weekend stuffing my face.'

'Unlike you, she can't just drop everything. She's a wife and mother.'

'I have responsibilities.'

His was sceptical. 'You're in your mid-thirties, unmarried, don't have children and I'm not sure you have a job.'

'You know I work as a freelancer. That's my job.'

He looked at me speculatively. 'Do you intend to freelance while you're down here?'

'Of course. I think there's a lot to write about.'

'Like what?'

'You mentioned that you'd like to see some reviews of your business and its produce. So, this is a great place to start.'

'Does your father read your journalism?'

'Don't know. It's doubtful, unless it's about his friends or acquaintances.'

'I'd be happy to host a gourmet weekend for Charles and his closest associates, if you'd like to set it up.' Brian was revealing his agenda and I wasn't going to play along.

'He's pretty busy and we're not that close. And, on your other point, being single is my choice.'

Brian, sensibly, did not pursue his Charles ambitions. 'What do I need to do to make you change your mind?'

'Give me more than cheese and biscuits.'

He fixed me with a ferocious stare that he'd probably practised in a mirror using a picture of Fabio as his guide. The port had done strange things to my brain and I barely stopped myself from giggling.

'There will come a time, Alex, when you'll hear the clock ticking. Then a husband will become important.'

'I see enough of Charles' new family to make me realise I'm not the mothering kind.'

'You haven't found the right man.'

The cheese had been delicious but talk of my love life was all I needed to end my visit.

'I'd better be getting back to Gracetown now.'

'Okay. I suppose you don't want to be driving at kangaroo time.'

Standing, he offered me a hand. I grasped it and staggered to my feet.

'Are you right to drive?'

'Sure. Not a problem.' We both knew that was a lie.

Brian raised his eyebrow when he saw the Jeep.

'I can't imagine your father appreciates his daughter going about in such a piece of junk. It doesn't look roadworthy.'

'My father isn't silly enough to tell me what to do.'

'Charles always seemed to be a very generous man. I'm sure he'd provide you with something more appropriate.'

'That proves you don't know my father very well.'

'I know he's held in high esteem. In your shoes, I'd value any input he had to offer. When I have a daughter, she'll always see me as someone she can talk to and consult.'

'Then I hope you never have a daughter.'

He winked at me. 'One with a little bit of you in her might be nice.'

Now was the time to run! I picked up speed and reached the Jeep well ahead of Brian. The cold started to clear my brain while I waited for him to arrive. It was when I opened the driver's side door that I remembered the dire state of my fuel.

'Shit! There's not enough fuel to get me home. Can I syphon from one of your vehicles? It needs to be diesel.'

'That's easy. We have our own tank around the back. If there's a few drops in that thing it should get you around there, otherwise I'll get my cousins and we can push.'

'Thanks so much.' I hopped into the seat, leaving the door open. I turned the key and the engine gave a tail pipe fart and started chugging. 'Looks like it's just enough if I go slowly.'

With Brian walking in front, I followed him along the building, turning left at the end. The car shook and creaked over the same road where I'd seen the ute. The shed with the sliding door came into view and we continued towards it before doing a sharp turn and following its front wall to where a bowser was set in a concrete stand.

'You'll need to pull in closely because the hose isn't very long.'

I jostled the Jeep back and forth until Brian held up his hand to stop. I got out and watched as he pushed the nozzle into the tank.

'Sorry about this. Dirt is the only thing that will come out of the pump at Gracetown.'

'Not a problem.'

I looked around, trying to be casual. 'What's this shed?'

'It's our warehouse. The cheese from Croatia is put directly into storage. It has stone vaults underneath where the air is kept exactly to the temperature needed to grow mould. Our soft cheeses love it. It's amazing how important they are for building the right type and depth of mould. Too much makes the cheese bitter and it overwhelms the creaminess.'

'They sound interesting.'

'Before you ask, no, you can't have a look. It's a very carefully controlled environment so only a small number of people go down there. Even breathing can upset the ecology.'

I immediately began to wonder how I might become one of that exclusive group.

'Who looks after the vaults?'

'Stephen's in charge and spends the most time in them. He turns and circulates the cheeses so they age evenly. Apart from that, they're not touched until it's time for distribution. Then Matthew lends a hand. When Marco is here, he checks the stock and makes sure the dummies have done the right thing. Although of course he doesn't get his hands dirty actually *doing* anything.'

'How about you? Have you been down there?'

'Of course. When I absolutely have to. I think I'm allergic to all the mould in the air. My nose itches and I can sneeze for days.'

Brian's nose expelling highly pressurised air made me think of the Manhattan Project and fake towns blown to smithereens.

'I'd love a little peek. I'd hold my breath.'

'No, Alex. You write your reviews of the end product. The rest is out-of-bounds.'

Jess would have recognised the changes in my expression: eyes narrowed, jaw thrusting forward, squared-off shoulders. Signs of a stubborn determination to do the exact opposite of what I'd been told. If he had known, Brian may have been less nonchalant. Thrusting his bony chest out and broadening his skinny shoulders, he continued filling the Jeep, looking at me from under his brow to see if I had noticed his machismo.

I leaned against the car, looking towards the warehouse, wondering what was going on within its walls and below its surface.

A grinding noise started up, and we saw the door of the shed slowly opening. With barely enough space, the same ute I'd seen previously drove out and started on the road towards us. We watched it get closer, then take a right turn to follow the road back past the creamery. In the tray was the same group of surfers, the Gracetown Surfer Dude leaning against the tailgate. This time he looked directly at me. For a moment he looked confused – I was familiar, but he couldn't place me. Then his expression cleared. He leaned forward and said something to his mates. They all turned and looked at me, their faces curious, yet guarded. They kept staring as the ute rounded the corner of the creamery and disappeared.

'Who are they?'

'A group of locals we get to help stack and store the product when it's cleared the port in Albany. Comes up by refrigerated transport and they help to unload it.'

'I thought they'd be out on their boards all day.'

'Even surfers need to eat.'

I'd imagined them getting by on krill. 'I thought you only used family.'

'Naturally our preference is family or, at least, other Croatians. We need more people and surfers are efficient, fast workers. Probably because they want to get back in the ocean. The problem is when the weather report tells them the waves are good. That's more an issue in spring and autumn. Then we bring over more Croats on two-month working visas to fill the void. The surfers want the money and they're willing to do afternoon and night shifts to get the product stored as quickly as possible. It's all in the timing.'

'No day shift?'

'When there are no waves it's bloody hard to get a surfer out of bed before eleven. In winter we aim for a two pm shift and another starting at seven.'

I looked back at the shed. 'Are you sure I can't change your mind about the vaults? Just our secret.'

'No,' said Brian. 'Even you can't make an interesting story about rows of shelving in a hole in the ground.'

'I don't know. I'm very interested in seeing the final product en masse. Vaults stacked full of cheese must be a wonderful sight and readers would be fascinated.'

'Well, your readers are going to be disappointed because I'm not taking you into them.'

'Maybe Marco will help me.'

'Good luck. After you broke into the lab in Croatia, I think even he will be wary about letting you see our entire business.'

'I didn't break into anything. The door was open.'

'May I suggest you don't do the same thing here?' Brian pulled the nozzle out of the tank and replaced it on the bowser. 'My cousin's smart, but he's an arrogant arsehole on a delusional power trip.' He closed the cap on the Jeep. 'There you go. Full to the brim.'

'How much do I owe you?' I opened the glove box to get my purse.

'Nothing.'

'No, that's too generous.'

'The company is paying. And there are no strings attached.' He looked at me ruefully and I felt a little pinch of remorse – just a pinch and not for long.

'Thank the company for me.' I kept my voice light as I climbed into the driver's seat and turned the key. After a bit of coughing, the Jeep was right to go.

'You'll need to come for breakfast on the weekend. Marie will probably be here, and Baba Tete does a breakfast you won't believe.'

'Sounds good. You have my number, so give me a ring. It's been really great.' My sincerity was genuine. 'A fabulous host and amazing food. What more could a girl want?'

'You're welcome. I'll see you over the next few days?'

I nodded and waved as I attempted a three-point turn that degenerated into a forward-back, forward-back hopping. Eventually I managed to get onto the road and drove away. Through the rear-view mirror, Brian was waving with a tragic expression on his face, as though farewelling a passenger on the *Titanic*.

~

As I drove north, I thought about the warehouse and the vaults underneath. Brian had banned me and that was all I needed as an impetus. I'm sure if Jessica had said I was *definitely not* allowed to be a surgeon, I'd have worked hard enough to become the first person to transplant faulty organs, while simultaneously playing 'Achy Breaky Heart' on the banjo.

Even if Brian's reasons about the vaults were valid, surely a quick peek in the shed wasn't unreasonable. He'd been happy to show me around the rest of the compound. Why was he so precious about that building?

I'd toured the catacombs in Paris and since then linked underground rooms with spaces full of skulls and skeletons neatly stacked on earthen shelves. Not that I thought the Puharich vaults actually held the bones of cheesemakers past. But the violence of Jure and Zorka's deaths had stayed with me and affected my perception of the Puharich clan.

Then there was the sophisticated 'food technician' laboratory in the highland backblocks of Croatia. Was there a similar set-up in the warehouse or vaults? Brian had quickly marched me out over there and made sure I didn't go back. The Puhariches were intent on letting me see what they wanted me to and nothing else

And what about the surfers? I understood they had to eat, but sticking beach-loving child-men into a refrigerator to haul cheese around didn't feel right. These were chilled guys with salt-cracked lips whose interests centred on boards, wetsuits and clapped-out station wagons. Every so often, they may hitch themselves to a chick, particularly if the waves were crap or she had a well-paying job. Doing back-to-back shifts in a cheese warehouse seemed dangerously close to a conventional working life.

Where did Surfer Dude fit in? I'd misjudged him. He hated the Puhariches, yet he worked for them. In fact, he looked to be the leader of the pack – giving orders to his surfer buddies in a way that suggested a familiarity with the role. It is a rare man who works for people he considers arseholes unless there is a significant upside. I was at a loss to see what that upside was for him.

From the top of my head, to the tips of my toes, my journalist's instincts were telling me that the warehouse and vaults had their own story to tell. I had to get in. Driving in a kind of cheese-infused fog, I arrived at the marvellous conclusion that I needed to find a way in without the knowledge of the Puhariches.

Never having completed Break and Enter 101, no idea on how to do an actual break and enter came to mind. In movies, tyre irons are a popular method of smashing glass, and credit cards are nifty lock openers. Knowing my luck, I'd knock myself unconscious with the former, and drop the latter under the door before getting it anywhere near the lock. Therefore I'd need to draw on my own latent abilities to creep and make the rest up as I went along. I peered through the front windscreen at the gathering dark. The tiny new moon meant the night was going to be at its darkest. If I put it off for another night, the moon would be brighter: easier for a gang of Croatians brandishing newly minted tourist visas to see me and bury me among the gouda.

It was a very short leap to go from these observations to the decision that the time to make my move was tonight.

The drive back to the holiday park was slow. The food, wine and port made my brain jostle about in my skull. My eyes spent more time peering up into my own eyelids than they did looking at the road. I relied on the rough edges of the bitumen and the click of the cat's eyes in the middle to keep the Jeep in a straight line. It was rudimentary, yet effective.

By the time I pulled up at the cabin, it was pitch black. The camping ground was deserted, and the manager hadn't wasted money on external lighting. I felt, rather than saw, my way to the door, running my hand along the wall to turn on a light. Nothing. The amenities didn't include lights inside the lean-to. Meaning a drunken stumble to the kitchen to find a switch. The light stung my eyeballs. I looked around, sensing that something wasn't right. The aroma of unwashed man and stale cigarettes hung in the air. I was still, listening. The sound of creeping feet and then the click of an opening door came from the bedroom. I could've charged across the room and confronted whoever was trying to leave but a sense of self-preservation made me stay put. I waited to hear the door close then ran to the bedroom and looked through the french window. Lumbering along the face of the sand dune was the vague outline of a man dressed in the kind of duffel coat stocked at army surplus stores. A gloved hand held the hood low on his face and his feet, clad in thongs, battled in the sand.

Shouting was pointless and it was impossible to run after him without scratching my boots on the prickly saltbush. No intruder was worth the sacrifice.

Further investigations could wait until daylight. In the meantime, I worked quickly to move two of the lounge chairs to the front and back doors, wedging them under the handles. In my bedroom I closed the curtains tightly and pushed the bed hard up against the french doors. The bathroom window was rusted shut and the louvre windows in the kitchen hadn't been opened in decades. I gave thanks that the camp manager was a maintenance lazy arse.

After a quick check of my valuables, I sat down, feeling ill. I've rarely had any man in my house, let alone a potential thief. Once a randy idiot broke in to steal my lacy undies, silky pieces set aside for occasions requiring something saucy. Now there was someone who who didn't seem to have taken anything. What was he looking for? And, more importantly, who was he? Dead bodies in Croatia made me think of the Puhariches. And I wouldn't put anything past the holiday park manager. Then there was Surfer Dude. In the tiny village of Gracetown it was an easy thing for him to find out where I was staying. Had my appearance at the creamery made him want to scare me off? It made me doubly determined to get back to the warehouse tonight.

Making a cup of tea, with the addition of a thick stream of calming honey, seemed appropriate. A syrupy hot drink was Jessica's answer to all calamities. In the sitting room, I turned on the TV and sank into the remaining armchair. I felt like pulling the cork on a bottle of red, but a drunk-fuzzy brain would upset my plan. Lying on the bed risked falling asleep, ruining the chances of me waking with my resolve intact. I turned up the volume on the TV and was thankful for a movie where explosions, gunfire and screeching voices were the main plot devices. I decided nine thirty was the time for action, giving me scope to get ready, drive to the estate and find a way into the building.

Doing something that some might consider illegal always made me think of Ben. He was my default conscience – mine being slightly underdeveloped. One one-hundredth of me acknowledged I ought to ring and give him the heads-up. The rest of me knew this was a bad idea because he'd make me promise to stay home. I'd have to break the promise and then his disappointment would cripple me for days. I have a very low care factor when it comes to disappointing almost everyone. But when it came to Ben and Jess, I always felt like I'd injured them – put a little tear in the bit of their hearts where I lived.

I didn't want to feel guilty before I'd even started. And with so many unanswered questions, there was definitely a big cheese-flavoured story to uncover. My instincts told me so.

CHAPTER FOURTEEN

The clock ticked over to nine pm. Going into the bedroom to consider clothing, I felt that the Hollywood version of a Ninja, all in black, was the most appropriate. Corduroy stirrup pants and a cardigan with a skivvy underneath was the best I could do when it came to black. There was something Beat poet mixed with librarian about the outfit. The only black shoes in my case were sweet ballet flats with a cute velvet bow on the heel. The mirror revealed a Stepford Wife rather than a Ninja, but it was all black. Jessica kept a beanie in the Jeep for her midnight moon ceremonies, so my hair was tucked away and, at least, my head kept warm. Navy blue gloves with pompoms at the wrist were the final flourish. There was always a torch in the glove box, although using it was dangerous: it screamed 'person trying to sneak in!'

After eating a chocolate bar and swallowing a lukewarm cup of coffee for courage, I left the cabin. A choking engine and shrieking brakes were the downside to Jess's car. It was not made for stealth. In the quiet night, it sounded like an airplane coming in for a crash landing. I drove slowly through the campground, doing the vehicular version of tiptoe. The manager's office was coming up on my left and, as I crept past, the silhouette of a fat man, cigarette smoke trailing away from the top of his head, was pressed against the window.

I didn't switch on the radio or put in a cassette. I didn't even talk or sing to myself. Silence made me feel suitably furtive, putting me in a Ninja mindset. The Jeep chugged along as fast as it could go without overheating. I slowed when I saw the large archway marking the entry to the estate then pulled over and peered through the windscreen. Going down the driveway was not the way to begin Special Operation Creamery. Looking at the Missus's map, I saw that all the roads in the area were arranged in a grid pattern. Reversing and turning down the road bordering the estate would probably lead to another road going along the back of the Puharich block.

I eased out onto the main road and found a smaller one running parallel to the estate driveway. The Jeep was at snail pace as I watched for the end of the fence line. After about half a kilometre, the fence took a hard right turn. Braking, I wound the window down and saw a well-maintained dirt track leading off the bitumen. I turned in, went a short distance and stopped, parking as far off the road as the vegetation allowed. Across the road was a tautly strung wire fence. Grapevines and olive trees sloped gently up and away from my position. Beyond the neat rows, barely visible in the night sky, was the gable of the warehouse.

'Righto.' I pushed my hair into Jess's beanie and pulled it low, making my head look like the top of a Sharpie. Getting out of the Jeep, I walked around the back, opened the tailgate and hunted for her torch. I found two: a small penlight and a heavy one of yellow plastic. Though bulky, it provided the best light and might come in handy if I needed to knock someone out: not a scenario I favoured. Luckily, my Brown Owl from Girl Guides had taught me to be prepared for anything. I shut the back of the Jeep and locked the doors. Across the road, I looked for a sign warning me the wire fence was electrified. Ten thousand volts charging through my body would probably blow a hole in my ballet flats. Someone told me that an electric shock could explode ovaries. It was likely that I wasn't going to use mine, but why take the risk?

There were no signs and no buzzing. I tipped my finger on the top wire – nothing. Reassured, I tucked the torch under one arm and held apart two strands of wire. A lady had the ability to step through. Me? I hopped, fell and rolled away like a black pudding. I got up and brushed myself off to find a tear in the knee of my stirrup pants.

'Shit!' It sounded so loud, I expected Puhariches and surfers to come running.

I kneeled low and waited. All was still.

Back on my feet, I hunched over and darted from tree to tree. It was better when the vines began. Although naked after their winter pruning, their thick trunks and canes provided useful protection. It didn't take me long to get to the back corner of the shed. From inside I could hear sounds of industry: refrigerators, voices, a radio and a clanging of metal against metal. With my back squashed hard against the side of the building, I moved along the wall, stopping about a metre from the front corner.

A band of light shone across the paving from the slightly open door. Squeezing my bum cheeks together, my sphincter made a vacuum seal, which sucked me tighter to the wall. I slid along. At the edge I flipped myself over and flattened my front against the metal and stretched my neck around the corner until one eye saw through the crack between the wall and the opening. Two covered trucks had been reversed into separate bays, ramps lowered, so they almost touched a wall that ran the full height and width of the building. This was the shed within a shed. I couldn't see anyone, but there were voices and the sound of trolley wheels at the back of the truck closest to me. Having a body bigger than a tent peg, I was never going to be able to squeeze through the crack.

Given that the trucks had to go in, they also had to come out. Straightening up, I moved back along the side wall away from the light to wait. Although determined to remain standing and on alert, it wasn't long before my legs and feet were too cold to hold me up. I slumped to the ground and pulled my knees into my chest, hoping to keep warm enough to stop frostbite.

It was about thirty long minutes before I heard the rumble of an engine. It wasn't from inside the shed. Unfolding myself, I crept back to the door. Another truck was coming down the road, passing the fuel tank where I had stood with Brian that afternoon. A replica of the two already parked, this one moved slowly towards me and sounded its horn. Immediately the giant door started to open. The truck came closer, turned around in front of the shed and reversed as close as possible to the building before it stopped and waited for a big enough space to drive through. As soon as he was able, the driver manoeuvred the vehicle into the shed.

Now was my Ninja moment!

There was one person in the cab: a surly-looking man who had the same proportions as the Puharich boys. He swung down from the cabin and went to the back of the truck, speaking loudly and crossly in Croatian. I heard a door opening and the rapid footsteps of other people, who gathered at the rear of the vehicle. While they were distracted by Surly Man, I shot through the door and threw myself under the truck, skidding to a stop with a jerk of my stomach, hitting my chin on the ground. I rolled over onto my back and moved my hands up and down my body, checking for torn clothes and bits of bared skin. I was intact. My nose was now pointed up and I felt the heat of the truck's underbelly. Smells of oil, dirt and rubber made me want to sneeze. I held my nose until my eyes were about to pop out. The subsequent 'tish' of air sounded deafening to me but passed unnoticed by the men whose legs I saw moving to-and-fro at the back of the truck.

I craned my neck and looked along the wall of the inside shed and saw a break indicating a door. I was too far away to see through it. The truck next to the one I was under provided me with the best view. I wriggled to the edge where the shadow of my truck ended. Waiting until a break in the movement of the men meant I could roll across the floor and underneath the other truck. Giving it more thought may have made me nervous. As it was, I was pumped full of adrenaline, feeling capable of great and dangerous things.

As they emptied the truck, the men took longer to move in and out. I tucked my arms tightly against my sides and with an enormous intake of breath, I rolled. Fast. Like a sausage rolling off a barbecue. I barely stopped myself before I popped out the other side of the second truck. My bum cheeks gripped the concrete and brought me to a halt. The rhythms of the men continued undisturbed. I shimmied to the back of my new hiding place and found myself close to the wall of the inner shed. Tipping my head to get one eye looking out, the open door was barely two metres away and it was thrilling to see a large window set into the wall directly behind my truck. It had a wide sill and was almost a metre off the ground. Double-glazed, the only noise came from the open door and the men unloading the truck. The lights in the shed were so powerful, every grain of dust was visible. No amount of black was going to camouflage me. While I was trying to make a plan, Surly Man yelled something, and his minions stopped. I saw legs, with their clunky steel-toed boots, cluster around and then split up, moving in a line towards the front of the shed.

Another pair of legs appeared, this time at the inner door. These ones were bare and wearing thongs. 'Where're you goin'?'

The footwear told me I was dealing with two separate groups of men: surfers and Croats. I took a little moment to reflect on the fact that shoes maketh the man.

A heavily accented voice replied, 'We finish unload. We have smoke.'

'Don't take too long. You've got to get these trucks back.'

Surly Man didn't reply, but there was much muttering as he turned and left the building, followed by his acolytes.

Thank god for smokers!

I didn't need to bother about using the open door as my spy-hole. All I had to do was get to the window. If anyone looked up, they might see an eye and a quarter of a beanie. My heart was beating so fast I thought I was going to vomit. If only Pop could see me now! Who knew that sheds and smelly old vehicles were so exciting. I rolled out from under the truck and crouched by its rear wheel. On all fours, I scuttled to the wall and splattered my body against it. With shaking knees, I rose and pressed one eye against the window.

Both peepers had gone murky in all the excitement. I blinked a couple of times to clear them. Once I could see, a room stretched out before me, white, shiny and gleaming. Long benches held large rounds of cheese, encased in bright yellow or red wax. Against the white, they looked like big jewels. At the bench in the middle of the row, four surfers were doing something to the rounds. I watched as they worked with a tool resembling a corkscrew. They turned it into the cheese and pulled out a cylindrical plug of the pungent edible. The wheels were then carried to the table closest to me. It was at this last table where Surfer Dude from the Gracetown general store was positioned. Next to him were three other surfers who fiddled with small weights that looked incongruously delicate in the enormous room.

They were tilting the cheese with the holes so that it balanced on its side. Working together, one held the cheese in place, while Surfer Dude pushed a narrow scoop into the hole. Moving with practised ease, he pulled the scoop out and a cascade of little white pills tumbled to the surface of the bench.

My instinct was to make all the noises of an extremely surprised person. I almost blew my face off holding it in. Since when was cheese made with tablets? Maybe this was a Croatian technique of preserving it for travel? It was a creative spin that allowed time for my brain to stop fizzing.

While my synapses were struggling to reconnect, the sound of shuffling feet signalled the return of the smokers. Instinctively, I dived back under the truck and watched their legs cross the floor. I'd be in serious trouble if they got back into the vehicles and drove away. I wasn't about to do a James Bond and hang off the undercarriage. Luckily for me, the feet passed between the trucks and into the open door of the warehouse. The last man closed it.

I'd been holding my breath until all the feet had disappeared. My heart had almost stopped, and my skivvy was soaked with sweat. I was in a state of disbelief: using cheese to hide tablets was a travesty, a crime against the ancient alchemy of turning white sour liquid into pieces of gastronomic art. And the foodie reviews had to wait. Here was a story to gladden even Pop's hardened heart.

This, coupled with an incendiary curiosity meant I had to take another look. Commando-style, I wriggled back to the window and once again stuck my eye just above the sill. The band of smokers were at the far end of the room where they were taking wheels of cheese from the benches, putting them onto trollies and then rolling them into a refrigerator.

At the table closest to my window, three surfers in charge of the scales had little plastic bags and were scooping pills from the bench top, weighing and sealing packs before placing them into metal cases the size of shoeboxes. They added these to a stack already on another trolley parked at the end of the counter. One of the Croatian squad picked up the emptied cheese and took it back to the middle table where the round cores were hammered back in and a wax seal applied to cover the telltale circle. Having clocked Surfer Dude and his mates, I wondered if anyone from the Puharich clan were overseeing the goings-on. I didn't have a clear view to the back of the room, so the cousins, for all I knew, could be sitting there calculating profits on ancient abacuses like four versions of Croesus.

It was a highly efficient operation where everyone had an established routine. Immigration would be amazed at how diligently the Croatians were making their visas work. Even the surfers were moving with a speed and intent that belied their laid-back vibes.

I found myself admiring the ingenuity of the Puhariches to hide pills inside cheese. I thought about the building at the back of the grandfather's mansion in Croatia. It had to be a laboratory, except, rather than developing innovations in mould as Brian had suggested, it was actually where the tablets were cooked, pressed and packed into great wheels of edam and gouda. Brilliant! It explained why the old man had such money and power. It made me ponder anew about Jure and Zorka. And about the four Puharich men who I'd judged either to be too handsome, too thick or too dorky to be bad. Ben always said my assessment of blokes was consistently off: it looked as if he was right again.

To my shock, out of the gloom at the back of the shed, Stephen Puharich emerged, a walkie-talkie pressed against his ear. He yelled something in Croatian before turning it off. Through eyes misted over with diesel fumes, I watched as Stephen stopped at the table closest to me. Surfer Dude indicated to his mates to group around him. Stephen counted bills from a wad of cash into their open hands, then pulled a plastic bag from a pocket. Inside were other smaller bags containing a number of the white tablets. He threw one to each of the surfers. Then they turned and ambled down to the back of the room before disappearing into the night.

When it felt as if my eye had turned into a marble, I shimmied back to my spot under the truck.

Almost immediately the door opened, and I heard Stephen turn the walkie-talkie back on and resume his conversation.

'They've got this load off, so do you want the trucks back now?'

Through the crackle of the handset, I heard the voice of Matthew and his tone suggested he wasn't happy. The brothers spoke in a mix of English and Croatian.

'Where the fuck are the trucks?' The distortions of the radio didn't hide Matthew's fury.

'Still here. How much is left on the boat and how much is at the beach?' Stephen's feet were pacing at the end of my truck.

'Too much for me to carry back, you dickhead.'

'Alright, alright. I'll send one to Prevelly now. Will we park up here or do you want them at the boathouse for tomorrow?'

'Park there. I'll bring the ute back after the last truck leaves. Can you get your shit together and send one back? Or do I need to give you instructions?'

Stephen stopped pacing and swore down the phone. He spoke these in Croatian, but I can recognise naughty words in most languages.

'I'll let them all know they've got to come back tonight, though I don't see the point.'

'You don't have to see the point.' If I wasn't mistaken, there were faint sounds of waves over Matthew's handset.

'If you keep yelling at me like that, I'll punch your head in.' Stephen switched off. Still mumbling a long string of invectives, he returned to the inner room.

It wasn't long before Surly Man's clumping boots emerged, stomped to the first truck and disappeared into the cab. A plume of black exhaust shot out and spread to my hiding spot. I was possibly going to pass out from carbon monoxide poisoning. All I could do was pull the neck of my skivvy over my face and squeeze my eyes shut. The truck moved slowly forward and chugged off into the night.

I heard the slam of a door from the far end. This seemed to be the signal for the steel-toed Croatians to stop their work and to move inside. I heard the sound of clinking glasses then the cry of '*Živjeli!*': it seemed drug-running was thirsty work.

It was time for me to leave. I didn't fancy becoming roadkill when my truck moved away. I had enough material to write a drug-smuggling exposé. Pop might even take me out for a celebratory burger. First, though, I had to leave the building.

With one truck gone, there was a large empty space for me to traverse. Doubling-up, I crept to the side of my truck. There was no point hiding underneath: my sneaking for the night was over. Standing straight, I pressed up against the vehicle, sliding along its surface before tucking myself against the front bumper. Moving to the corner closest to the exterior door, I peeked around. If I could see through the inner doorway, then they could see me scoot across the shed. The loud talking and even louder laughing coming from inside gave me the courage to make a run for it. I had no other plan.

Keeping my skivvy over the bottom of my face and the beanie low over my eyes, I bent over almost with my nose to the floor. I felt like Quasimodo with my back humped over and my knuckles dragging along the ground. I was out the door and toppled face-first in the dirt at the side of the shed before panic set in. Lying still, I waited for a horde of grumpy Croats to drag me back. All was quiet. My skivvy had slipped off my face and spit was mixing with dirt to form a crust of mud on my chin. To make me feel extra special, I'd ripped the crutch out of my stirrup pants and the cold air was wafting around my nethers.

It was about five minutes before I had the wherewithal to get to my feet and head back to my car. Unlike the excited Ninja warrior who had stealthily moved through the estate on the way in, I was now a cold and tired woman as crinkled and shrunken as a raisin. The sight of the Jeep almost made me shed a tear. It was good to be back behind the wheel. The car smelled of Jessica: it closed in around me, feeling like one of her sweet hugs. The rabbit's tail bobbed about as I turned the key. I swung the car around and drove back to Caves Road. The clock shaped like a unicorn Jess had hung from the cigarette lighter indicated one o'clock: three hours since I'd left the cabin.

I couldn't remember the drive home. The little cabin seemed to simply appear in the headlights. By the time I opened the door and stepped inside, I was on the verge of collapse. If the intruder returned, I would probably just wave and tell them to help themselves. I managed to light a burner on the hob to boil the kettle before collapsing onto a dining chair. I didn't move until steam shot out into the room and a feeble whistle broke the silence. I made a cup of tea and limped to the bedroom. It was a shock to see myself in the mirror. The beanie was high on my head, with my hair sticking out around the edges, creating a monk's tonsure, and there were enough holes in the jumper for it to be called crochet. Crusts of mud were lodged in the corners of my eyes and two dark brown lines like the ruts on a road went from my nostrils to the cupids bow of parched lips. A muddy beard, looking like a cheap prop from an Errol Flynn pirate movie, caked my chin.

The true tragedy was on my feet. One ballet flat had lost its bow and they were both browny-black with small pebbles embedded in the toes and heels. For parading down the highways and byways of civilisation, their life was over. Removing them gently, I tucked them under the bed.

With all the nervous energy drained from my body, every fibre began to ache. Gingerly, I pulled everything off and got into the shower. A brown puddle formed at the bottom as the water ran off, creating a little whirlpool as it struggled to drain away. The hot water had run out before I sprinted to the bedroom, picked up my sleepwear and returned to the lounge where a little electric heater provided a meagre warmth.

It took me a while to dry properly and get dressed. Everything hurt. I'd clenched my bum cheeks so tight and for so long it felt like I had boulders in my knickers. My knees and elbows had bloody grazes and my chin had gravel rash. I wallowed in self-pity while I re-boiled the kettle, filled the hot water bottle, locked doors, turned off lights and climbed between the comfort of old-fashioned flannelette sheets. My sleep was so deep, it verged on a coma.

CHAPTER FIFTEEN

The next day it took a while before my brain registered daylight. Through artic air I staggered to the kitchen to make a coffee. With a scorching drink and wrapped in one of the extra blankets, I sat in front of the heater like a woolly King Tut. As my brain made the slow grind into awareness, I returned to the adventure of the previous night. Drugs smuggled in cheese – what a story! My next move required careful thought.

There were two options: ring Ben and tell him about the drug operation and let the police take over, or dig around a bit more and *then* turn it over – after I'd sent a story through to Pop. The first option made good sense. The second option was daft and dangerous. But it was better suited to the chaos principle that governed my life. And I needed to know if all four Puharich men were involved. I was now certain the grandfather was at the top of the drug heap – the lab was on his property and if he wasn't squeezing the pipettes, he controlled who did. Who was the kingpin here? Or maybe it was a queenpin and Marie's affability hid a calculating drug tsarina. I hoped not: I felt a protectiveness towards her based on those record-listening, hairbrush-singing days in her bedroom. After all, she was going to be my bridesmaid when I married David Cassidy. Or maybe a baba was behind it all – a pint-sized puppet master.

Sipping my jug of coffee, a number of plans came to mind, most of which verged on the ridiculous and were bound to end in tears. For the purpose of journalistic verisimilitude, I wanted to get a hold of one of those tablets.

The bloodied room in Croatia suggested that the most dangerous plans involved the Puhariches. This meant Surfer Dude at the Gracetown general store was probably the best opportunity to get a tablet. His part in the entire operation was still unclear. Was he involved more than as a surfing supervisor? Last night I'd been struck by his demeanour – lethally concentrated on his work. I imagined him staring down a shark long before it had a chance to nibble his toes. It was very possible the Surfer Dude was the apex predator. Yet the fact remained he was one person living in a run-down shop: the Puhariches were a whole clan lording it over a secure compound.

My aching body meant it was slow work getting ready. The ruined clothes were a sad heap and I didn't dare look at the heartbreaking ballet flats under my bed. Not wanting to kill off another good pair, I found the ones I was least attached to – platform runners that had seemed a funky purchase at the time but made me feel a bit too fashion-victim when they were on my feet. I always packed a sacrificial pair. Inevitably because there were times when the extravagance of my shoe shopping meant taking things out of my suitcase to make room for new purchases. In this instance it was platform runners. The fact they were lime green added to their expendability. Kitted out in another pair of stonewashed jeans and a thick parka, I locked up and headed out.

It was when I got into the Jeep that I remembered my visitor from the previous evening. I retraced my steps, paying careful attention to disturbances on the ground. There were clear footprints. Oddly, one had the imprint of a thong, the other had the depressions of toes and a heavy heel. So, either the intruder had got a discount by buying one thong rather than a pair or they'd lost the other while escaping. On turning the corner of the cabin, I saw the missing piece of rubber outside my bedroom door. A thong of yeti proportions was resting in a saltbush. I picked it up with the tips of my fingers. To my practised eye it was a well-worn rendering of a size twelve foot. I dropped it back into the bush and rubbed my fingers on my jeans. No time to wash them now, a disinfectant bath would have to wait until after my visit to Surfer Dude's.

Driving out of the camping ground, a thin woman in jeans and a misshapen t-shirt was sweeping the veranda of the manager's cabin. She stopped and leaned on the broom to watch me, giving a tired wave as I drove past. That must be the Missus.

I turned the Jeep towards the Gracetown village and was at the general store in less than three minutes. Unsurprisingly, mine was the lone car parked at the front. The shop seemed deserted. But the door was open, and the shell curtain hung at a droopy angle across the top. I wasn't sure if it was a half-hearted attempt at home beautification or a control measure for flies in summer. The shells made a desultory clicking as I walked through. A young woman wearing a sundress with a red-checked flannelette shirt over the top was standing behind the counter. She was flicking through a surfing magazine and sucking on a greasy dreadlock. Looking up, she gave a start as though she was shocked to see an actual customer in the shop.

'Hi.' My aim was to be lighthearted and chummy.

'Hi.'

'Your blackboard says I can get breakfast here.'

'Yeah.'

'I'd like to order. Been a late night.' I tried to sound cool. 'What's on the menu?'

'Egg toasted sandwich, egg and bacon toasted sandwich.' She paused.

'What else?'

'Nothing.'

'No toasted bacon sandwich?' My joke was lame. It was me trying to be friendly; a happy distraction from the snoopy intrusion I was hoping to pull off.

She shook her head. 'Just what I said.'

'Okay. Give me the egg and bacon one. Do you make coffee?'

'Yes.'

'Then, I'll have a cup of that as well.'

'I'll get the coffee first cos the other stuff will take a while. Butter?'

'Yes please.'

'Tomato sauce?'

I rolled my eyes at the culinary travesty. 'No, leave it off.'

As she turned to throw bacon on the grill behind her, the clicking of shells announced another customer. It was Surfer Dude.

'Hey, Sue,' he said. And then he looked at me. 'You here again?' His face was as expressionless as his voice.

'Breakfast this time.' I sounded ludicrously perky. 'Hey, didn't I see you at the Puhariches?'

'So?'

'I was surprised. I got the impression you didn't like them.'

He narrowed his eyes. 'I don't give a fuck about your impressions.'

My interviewing skills were not working on Surfer Dude. 'Hang on. I'm making polite conversation.'

'Really? Feels more like stalking.'

'Don't be ridiculous. This is the closest place to get a feed.'

'Well you can get your breakfast, stick your questions up your arse and fuck off.' He turned to Sue. 'Easterly's in.'

She didn't turn around. 'When will you be back?'

'Dunno.'

Surfer Dude went to the back of the shop. I heard him stomp up some stairs before he returned carrying a surfboard, a wetsuit draped over the tip. 'We're at Main.'

Sue seemed to know what this meant. 'Okay.'

He swivelled the board around, the tip almost swiping the side of my head. His smile was cruel when he saw my shock. 'See you round.'

With his surfboard tucked under his arm, he strode through the door.

Sue continued frying. The silence was broken by the popping of bacon. Now was my chance.

'Is there a bathroom I can use?'

She lifted the spatula, swishing rancid oil across the floor. 'Up the stairs. Loo's on the left.'

I walked among shelves of cans and packets of dried food, much of which, I was sure, were beyond their use-by dates. A dirty glass-fronted fridge at the back held cartons of milk, yoghurt and an abundance of Puharich cheese. I wondered in how many ways Surfer Dude was paid: money, mozzarella and drugs. I trod lightly on the stairs covered in lino squares, most of which had come unglued. The toilet was where Sue said it was. The seat and basin were stained with unmentionables and a high stack of *Tracks* magazines on the floor threatened to tip into the bowl. The smell was chunderous. I didn't care. My bum wasn't getting anywhere near its porcelain rim. It was the room across the hall that held more interest for me.

It looked like someone else had turned it over before I got there. The room was completely destroyed. Detritus from the kitchenette was spread across the floor and onto the couch which doubled as a bed. I couldn't think why anyone needed a blender and electric frypan where they slept, but then, I don't cook. Clothes were everywhere: t-shirts and board shorts lay on the floor like multicoloured cow pats. A damp wetsuit was dripping from the curtain rod, sending dirty smears down the orange sheet acting as the curtain. On a small dining table squashed into a corner were a range of pot-smoking implements and a sad-looking plant. The fetid smell suggested the room had probably not seen an open window since 1955. As I moved to the table, small clouds of dust puffed up, coating my jeans in fine particles of germ flora.

There was a real advantage in Surfer Dude not being houseproud. Sitting in the middle of the catastrophe on top of the dining table was a tiny bag of pills. I bent low to study the half dozen or so little white discs. Wiggling my pinkie finger into the bag, I pressed it on one of the tablets and slid a pill out. Using the tips of my fingers as tweezers I picked it up, wrapped it in a tissue from my pocket, and put it carefully into my jeans.

It's amazing how one small act can make you feel like a major criminal. I carefully walked back to the loo. With much fanfare, I flushed the toilet, opened the door and slammed it shut. Then I stamped down the stairs and returned to Sue, who was busy creating a fire on the grill.

'How are you going there?' My eyes were watering with the smoke.

'Okay. You happy with well done?'

'Yeah, that's fine. Starving, so anything is good.'

'Your coffee is near the till.'

A tall cardboard cup was filled with a black liquid smelling of charred forest. When I took a sip, bits of fine dark powder coated my teeth.

'It's hot, so be careful.'

'Thanks.' I wanted to point out she must have boiled up the burnt remains of a tree, but demurred. No point in getting Sue offside. It was more important to keep her talking to see what she knew of her boyfriend's working life.

'How long have you lived here?'

'Ages.'

'Do you like Gracetown?'

'Yeah. I mostly live in town. Just come here to cook and stuff.'

The bacon fat was spitting like fury.

'Do you surf too?'

'Do I look like a fuckin' idiot? A shark will bite Pete's arse one day.' It was nice to know Surfer Dude had a name. Sue's tone lacked the affection towards him I expected from a woman who exposed herself to the pathogens floating around the flat. God only knew what kept her there.

'Are sharks a problem?'

'It's the ocean! Of course, they're a problem. Some dickhead got his guts ripped out a couple of months ago.' She came to the counter and handed over a toasted sandwich that had shards of bacon sticking out, dripping with fat. 'That'll be five bucks.'

I pulled out my purse and handed over a ten-dollar bill. 'Sorry, I haven't got change.'

Sue shrugged and moved to an old till set on the right-hand side of the counter. 'I've only got coins.'

'That's okay.' Sue dropped a number of sticky discs into my palm. 'I s'pose there's not many people this time of year. It must be hard on your cashflow.'

'Winter's for surfers. Main Break is pretty wild this time of year. Fuckin' stupid if you ask me.'

'Why?'

'Cold as! And they all want to come in here and use our shower.'

'Don't they all have homes to go to?'

'Course. But sometimes they come here to get cleaned up before they go to work. It's closer.'

'I may have seen some of them at the Puhariches' creamery.'

'That's them.' She pushed the till shut and gave a breathy grunt. 'Fuckin' arseholes.'

'You don't work for them?'

'No way. I won't work for someone I can't trust. I've got standards.' She absently twirled her nose ring. 'The Puhariches would tear the heads off babies if they thought it made a buck.'

'Really?'

'They're nasty and rich as fuck. No one else makin' cheese is like them.'

'Why do you reckon they're so rich?'

'Dunno. But how many cheese factories work three shifts? We're in fucking Margaret River, not the city. And they've got half the Croatian mafia working for them.'

'I thought they do a lot of import–export.'

'Says who?' Sue's voice was changing. There was belligerence and something else. A hint of fear?

'I read a story about them,' I lied.

'Then you know jack shit. You'll get their side and nothing else, 'cause no one will say anything against them.'

'You and your boyfriend do.'

For the first time she looked me straight in the face. 'Come to spy, have you? Well, you can take your sandwich and your coffee and fuck off.'

'Anywhere nice I can park while I eat?' I had the ridiculous impulse to part on polite terms.

'End of the street.' Sue disappeared among the shelves.

As I got back into the Jeep I wondered about Sue. Even in all the domestic chaos of the flat, she must have seen the pills and known, or guessed where they were from. And maybe it was actual fear of the family and their power I'd sensed in her tone.

I followed Sue's directions and parked with the nose of the Jeep almost touching the sand. The cold wind was now blowing from the south. The waves were even, neat rolls that collapsed into foam runnels as they hit the beach. There were about a dozen boys in wetsuits on small boards, flippers on their feet, throwing themselves against the waves and riding them in. Their huge grins and loud laughing made me smile. I was amazed at their persistence: swim out, grab a wave, hit the sand, stand up, turn, and do it all again.

The smell of the egg and bacon toastie was making my stomach juices burn a hole in my belly. I unwrapped it and took a sizeable bite. Wow! Through all the smoke, Sue had created something that tasted absolutely wonderful. She had managed to grill the bacon to the right level of crisp and the egg was firm on the outside and soft in the middle. The slices of toast were so thick, they soaked up all the fat and yolk without losing their texture. I sat and watched the boys on the water with bits of bacon and egg dripping down my chin, feeling like a kid on holiday.

The coffee was still a step too far. Although the black dust had settled to the bottom of the cup, the taste remained more akin to charcoal than café au lait. I opened the door of the Jeep and tipped it out. In the glove compartment I found some tissues and tried to clean my face and hands. Little bits of tissue stuck to my cheeks and caught on my eggy lips. In the rear-view mirror I looked like I'd been caught in a snowstorm.

Settling back in the driver's seat, I put fingers in my jeans pocket and carefully pulled out the tablet. It was the size of an aspirin, yellowish white, flat on one side and slightly convex on the other. The flat side had been stamped with an image. Looking closely, I saw the shape of a cat's head.

'Great.' Here was confirmation the little pills came from the dark side. After a moment's hesitation, I tapped it on the very tip of my tongue and winced at its bitterness. Pop was always pleased when I substantiated my work with primary research. He liked authenticity to investigative pieces. Ben on the other hand would have a fit if he knew I'd licked the evidence. But when the whole thing blew up – a certainty in my mind – the police still had thousands of other little pieces of evidence to work with.

I sat and looked out the window, back to the boys and their boards. Their exuberance, the blue of the sea and the stretch of magnificent coastline were incongruous with the poison in the palm of my hand. Part of me wanted to charge into the police station in Margaret River, hand over the pill and demand a raid on the Puharich house, creamery, warehouse and every other building owned by the family. I imagined high-stakes action, charges laid, and a big, loud trial where I'd take centre stage and bring down the entire Puharich drug cartel. I imagined being feted like a female Eliot Ness.

This was going too far. I decided to drive back to the cabin and ring Ben.

Gathering up the leftovers of my breakfast, I climbed out of the car and went to a bin attached to a pole by a rusty chain and padlock. Why would anyone want to steal a bin?

As I was dumping my garbage, I was shocked to see Surfer Dude standing about six feet away at the bottom of the dunes, his surfboard at his feet. He'd pulled down his wetsuit to hang from his hips, the rubber torso and arms dangling like a melted body.

He stared – and watched as I got befuddled in the way of children who've been caught doing something wrong. I wondered if he had been close enough to see me clearly in the car. Had he watched as I unwrapped the tissue, and raised my fingers to my mouth? Looked as I held the tablet up to the light in order to see the cat?

I returned his stare with a look of trepidation, unsure what to do next, so I gave him a wave and a half-witted smile. He remained still, silently watching as I finished with the bin and scurried back to the Jeep.

CHAPTER SIXTEEN

I couldn't get out of Gracetown fast enough. I had visions of Surfer Dude getting on his board and being blown up the coast to meet me at the cabin where he'd threaten to turn me into shark bait if I didn't hand over the tablet. Fanciful? Maybe. I had told him where I was staying. And, the thought crossed my mind, he might already have been there. Was he the person whose thong was embedded in the salt bush outside my bedroom door?

By the time I turned into the holiday park, it was eleven o'clock. Being a Friday, I could phone Ben at work and get him to do whiz-bang things on his computer while I stayed on the line. The challenge was to get a connection on my mobile. I climbed onto the kitchen table, TV and even managed to balance on the bedhead, but there was no signal. I put on my coat and ugg boots, going outside to climb the sand dune sheltering the cabin from the wind. I scrambled up the slope, cursing like a sailor. At the top a ferocious south-easterly was blowing. Struggling against it, I did star jumps to try and get a connection, before a final gust blew me over and I tumbled down to the beach. Pulling up just short of the water, my coat had torn and was vomiting its nylon stuffing. I charged back and forth along the beach watching for the illumination of the little lines indicating a connection to the outside world. Nothing. So much for technology.

I wondered at the perversity of nature that Brian Puharich got through to me, yet I couldn't talk to Ben.

I climbed back up the dune, fell over the top and, with my arse pointing to the sky, I slid all the way home.

On returning to the cabin, my desire to contact Ben had increased exponentially. The more times I didn't connect, the more I needed him to know about my discoveries. I was alone in a situation that felt increasingly threatening.

My options were limited. There was the phone attached to the manager's office. It was an internal line and I wasn't keen on asking him for access to his landline. If the Missus was about, I'd feel better because talking to her husband didn't tickle my fancy.

I shook as much of the sand out of my clothes as possible and pushed the wadding back into my coat sticking, it down with cellotape from Jess's emergency kit. My ugg boots were sodden from running along the shoreline and now smelt like wet wool with overtones of sheep dag. Their life was over and they now belonged in the garbage bin. Ballet flats and now uggs: at this rate I'd be shoeless by Wednesday. I put on the show-stopping platform sneakers, locked up, got back into the Jeep and drove to the manager's office. It was shut and the sign about after office hours was up in the window. I picked up the phone and dialled. It rang out. I dialled again. It rang out. This was going to be a battle of wills between me and the manager. I dialled again. Clearly the ringing was too much to bear and the phone was picked up.

'What?' It felt satisfying to hear his irritation.

Putting on my sweetest voice, 'Hello, this is Alex Grant, I'm staying in cabin five.'

'I know who you are. Whaddya want?'

'There's no mobile phone connection.'

'Go to the road. Head north. Might get lucky.'

I sensed he was going to cut me off. 'Wait! Is there a public phone here?'

'On the wall of the dunny block.'

The phone went dead.

The dunny block turned out to be a long, brown brick building, stuck in the middle of a dusty patch behind the manager's cabin. Hills Hoists looking like steel daisies were planted along one wall, and the phone was sheltering under a plastic dome that hung sideways on one screw. I'd crawled all through Jess's Jeep to find every dropped coin until there was enough money to make my phone call. By pushing the plastic canopy up and resting it on my shoulder, I was able to dial Ben's number.

'Detective Brown.'

'Ben, it's me.'

I heard a deep sigh. 'Have you done something?'

'Maybe. Can you talk?'

'I'm on my own, if that's what you're asking.'

'Great.' I shifted the weight of the plastic bubble.

'Where are you? You sound like you're in a tunnel.'

'In a phone booth that looks like an oversized motorbike helmet.'

'What have you done?'

'I may have, on the off chance, got my hands on some drugs.'

'You cannot be serious!'

'One little pill. It has a cat's face on one side and it tastes bitter.'

'Jesus, Alex. You tasted it?'

'On the tip of my tongue. For research purposes.'

'Research?' He was winding up to lecture. 'This is exactly the kind of stunt you've pulled in the past and it has always ended in trouble for you and for Pop.'

'He thinks the risks are worth it and so do I.'

His barely suppressed frustration was coming down the line.

'Where did you get it?'

'You don't want to know.' I sensed a faceplant on his desk.

'Do you want to send it up to me for testing? If you go to the local police, they'll put it in an overnight bag and I'll pick it up tomorrow.'

'Not such a good idea. They'll want to know where it came from.'

'Pack it up, put it in an envelope and tell them it's urgent. They won't know what it is. I'll ring down and let them know you're on your way.'

'Okay, there'll be a post office in Margs.' Which I had no intention of finding. 'In the meantime, I'll describe it to you. Maybe you can ask the drug guys if they can guess what it is.'

There was silence on the line. It was the quiet moment before Ben gave in. 'Alright. Tell me what it looks like.'

'About the size of an aspirin. Flat on one side, convex on the other. And it's stamped with the head of a cat. Just the outline, but it's pretty good.'

'What colour?'

'Yellowy-white.' I heard him writing.

'I'll go downstairs and hunt down Ian. He's usually up to date with what's on the market.'

'Thanks. Have I told you that I love you?'

'Only when you want me to do something.'

'How long will it take? I'll have to call you back from this telephone.'

'Give it half an hour. It'll take two minutes if he doesn't know anything. If he does recognise it, then that's another type of conversation.'

I moved the plastic dome to my other shoulder. 'Can't you be quicker?'

'Take it or leave it, Alex.'

'Okay. Exactly thirty minutes.'

He put the receiver down.

How to fill in thirty minutes? I have absolutely no waiting skills. Jess often describes my birth like this: 'You were so impatient, you cut your own umbilical cord.' Every time she tells it, she laughs like a hyena.

I didn't want to go too far and I was sick of the inside of the cabin. Instead, I returned to the car. The insipid morning sun had disappeared, and the air had turned even colder. The inside of the Jeep was a fraction above zero. I rummaged around in the junk on the back seat and found a picnic blanket. I wrapped it tightly around my body and considered my findings.

The tablet presented all kinds of new theories about the Puhariches. There must be a very big story behind its cat face. I wondered who, out of the family, was involved? So far I didn't have any evidence that Marco or Brian were in on it. Though I had to consider that despite the gorgeousness of one and the aesthetic deficits of the other, under the surface these men might well have the cunning and brains of a drug baron. As for Stephen and Matthew: Brian and Marco had been scathing of their intellectual capacity. However, it was possible that they were under the careful supervision of their grandfather, who, in turn, was the Don of Dalmatia. Now that I could believe.

Apart from Stephen and Matthew, there was Surfer Dude and his buddies and Surly Man with his gang of steel toes. Surfer Dude didn't strike me as someone to waste energy thinking about legalities. Watching him proved he was capable of managing his own gang and he had no scruples in taking wads of cash and bags of drugs. My impression was that he'd do whatever was needed to protect the source of income that supported his supposedly carefree lifestyle.

Surly Man and the steel toes were as problematic. They sounded like an angry rock band, but maybe they were much more dangerous. Sue had called them the Croatian mafia and I didn't think this was too far from the truth. There was a Russian mafia and an Italian mafia, so it stood to reason that a country squished between the two would also have some form of established organisation capable of drug-running and resting horses heads in clean sheets.

It didn't take long for my fingers and toes to start tingling with the first signs of hypothermia. Turning on the Jeep meant running down the diesel and I didn't fancy having to call on the Puharich bowser again. I'd have to go back to the cabin to wait. Once in the kitchen, I put the kettle on then sat at the table hugging my coffee jug and watching the hands of the clock that hung on a nail above the stove. By the time it ticked over the half hour, my head was pounding and a nerve under my left eye was twitching.

I optimistically grabbed my phone: one small stripe suggested the twin towers of Bunbury and Busselton were sending out the requisite beams. I rang Ben and he picked up immediately. His voice was faint and crackly.

'Right on time. It's amazing what you can do when you want something.'

'You know I –' The line disconnected. I swished the phone in the air and a stripe came back. I rang again. 'Hold on a minute. I'll go outside and see if I can get a better line.'

Ben's reply was lost.

I raced out the front door and started to climb the dunes again. I scrambled upward, holding my phone high, watching for those extra little lines to appear. At the top there was still no signal, so, like a dog with worms, I slid on my bum all the way down the other side. With a wet behind and platforms full of sand, I got to my feet and stepped into the shallows. Two stripes indicated I had reconnected.

Once again, Ben answered on the first ring. 'Where are you? I can hear waves.'

'I'm sort of in the surf.'

'Really?' He was incredulous in an unsurprised kind of way.

'Can I get electrocuted using a phone in water?'

'No, Alex, not even you can get electrocuted by a mobile phone.'

'Right. What did you find out?'

'John has come across something that sounds the same as your pill. Apparently, it's the latest drug of choice at raves.'

'What the hell is a rave?'

Ben laughed. 'It's the younger generation's version of dance clubs, except they are organised at short notice, are usually held at huge venues like warehouses and go all night. Hence the need for happy, energy pills.

The one you have is potent, so don't lick it again.'

'What's special about this one?'

'It's primarily a substance called MDMA. I won't bore you with the chemical details. Ketamine is the secret ingredient; it's been around since the early sixties and became a quick high for the hippies in the seventies. Nowadays it's sold as Kat, hence the stamp. Eastern Bloc countries divert the ketamine from pharmaceutical companies and from bulk chemical suppliers. Easy thing to import if you're in Croatia and there's an endless amount. For the ravers it's both an hallucinogen and an energiser.'

'So, they see pigs flying very fast?'

'It's more likely they think they're the pig flying.'

'Dangerous?'

'Very. Can be more deadly than either of the ingredients on their own. And extremely popular. The market can't get enough of the stuff and a tablet costs twenty-five bucks. It's top of the range. Are you going to tell me how you got it?'

I paused to think. 'I don't want to yet.'

'Why?'

'I need some time to work it out in my head. If I told you, then you'd have to do something. I want this story. Pop will be furious if I don't give him something substantial.' And Carly would make me give the petty cash back. 'Another twenty-four hours should do it.'

'Short of having you arrested for possession, I can't make you do the sensible thing and let the police take over. Am I right?'

'Pretty much. I want to know who's behind it all. At the moment I've got two dim Puhariches and a dubious bunch of surfers and Croatians. There's nothing El Chapo about any of them. I'm determined to get a kick-arse piece out of this.'

I could almost hear Ben scowling. 'This is a dangerous drug and the people behind it are probably as lethal. You're making a dumb decision.'

I held the phone away from my ear and yelled in its direction. 'Losing connection. Can't hear you ... breaking up.' I cancelled the call.

By now my feet had sunk into the sand. The heels of my platform sneakers, like the footings of a skyscraper, had cemented me into the seabed. Each wave hit my legs harder, sending spray flying up to wet the bottom of my coat. I was freezing cold and hungry. I tried to pull my feet out of the water. They were firmly buried, the sand sucking them deeper and deeper. At the point when the waves were furthest out, I bent down and untied my shoelaces. Pulling my feet away, I ran out of the water and watched as the waves came back in and swallowed my shoes. Killing three types of footwear in two days was a moral travesty. I'd have to find a shoe store urgently.

Climbing back up the dune and going down the other side took all my residual energy. In the cabin I boiled water for my Cup Noodles, a culinary travesty invented by the Americans. Shaking in two little packets of flavoured MSG, I turned on the TV and slurped my way through an 'Asian Experience' infused with a polystyrene aftertaste.

It was inevitable I'd have to go back to the creamery: to indulge in more fromage and to find out why wheels of cheese were spewing up little white pills. There were two critical questions I wanted answered: who was at the top and how wide did the organisation spread? How great for my story if I were to stumble upon the family huddled over piles of loot, throwing it around like Scrooge on a boozy Christmas Eve. Brian had mentioned a high tea taking place every Friday, Saturday and Sunday. This was perfect!

My jeans were wet and had a tear across the bum revealing red, scratched skin that would soon start to sting. I pulled them off and replaced them with corduroy trousers that seemed to have shrunk since I'd last worn them before my Croatian holiday. I disconsolately looked at the three shoeboxes standing empty as coffins, then slid my feet into a pair of leopard-print mules, fortifying myself to face whatever the Puhariches might serve up.

CHAPTER SEVENTEEN

The drive south that afternoon turned out to be very pleasant. The wind had dropped, and the sun emerged from the puffy grey clouds that had dogged the morning. The light shone through the canopy of the gum trees bordering the road, making them shine with an orange luminescence. The giant trees made me feel like I was in the presence of a majesty whose purpose was to remind me of my microscopic importance. Thankfully, glimpsing my gorgeous shoes on the pedals of the Jeep distracted me from any further introspection.

When I turned into the Puharich driveway, I was stunned to see the carpark full of police cars and an ambulance. My first thought was one of the boys had upset Baba and she'd unleashed her temper with calamitous consequences. I half-expected to see her wizened body being locked in the back of the paddy wagon, screeching and spitting insults in Croatian. Apart from the cars, no one seemed to be about.

I pulled to a stop at the furthest point along the creamery veranda. The police had either been in a rush, or they hadn't been taught how to park. Cars were pointing in all directions and an ambulance was stopped up against the trellis connecting the creamery to the house. I felt like the single survivor in a very large car crash, something akin to standing in the middle of a scene from the *Blues Brothers*. The only thing missing was a saxophone and drum kit.

It took a moment for me to hear voices coming from behind the creamery. Walking to the corner of the building – a half-tiptoe-half-sashay to stop the mules from flying off my feet – I turned in the direction of the warehouse. At the end of the wall I stopped. It was clear from the echo of voices that a large number of people were inside. Outside, half a dozen police were spread out in a line looking intently at the ground as if someone had dropped an earring.

Then I saw Marie. She was standing alone to the left of the warehouse door and she was dabbing her eyes, her shoulders doing those odd little shrugs that happen when crying has become less water and more chest spasm. Seeing her made it much easier to step forward. The police were so concentrated on looking down they didn't notice me going past. Even Marie didn't register my presence until I was about a metre away.

'Alex!' Her face was red and scrubbed of all its make-up, the only remnants an ant-trail of mascara down her cheeks and a smear of lipstick going from the corner of her lips to her right ear. It looked like her mouth had shifted to the side of her head.

'Marie!'

She held her arms out, signalling a hug.

I have never been a hugger, or a kisser, or a giver of any type of physical exchange in public. Now, under the prevailing circumstances of tears and outstretched arms, I had to do the right thing.

I leaned forward and lightly put my arms around her back. She pulled me in so hard her boobs pushed mine off my chest and into my armpits. Her chin dug into my shoulder. Wet tears and snot rubbed into my hair.

'I'm so glad to see you. It's unbelievable.'

'What's wrong?' My lips were right near her ear; all I could think of was earwax.

'Horrible. A horrible, horrible thing.'

'Tell me?'

'Something so dreadful. So dreadful, you won't believe it.' She did another big sob that shook us both: another squirt of tears in my hair.

I put my hands on her upper arms to push her away. 'I just got here, so I have no idea what's going on.'

'There's been an accident. That's what they're saying.'

'What kind of accident?'

'My cousin was down in the cheese cellar and a shelving unit collapsed. Stephen was hit by wheels of parmesan. He's dead.' She burst into another round of tears.

A little giggle almost burst from my lips: death by flying cheese sounded so absurd.

'Oh, Marie, this is awful.'

She looked at me miserably. 'I drove down this morning, pulled into the yard and Baba was coming up from the warehouse screaming. I thought something had happened to Marco because she was yelling 'my poor Marco' over and over. She was absolutely hysterical.'

'Marco has had an accident as well?'

'No, no. Only Stephen. Marco found him.'

'So, Marco is alive?'

'Yes, but Baba thinks he's worse off because he found Stephen and apparently it's an awful sight.' Marie pulled another tissue out of her handbag. 'Marco has always been her baby. Stephen and Matthew are Zorka's. Or were Zorka's. I can't believe he's dead!'

We stood silently. I wasn't sure what to say and Marie looked too wrung out to carry on any further conversation.

'Maybe we should go into the house and get a cup of tea.'

'No, Baba's in there howling and I can't bear it.'

'What about the creamery? A little port might help.'

I put her arm through mine and guided her around the clump of downward-looking coppers and through the back door of the creamery. It was a bit of a squeeze walking side-by-side down the corridor and the renewed proximity of our bodies unsettled me further.

I sat Marie down on a couch and went to the bar to find sustenance. The port was on a shelf above the cheese fridge. I filled two wine glasses almost to the brim. For good measure, I cut a large piece of brie off a round from the fridge and grabbed a packet of crackers before returning to the sniffing Marie slumped on the chesterfield.

'Here you go. Drink that, then have a bit of cheese. It'll make you feel much better.'

Like a dutiful child, she took a slug of the port, followed by an equally large bite of the cheese.

'Feel a bit better?'

Marie nodded, causing a little bit of snot to dribble down to her top lip. I wondered if it was too harsh to pass her a tissue and ask her to blow her nose. Deciding to say nothing, I was completely distracted by the drip as it teetered on her cupid's bow. The more I tried not to look, the more my eyes fixated on the teetering droplet. It took a few seconds for me to register that she was talking.

'… anyway, it's nice to see you.'

The drip splashed down the front of her shirt. Relieved, I refocused.

'Why are you here? How strange is it that you've turned up at another one of our crises? I'm glad.'

'I came to try a high tea. Brian told me it's a wonderful experience.'

'Everything is wonderful according to Brian.' It was the first time she'd criticised, albeit mildly, Brian's view of the world. 'There's been another death in the family and he seems to think it's nothing out of the ordinary.'

'Another death? Isn't it only Stephen who's been killed?' I was getting more confused by the minute.

'You're forgetting Jure and Zorka.'

'Marie, Stephen's death was an accident. It's totally different to what happened to Jure and Zorka.'

She shook her head. 'I told you in Croatia that something wasn't right. Jure's brother was obviously insane and Brian, Marco and I had to leave my grandfather exposed. The boys think they're the ones capable of protecting him. I think a woman can be as fierce when pushed.'

'The only time I get really ferocious is at a shoe sale,' I said, but Marie was not to be diverted.

'I was worried about Dida, but maybe it's not him we should be thinking about. Now this has happened! I don't know what's going on. I think –' She stopped talking as we heard hurried footsteps approaching from behind. We swivelled on the couch to see Brian coming towards us, flushed with self-importance.

'Here you are, Marie. And Alex – I wasn't expecting you.'

I got up to face him. 'I thought high tea would be nice. But it's a bad time.'

He stopped in front of me and slurped a kiss on each cheek, his nose making indents on my face so deep I could call them dimples.

'Death is rotten at the best of times. To have one happen here at the creamery is the worst. Absolute PR disaster.'

'Surely it won't affect your sales. It's not as if your cheese killed him.' I shook my head: that was, precisely, what had happened. 'Sorry. It literally was your cheese.' I sounded ridiculous. 'It's unlikely any of your visitors might get sconed.'

Brian didn't reply as he moved around me to stand in front of his sister. 'You'll have to cope and deal with the media and with our buyers. We can't have the business ruined by something like this.'

She looked up at him, slightly stunned. 'I can't think about the media at the moment. Our cousin has just been killed. By our cheese. In our vault.'

'We have a situation that has the potential to destroy us. And you're the one with the marketing degree.'

'I didn't do a unit in marketing after death, Brian.'

'Then you'll need to pretend.'

The bluntness of his words chilled me.

'I'll let you get on with it then.' I stood up.

'No.' Brian gave me a look that made me sit back down. It was like a non-verbal shove. 'We can have a talk while Marie goes into the house and composes herself.'

Without a word, Marie got up and left the room.

'Can I get you another drink?'

'I'm fine.'

'Then I'll fix myself one and we can have a chat.'

Brian now sounded like we were going to exchange recipes or knitting patterns. It made me feel nervous. Had he somehow found out where I'd been last night? My story for Pop was getting edgier and my brain was fizzing with questions.

The leather of the chesterfield wheezed when Brian sat down next to me.

'Did Marie fill you in with the details?'

'No, she was pretty much in shock about the whole thing.'

'My sister doesn't really have the stomach for it.'

I didn't know what 'it' was. Surely most normal people would be equally rattled. 'Marie said something about an accident involving Stephen.'

'He's dead.' Brian's voice was dispassionate. 'And the police are suggesting the shelving in the vaults failed, sending the cheese flying.'

'You don't think so?'

'Of course I do. And we'll probably have to pay a fine and make some changes to the way we shelve our products. Nothing more.'

'Do you know how it happened?'

Brian looked at me speculatively and took a long sip of his wine. 'Are you being a journalist or a friend?'

'A friend of course.'

'Then as a friend I can tell you that Stephen took himself into the vaults last night. God only knows why.' I could guess, but I held my tongue. 'He was probably drunk and has, somehow, made a shelf collapse, sending dozens of cheese wheels crashing.'

'It's horrendous.'

'Worst thing possible for the business.'

Wasn't too flash for Stephen either. 'I suppose the police will be around for a while?'

'Probably.'

'I'm happy to listen if you want to talk about it.'

Brian looked at me, trying to gauge my motivation. I wondered who was playing who.

He sank further back into the sofa and spoke, his voice low. 'This morning, Marco went looking for Stephen because he wasn't at breakfast and Baba said his bed hadn't been slept in. Marco said to wait for a while because Stephen may have stayed over at someone's house.'

'A girlfriend?'

Brian raised an eyebrow. 'I doubt it. Anyway, in all the years he's been here, Stephen has never missed breakfast. We waited for a few hours, then I started ringing people he knew. Matthew took a ute to go and look for him at Prevelly Beach, although why Stephen would be there is beyond me.' Brian paused again, this time to balance a piece of brie on a cracker. He stuck his tongue out, put the biscuit on the tip and curled it back into his mouth. 'Marco and I looked around here. It took twenty minutes or so before he found Stephen. He phoned from the warehouse and told me. Then I rang the police.'

'What was Marie doing when all this was happening?'

'She hadn't arrived. I told Baba and she got hysterical because her precious Marco had found his dead brother. By the time Marie got here, Baba had her rosary out and was doing the full-on wailing and screeching like she was being attacked.'

His cruel tone made me like him even less. At least the baba had feelings.

'Marco said it looked like Stephen had been dead for hours. All the blood was dry. Apparently, his head was completely caved in. The police told us that the falling shelves didn't make any difference. He was dead before they hit him.'

I shuddered, picturing a skull with a wheel of cheese wedged in its forehead, brains pushed out, grey and bubbly around the smooth yellow surface of the wax.

'I had to step up, of course,' Brian said. His egocentric preening, under the circumstances, was slightly grotesque. 'I came up here to wait in the office for the police, while Marco went back to the house. He wanted to be fussed over by Baba. It was up to me to hold the fort. I didn't want anyone going down into the warehouse to poke around. Plus, Marie was due and she needed to be stopped before she got anywhere near the warehouse.'

I wasn't sure why Brian thought Marie would want to go to the vault. She'd stop the minute she heard Baba's wailing.

'When did Marie arrive?'

'After the police. Baba told her what was going on. And Marie, like all women, fell apart immediately.' He shook his head and pinched his epic nose in a way that made me want to punch him.

'When the authorities arrived, I told them where to go. The body hasn't been moved yet. It shouldn't be too long. They've been down there for about four hours.'

'Stephen is still down there?' The thought made me queasy.

'Yep, and we won't be able to go back into the vault for a couple of days. Apparently, there'll be a police crime scene team coming down from Perth as well as the one from the coroner.'

'So, the local coppers have decided it was a crime?'

'Of course not. It's a workplace accident and the police down here need to make sure everything is done properly. There'll be hell to pay if they cock things up.'

It was easy to imagine Grandfather Puharich brandishing his cane, leading a phalanx of QCs to invade the Margaret River police station.

Sipping my drink, I considered my experience of police processes. 'If it looks like a workplace accident, they'll give it a cursory look-over and leave it all for the coroner.'

'Obviously.' With an unexpected pivot, Brian turned his body and looked me squarely in the face. He pursed his lips in a moue. 'Maybe you can stick around for a while.'

He rapidly blinked his eyes. For a moment I thought invisible dust was affecting his vision. Then I realised that he was fluttering his eyelashes at me.

He stretched an arm along the back of the sofa. 'Speaking to you now as a journalist – maybe I can arrange for you to get the scoop. Isn't that what they say in your circles?'

'I suppose if I was Lois Lane.'

'Does that make me Clark Kent?'

Flee! my instinct advised. But I sat, resisting the urge to tell Brian he would never be Clark Kent while his delicious cousin was still around.

'You might be the one to rescue me –' he blinked, 'to rescue us.'

'What do you mean?'

'Write something, Alex. You've seen what we do, our product. There's lots to say.'

'I'd be more than happy to do a piece on the Puhariches,' I said. 'Maybe more than one. It all depends on how deep you'll let me go.'

Brian looked thrilled and I feared he'd grasped the wrong end of the stick, but approaching voices halted our conversation. The police, who had been wandering in and out of the warehouse all afternoon, were returning to their cars, their feet moving in desultory steps across the gravel. City police always seemed to move fast, weighed down with their authority. It was as though being in the great metropolis meant they were expected to be examples of diligence, of taking their jobs seriously, and of being tough under any circumstances. Country coppers, on the other hand, wore their authority lightly; uniforms a bit stretched across well-fed midriffs and bleary eyes on a Monday morning after Saturday night barbies which stretched too far into Sunday. And they drove cop cars that popped up at school cake stalls so that kids could turn on the siren. This group sauntered past the window, faces grimmer than usual. We listened to their quiet banter as they dispersed to find their cars.

After they left, we heard the sound of rattling wheels. Through the window, a gurney appeared, being pulled by one paramedic and pushed by another. Strapped to the top was the black bag containing Stephen. His body jostled slightly as the wheels bounced on the gravel, as if he was trying to get out.

CHAPTER EIGHTEEN

It felt like Brian and I were in a theatre where the protagonists were entering on the right, then exiting stage left. The mood changed. He shifted his arm from the back of the sofa and sat forward.

'Well, that's that then.'

I nodded.

'Thank god they've gone. Hopefully they won't need to come back and we can open as usual. Stephen understood that the business has to keep running no matter what.'

'You said you won't be able to use the warehouse until the investigation is over.' I wondered afresh what Brian did or didn't know about the drug arm of the Puharich operation.

He shrugged. 'We can keep making cheese and temporarily put our stock elsewhere.'

'Will you ask other creameries for storage?'

'Hardly. Do you really think we'd let our competitors have the chance to find out what makes our product different? We have a unique process we won't share with anyone.'

'I was just thinking that it's the most convenient thing to do.'

'Convenience doesn't come into it. You're like Marie. Neither of you think like a proper businessman.'

I was being put in my place. Again I was struck by the cold-blooded nature of the Puharich clan. It was easy to imagine that their preferred way of dealing with Stephen's remains was putting them in cold storage until it was convenient for them to bury him. He could stay frozen if they chose cremation. Once in the furnace, his body would be reduced to puffs of steam, soon dissipating like a morning frost. Knowing the Puhariches, they'd probably put him in an esky and ship him back to Croatia, where they'd bury him in the family body farm out of reach of Australian authorities and their pesky coronial investigations.

'So, what will you do with your cheese?'

'We have a couple of boatsheds over at Prevelly Beach. They've been converted to temporary storage for when we have excess. They're the domain of Stephen and Matthew, so I've got no doubt they'll be a disorganised mess.'

Given the slick way they managed the warehouse, I was fairly confident Brian was selling them short. Was their dopiness a cover for something more nefarious? Maybe Matthew gave his brother a cheesy send-off, masked as an accident, leaving him to assume the role of 'the katman'.

Brian's mood switched again, and he slid his hand down the sofa towards my thigh. His fingers stopped millimetres from my jeans. I wanted to scream – nothing fancy, just loud and shrill. Instead, I squeezed myself into the corner of the leather seat.

He didn't seem to notice. 'There's a fair bit to do, and we've had to cancel high tea. Which is a pity. It can't be helped,' he sounded almost jolly, 'we don't want our customers spooked by a herd of country coppers. But I can give you some cheese and other things to take with you.'

Maybe, after all, I might tolerate a little thigh touching. 'Thanks. Takeaway is lovely. Yours is some of the best cheese I've ever eaten.'

'Of course.'

Brian stood. I could see right up into the dark recesses of his nostrils, the abundant hair swooshing back and forth with each breath, reminding me of the swirling bristles of a car wash.

He walked away and I heard him moving around at the back of the room. As I sat on that comfy couch, in that beautiful room smelling of soft cheese and vintage port, I considered Stephen's death. How likely was it that a shelf would collapse at exactly the moment when Stephen was standing under it? And why was he down there so late at night? I'd watched the end of the 'putting drugs in little bags' activity, and I didn't think the band of happy Croatians hung around for hours drinking, given there was more drug smuggling to do over the following nights. So why did Stephen stay after everyone else had left?

These were questions I didn't want to ask Brian. But I needed answers.

And I needed to see that shelf. The story I was writing for Pop was going to be a corker if it included a murder.

If an investigation team was being sent down from Perth, Ben was sure to hear about the 'accident'. He'd ring to tell me to mind my own business. All the while bickering and wasting precious time when we both knew I'd ignore him. Therefore, I had to get into the vault before he and his squad arrived. I never fancied lying to Ben; it stirred up my conscience, so it was always better he didn't know what I was up to.

Brian came back with a paper bag that was satisfyingly heavy.

'Wow, you've put a ton of stuff in there. Thank you so much.'

'That's okay. There's more where that came from, if you want to hang around.' He winked at me. 'I always take care of the women in my life.' He bent forward and put his hand under my chin, tilting it up towards him.

I gave a nervous laugh and tried to focus on Pop, the kicking good story I was going to write, and the goodies in the bag. His mouth was moving closer to my face. Quickly I turned my head and he ended up smearing spit on my ear.

Standing, he gave me another eye flutter. 'We've got plenty of time.'

I would've been out of there like greased lightning if I hadn't been so curious about Stephen and the drugs. And there was Marco to consider. I was eager to see whether he was in need of a little comforting of the kind a baba couldn't give.

Brian pulled me to my feet and escorted me to my car.

'Do you mind if I sit out here in the sun and have a snack?'

'Not at all. I've got work to do in the office, so take your time and enjoy.'

'Thanks.'

He gave me a wink and returned to the creamery. I watched him climb a set of stairs and disappear through a door at the top. He appeared at a window above my head and gave a wave, before turning back into the room.

~

I opened the door of the Jeep and put the paper bag gently on the floor of the passenger side. The weather was cold enough to ensure it stayed at peak lusciousness. I waited for a few minutes to make sure Brian was occupied, then walked to the end of the building and followed the path

I had taken the day before. All the police vehicles had gone and there was no sign of the workers or of Marco and Matthew. With the heel–toe motion of a competitive walker, but without the finesse, I stopped at the end of the wall, leaned forward, pressed one eye against the concrete and dipped the other eye so that I had a clear view of the warehouse door. To my surprise there was no cop on guard, although there was enough police tape to inspire Christo. With all the forensics collected and photos taken, maybe the sergeant was happy to leave it unattended, saving his scant resources for the filling in of forms and the cracking open of King Browns to celebrate a job well done.

Bent over, I ran across the open space and flattened myself against the metal of the warehouse. Of course, no matter how much I sucked in my stomach and held my breath, I remained in full view of anyone who might be going into the house or creamery. But there was a reassuring sense of invisibility with my back pressed against the tin.

I crept along to the door, and pulled on the handle. It slid smoothly along its tracks. I turned in with all the stealth of a thirty-three year-old woman who knew she had no right to be there. A more sensible person would have stopped there, respecting the purpose of the police tape and made an exit. For me getting the story had always overridden little things like contaminating a crime scene. On another level, the stretch of plastic ribbon bought out my inner rebel – the part of my temperament that Ben said was an immature response to a powerful, authoritative father; he had taken his university psychology units far too seriously. I shrugged away thoughts of Ben and resumed my mission.

Traversing the empty space where the trucks had been, I ducked under the tape and slunk into the inner room. The long tables were bare and everything was preternaturally clean. Even the concrete floor looked as though it had been scrubbed by a platoon of babas.

I sped down the length of the tables and stopped at the door where I'd watched Stephen disappear. Ducking under another useless bit of police tape, I climbed down the steel steps leading to the vaults, my hands scrunched up, clutching the cuffs of my jumper. In *Midsomer Murders*, it was a proven way of not leaving fingerprints.

'Vault' was an entirely appropriate word to describe the enormous coldroom at the bottom of the stairs. The ceiling was at least six metres above my head and lined with bricks arranged in a basket weave pattern stretched into four concave sections that met in the middle. Here a shield stamped with the Puharich family crest held the sections in place. Enormous steel shelves spread out to my left and right and on them were arranged the red and yellow waxy rounds of Puharich cheese. It was wonderfully atmospheric. I stuck my nose in the air and sniffed with pleasure the creamy, piquant aroma.

Moving along the rows, it was immediately obvious where Stephen had died. Police tape made a large square barrier around a section of concrete floor. I saw small pieces of yellow wax left behind when the cheese wheel had been removed. I was disappointed not to see a white outline of a body painted on the floor – like those left for Phillip Marlow to ponder through the twirls of smoke coming from the cigarette glued to the corner of his mouth.

I bent over the tape to take a closer look. A large dark smear was all that was left of the blood that had flowed from Stephen's head. It had obviously been catastrophic, as spatters of rusty red extended outside the taped boundary and sprayed the wax of the cheese on the opposite shelf. At intervals, tall ladders hung from railings with wheels affixed at the bottom, allowing them to be pushed along the shelves to give access to the uppermost cheeses. I went around to the back of the shelf from where the parmesan had fallen. My hands were clumsy bundles in my sleeves, but I managed to push a ladder to the right spot. Then I gingerly climbed up, fighting Hitchcockian swirls of vertigo.

Reaching the top, the reason the local police had called for the Perth homicide team to attend the scene became immediately obvious.

The shelf hadn't broken. Instead, the four screws that held it in place on the edge closest to me had been removed. It would have been easy for someone to tip the shelf and let the cheese slide off. Unless he was looking up at that precise moment, Stephen wouldn't have known what hit him. It was easy for someone to climb up, lie unseen along the top shelf, watch for Stephen to walk underneath, then stretch their arm down and pull the side of the lower shelf towards the ceiling. So simple. Anyone could have done it. Even Baba. I'd watched her thin, yet muscular, arms carry heavy dishes with ease. Was she protecting the interests of her favourite by getting rid of Stephen? If this was the case, I'd be shitting my pants if I was Matthew.

Or Matthew himself? He definitely had the strength to do it and only last night I'd heard his fury as he spoke to his brother on the walkie-talkie.

He had been a different man to the docile eating machine who'd sat across the table from me at lunch.

Maybe it was an outside job. I thought about Surfer Dude and his tribe. Their lithe surfer bodies were fit enough to do the deed. Surely they had too much self-interest to protect? The Puhariches were an ATM for cash and Kat. But I couldn't stop thinking of Surfer Dude and his detached insolence.

Brian and Marco were preoccupied in competing with each other in the cheese business. I wondered if they had time to plan and execute a murder. The manner of Stephen's death suggested someone who knew the vaults. The cousins clearly fitted the bill. Like Matthew, they were on site, so it was easy to go from the house to the vault and tip the shelf, releasing the cheese to crack open Stephen's forehead like an axe through a coconut.

I thought of Marie. Maybe she was making room for herself by getting rid of her cousin? I found it hard to believe a woman could gushingly show off pictures of her daughter one minute then turn around and commit murder the next. Then again, history is littered with mothers who slit throats and kill husbands to run away with toy boys or to make more room in the walk-in robe for their shoes. And Marie shared the same DNA as the malevolent old man in Croatia. It was conceivable that he was pulling Marie's string from afar, keeping his hands clean while his granddaughter risked everything.

Thinking of the scenarios was making me feel ill. I climbed down the ladder and returned to the stairs leading back to the warehouse.

Once outside, I leaned against the wall. The sun's rays put some warmth back into my bones. I knew everything and nothing. Pop's fat face appeared in my mind's eye. Stick your nose in as far as it can go, he'd say. Take no prisoners. And make your fucking deadline!

It was then I remembered the bug Ben had reluctantly given me. My brain registered the same skittish sense of naughtiness I got as a child whenever my plans included something really bad, where I might get caught, but the punishment wasn't going to outweigh the excitement of the crime. The device, and all its bits, was in the glovebox of the Jeep. Where to put it was the problem. The maximum distance between the receiver and the transmitter was five hundred metres. The back road where I'd previously parked was perfect if the bug was in the warehouse.

That, however, had the big downside of being shut down by the police investigation. Besides, it was so vast I wasn't sure I'd hear anything other than echoes and distant mumblings. Trying to get past the old witch in the house was terrifying. If she caught me, she'd probably cut off the fatty parts of my body and boil them up to make fancy soap or scented candles.

The only place that was small enough, and with probably the most hidey-holes, was the office, which I surmised Brian and now Marco used to manage the business.

Trying to look casual, I sauntered back to the Jeep, where I opened the glovebox and pulled out the bug. Holding it under the dash so no one on the outside could see, I was struck by how the little tangle of wires and black plastic actually looked sneaky. As though the arrangement of inert parts had taken on the aura of its purpose. I separated out the bits and put the transmitter in a pocket of my jeans and placed the receiver back in the glove compartment. On the count of three, and then on the count of an extra ten, I got out of the Jeep and scuttled into the creamery. In a quick trot, I crossed the floor and went up the stairs Brian had climbed a short time before. The door to the office was shut. My attempt at a knock was a pathetic little tap that expressed all my fear and guilt. I sucked in a big breath and knocked with more force.

'What?' Brian's voice was frosty.

'It's me. Coming to say goodbye.'

There were the sounds of a rapid shuffling of paper and a chair rolling across the floor. Then footsteps. Brian pulled the door open too quickly, not giving himself enough time to rearrange his face from a dark snarl to his happy face. I was unnerved.

'This is unexpected.' It seemed to me his voice was forced-pleasant.

Maybe he'd seen me fiddling with the bug from the office window.

'I wanted to say thanks for all the lovely things you gave me.'

'That's all right. Come in.' He stood to one side as I walked past, then shut the door behind me.

An enormous desk was in the middle of the room. Along two walls, four-drawer filing cabinets were lined up, topped with archive boxes. The space was neat and precise, with one chair other than that behind the desk.

'So,' I said, 'this must be the nerve centre.'

'Sit down. Care for a drink … one for the road?'

'No, that's fine. I don't want to interrupt, just say goodbye.'

'I'm glad you took the time.' He leaned against the desk and folded his arms in a way that suggested the opposite.

'Yeah, well, I really appreciate your hospitality. It's been so long since we've seen each other.'

'Apart from in Croatia.'

'Yes. Apart from there.' I was sneaking looks around the room to find a spot to put the transmitter. A large pot holding the ugly sinews of a yucca was my best shot. 'It's a great office; so light and airy.' I sounded completely daft.

'And just as well, considering the amount of time I have to spend here.' He was impatient.

I got up and moved towards the pot plant. 'My mum has one of these in her conservatory. She loves it. I think they're a bit creepy.'

'It's not my favourite, but it's a plant that grows well indoors and Baba says we need plants to keep our brains in good order. According to her, plants suck in all the bad air and spit out the good air for us to breathe.'

My casual laugh sounded like a demented snigger. Taking the bug surreptitiously out of my pocket, I leaned down into the plant as though I was going to sniff it. 'The leaves are amazing, almost fleshy.'

Brian stood and moved towards the door. With his back momentarily turned, I shoved the bug deep into the leaves of the yucca.

'You'll have to excuse me. There's a lot to do before I can even get around to dealing with the Stephen thing.'

I followed him and turned as I stepped over the threshold. 'That's okay, I wanted to say thanks and goodbye for now.'

Because I was feeling like a guilty sneak, I let Brian bend and kiss me on the lips. It was a peck, but it felt sticky and too moist.

I almost ran back to the Jeep, where, in my hurry to get away, I spun the wheels causing a cloud of gravel to rise up. Looking in the rear-view mirror, I saw through the light of early evening the figure of Brian at his window watching me go.

CHAPTER NINETEEN

Finding a place to hide within a five hundred metre radius of the bug was easier than I thought. Before the gates opened onto Caves Road, a track ran off to the right and disappeared into a stand of gum trees. I guided the Jeep along the bumpy road which then veered to the left, taking me back in the direction of the creamery. Before popping out in the clear, I pulled up and buried the nose of the car in an enormous shrub covered in flowers that looked like loo brushes, but were something native coveted by foreign tourists.

Settling back in my seat, I twiddled with knobs on the receiver, listening for the clear air that indicated the successful identification of the correct frequency. Almost immediately I heard Brian doing businessy-type things: paper being shuffled, a bum moving around in a chair and, every so often, a giant snort that probably rattled the drawers of the filing cabinets. It felt like hours before I heard the phone ring.

'What?' Brian's voice was clear over the transmitter and its tone was icy. 'I'm busy, Marco. What do you want?'

A pause.

'I have no idea where Matthew is. I'm not his keeper.'

Brian was quiet as he listened. 'Fine, and when you find him, let me know because I want to kill him. There's something dodgy with the stock. Nothing reconciles. He has to get his stupid arse up here and give me some explanations.'

He was banging the desk for emphasis. 'I don't care what you think, it's my reputation on the line if we get audited and some tax office jerk finds something's not right.'

Whatever Marco's reply, it made Brian incandescent.

'I'm warning you and Matthew: don't fuck this up. I'll have you both sent back to Croatia before you can blink. You can come here tonight and go through this shit with me, then you can find your idiot brother and get things fixed.'

I heard the phone handset fly across the room and slam into the wall. For the next half hour, I listened as Brian tossed paper about, yelled at his absent cousins and slammed drawers, his fury almost creating a physical heat as it came over the receiver. Then, with a stomping of feet and a loud slam of the door, Brian left.

~

Eavesdropping was a hungry business and Brian's brown bag was sitting on the passenger seat. I pulled it over and sat it on my lap. Inside was a collection of Puharich cheeses, cracker biscuits, some dried fruit and a little bottle of port. There were no utensils, so I had to break off pieces of cheese and sip the port straight from the bottle. It was the poshest stakeout ever.

After an hour of radio silence, the glamour had worn thin. My legs were restless and my over-full bladder pressed against my liver. After jiggling about for another hour, I knew that if I didn't go to the loo, my abdomen would explode, spraying all that glorious cheese across the windshield. Driving to the closest toilet put me out of range and I was bound to miss something. So, faced with the inevitable, I climbed out of the car and trudged into the bush.

I've never had the ability to use nature as a toilet without splashing the legs of my trousers. Hence, I took them off and looked for a place to pee in only my underpants. Men cannot understand the terror of squatting in the kind of landscape that hides deadly snakes and long-tongued lizards. A rustle in a tree and a tickle of grass on my bum cheek quickened proceedings and I returned to the Jeep in my knickers and with my corduroy trousers in my hand. As I climbed into the car, the receiver came to life and all thoughts of pulling on my pants evaporated in a surge of excitement. Was a confession on the cards?

The office door opened, footsteps tapped on the floor and a body dropped into the desk chair. The unknown person picked up papers and pulled the desk drawers in and out. Then they got up and walked to another spot in the room where something was moved and then a clicking sound that I couldn't identify.

Suddenly the office door was pushed open so fiercely it slammed against the wall.

'What are you doing in here, Marco?' Brian's voice cut the air.

'I don't have to explain myself to you.'

'Who gave you the combination of the safe?'

'Dida.'

'How did he have it?'

'You've got to be joking. The old man knows everything.'

'Close the door and get away from the safe. Dida didn't tell me you had access.'

'Why should he?'

'Because ...'

'You can't even come up with a reason. You're pathetic.'

Brian's voice dropped to a snarl. 'I said, get away from the safe. This is my office.'

'It's the property of our grandfather and I'm here at his behest.'

There was a long, dreadful silence. I imagined the cousins regarding each other with unalloyed hatred.

When Brian spoke again his voice was bitter. 'What do you want from the safe, anyway?'

'The deeds to the boat houses.'

'Why?'

'Dida wants them. He's thinking of buying a storage facility at the dockyards in Albany.'

'What possible reason can he have for doing that? Those boathouses are empty for most of the year.'

'I don't question his reasons. All I know is that the old man wants to use them as collateral for something similar in Albany.'

I heard the 'pffft' of the desk chair cushion as somebody sat down.

Slower footsteps crossed the floor and chair legs scraped.

'Dida hasn't said anything to me about an Albany purchase.'

'I do as I'm told.'

'Did he tell you to come here and undermine me? I want to know straight from him that he's asked for these documents to make that purchase.'

'Don't you trust me?' Marco's voice was mocking.

'Not for one minute.'

'He may be a long way away, but Dida owns us and we're only valuable to him if we toe the line. Otherwise, we're dispensable. Like Jure and Zorka.'

'What have they got to do with it? Dida knows he can trust me.' A desk drawer opened and closed. 'Get lost, this is my business. I sign off on everything, including those boat sheds. I suggest you piss off back to Croatia.'

'Now, now. Be nice.' Marco was contemptuous. 'And don't worry, I'll be going back to Croatia on Wednesday.'

'What? You said Dida sent you here long-term.'

'I lied. He sent me here with the purpose of getting the Albany purchase underway and to check on my brothers. He wants to know they're under control and that they stay that way while we restructure.'

'Then he won't be happy Stephen had an accident under your watch.'

'He'll sort it. Dida will have spoken to the Croatian police by now and they'll speak to the Australians to move things along.'

'I don't think the system works like that.'

'All systems can work like that. It all depends on how well you grease the wheels.'

'Sounds like you won't be missing Stephen.'

'Probably not.'

This was a 'wow' moment. In my world people grieved the dead. But these two men were dismissing Stephen as though he was a distant, insignificant relative rather than a sibling and cousin.

I understood they both considered Marco's brothers to be intellectual minnows. Apart from eating, shitting and sleeping, people had been hard pressed to think of anything else they were capable of doing well. It sounded to me as if Brian and Marco were oblivious to Stephen and Matthew's night-time enterprise. I realised Zorka was probably the only person capable of truly mourning Stephen, and she was already dead.

'I'll do what Dida wanted and then I'm leaving,' Marco said.

'Can't wait.'

'Of course, I might stay longer. Maybe get to know Alex better.'

'She has finer tastes.'

'You're kidding yourself if you think you've got a chance with that one.

Stick to boring and stupid. Now give those deeds to me or speak to the old man tomorrow. And he won't be happy if he has to phone.'

It was a threat Brian couldn't ignore. I heard him walking then the clicking of the safe's combination and the metal whine as he pulled the door. Rustling paper, more footsteps and the sound of Marco pushing back his chair came through the transmitter.

'Thank you, cousin. It's not wise to refuse our grandfather's request.' The opening and closing of the office door indicated Marco had left.

Brian moved around, yelling obscenities. I heard the clicking of the lock as he secured the safe and the opening and closing of filing cabinet drawers. His movements got more agitated.

'If that prick thinks he can take over.' More crashing about. 'He's making a big mistake. I'm as much Dida's man as he is.'

A final bang indicated Brian had left the office.

These Croatian men were very angry people. Of course, I'd seen anger, even experienced it myself. This, though, had an unfamiliar intensity. There was so much venom in the conversation. Everything was supposed to be about family. Yet the cousins distrusted each other; their fathers were dismissed as anachronisms; and their grandfather was revered like an ancient deity. Would he be revered more or less if Marco and Brian knew what he presided over? What kept them together? In my family it was generally accepted that I saw Charles when I needed something or he wanted to watch the big TV. I never saw Trophy Wife, other than in the society pages whenever she was attending the ballet, the opera or the opening of an envelope. They kept the twins away from me in case I dropped one on its head, and I missed them as much as they missed me. And my brother, James, in far-off London, had probably forgotten he even had a sister. We didn't pretend to be close and this was what distinguished us from the Puhariches.

Starting the Jeep, I drove down the gravel and turned onto Caves Road. The receiver gave a final crackle as I went out of range. Now was the challenge to get back into the office and remove the transmitter. I didn't fancy trying to make up another excuse to get in. Brian might become suspicious of me doing so much hanging around, especially when he thought (with some justification) that my motivation was transient lust towards his cousin.

My freezing bum had thawed out by the time I turned into the holiday park. Who'd have thought that returning to the bleak little kitchen could give so much comfort? I double-checked the locks and climbed into bed, fully clothed, my coat spread across the bottom of the bed to give extra warmth to my feet, and fell into a feverish cheese dream of a fiefdom in which there were competing vassals and an overlord who might destroy any one of them if it took his fancy.

CHAPTER TWENTY

Sleeping in clothes is best left to the under-thirties. When I awoke, my jeans had pushed up, making a painful camel toe, and my bra had moved to my chin, making an elastic bow tie. Through the windows of the french doors, I saw that Saturday morning was well advanced. The noise of crashing waves indicated a strong southerly wind, which would be freezing, but probably made surfers delirious. It wasn't until I sat at the table with a jug of coffee, and a quilt around my shoulders, that I was ready to think about the previous evening's clandestine operation.

There was a knock at the door as I was drinking the dregs of International Roast. Clutching the quilt tighter to my chest, I opened it to see a pile of blankets with two legs encased in gumboots emerging from the bottom.

The blankets spoke. 'I thought you might freeze tonight. It's going down to zero.'

As I removed the top blanket, the face and dishevelled hair of the Missus was revealed.

'That's great. Please come in. I'll put the kettle back on.'

'No, I won't stay.'

'It would be lovely if you did.'

She looked disproportionately pleased at the offer. I dumped the blankets on one of the lounge chairs. She followed, walking right behind me like a sad little puppy.

'Tea or coffee and how do you have it?'

'Coffee, strong with a splash of milk. No sugar.' She pulled out a chair and sat down.

I filled two cups and joined her at the table.

'Thanks for bringing the blankets. I'm feeling the chill.'

'Most people from the city do. You underestimate how cold it can get down here.' She stopped and took a breath as though speaking such a long sentence made her tired.

'My name's Alex.'

She nodded. 'My husband said. Mine is Valerie.'

The lines around her eyes extended to her hairline and the skin of her cheeks dragged down to merge into the sagging skin of her jowls. It looked like melted wax.

I touched the quilt. 'Did you make this?'

'Yes. Sewing is a wonderful way to be happy.'

'It's absolutely beautiful.' I sipped my drink. 'Have you lived here very long?'

'All my life.'

'Wow, it's not often I hear that.'

'Never wanted to leave. My three kids are here, and grandchildren as well. My daughters work in administration at the shire offices. My son,' she shook her head, 'hasn't found his niche yet. He spends most of his time surfing and that's enough to make him happy.'

I hoped he wasn't Surfer Dude. 'Does he live here?'

Valerie shook her head. 'He has a shack at Prevelly. Do you surf or watch?'

'Neither. It's too cold for me. I don't know how they do it.'

'Most of them have been surfing since they were toddlers so their bodies can't feel the cold like we do. My son practically came out of the womb surfing.' Her smile was shy and sweet.

'I've always been a bit afraid of the ocean.'

'Not my boy. The bigger the wave, the better. He always tells me, "Mum, it's like skimming across the sky."'

'The Puharich creamery seems to employ surfers,' I said. 'I got to see a few of them when I visited.'

Her expression changed, becoming wary. 'Do you know that family?'

'I went to school with Marie Puharich and I know Brian from back then as well.'

'I see.' She started to gulp her drink.

'Does your son work for them too?'

'Not really. He gets his shack for free because he looks after the two sheds they own at Prevelly. He gets extra money by unloading the boats that come in there.'

'I didn't realise there were areas around here deep enough for boats to moor.'

'They don't come right in. Larger ones – mostly old whale watching boats – anchor offshore and smaller boats unload the cheese and bring it to the jetty.'

'It's a long way to come from Perth.'

Valerie stood. 'The boats don't come from Perth. The Puharich cheese from Croatia comes in at Albany port, most comes up by road. And what they can't fit into the trucks, comes up by boat. I understand you're friends of the family. To be honest, I'd prefer it if my son didn't work for them.'

'Why?'

'Those two boys are bullies. They treat my son like a slave, and they get away with it because he needs the money and unskilled jobs are scarce. That family owns everything and everyone.'

'Did you know that Stephen Puharich was killed yesterday?'

Her head tipped back as though I had slapped her. 'What do you mean?'

'There was an accident at the creamery.'

A drip of water plinked into the sink. The face of the Missus was blank.

'Bad things happen to bad people. I can't think of any locals who'd miss him.' She stood. 'I've got to go. My husband will wonder where I am.'

'Just another thing.'

'Yes?'

'Is there any reason for your husband to come into the cabin while I'm away?'

'Sometimes he likes to check things ... for security.' Her eyes had the same look of wariness I'd seen in Sue at the Gracetown store.

And, like Sue, I sensed in Valerie the same desire to see only what she wanted to. Better to believe their men acted with good intentions than to recognise them for what they were – bullies and possibly criminals. Before I had the opportunity to ask anything else, Valerie walked away.

Knowing the identity of my late-night caller didn't make me feel any better. I wasn't about to accept Valerie's delusions. I doubted my safety was uppermost in the manager's mind. Was he looking for something specific? Or was he a garden-variety creep who got off going through the silky smalls of his female guests?

Prevelly Beach had now been brought up by almost everyone I'd spoken to. The link joining the beach and the Puhariches was particularly interesting. I knew that Albany was a port that handled massive amounts of overseas trade, exporting various minerals and importing vast numbers of shipping containers. With fewer import agents and less security than the city ports, it was easy to imagine mountains of illegal material getting through undetected. Hiding drugs in cheese was genius. Putting it on smaller boats to be unloaded at a remote beach was stunning in its arrogance. My next move had to be to Prevelly to have my own look around.

Firstly, I had to deal with three things: cleaning my body, which was starting to smell like blue cheese; a rumbling stomach that wanted breakfast; and, most importantly, buying some shoes. Too many of them had become collateral damage. Maybe I could put in a claim as expenses incurred while investigating. But my chutzpa would wither under Carly's steely eye. With an empty stomach and empty shoeboxes, a visit to Margaret River had become urgent.

Because the water was barely lukewarm, my shower was a quick lather, a quicker rinse and a hasty dry-off in front of the heater. I was still shivering when I got into the Jeep and turned south on Caves Road.

In thirty speeding minutes I was in Margs and heading to the pub for brunch. There were two choices: the upmarket heritage pub where out-of-towners enjoyed cappuccinos in a new 'bistro-style' dining room, or the pub where the locals congregated to talk about surfing, footy and remedies for blocked udders. It would be perfect for eavesdropping so I could add some Margaret River flavour to my journalistic stew.

Country pubs have a special place in my heart. They are noisy with talk and laughter. More often than not, the carpet smelled of beer spills and deep-fried food. When I ambled into the pub in town, it was like returning to the house of an old friend. The same old blokes, ubiquitous in every country pub, were perched on high vinyl stools at the bar where they tapped the ash off their cigarettes and blew smoke into each other's faces. Among these regulars, teeth were in short supply and conversation followed age-old patterns of silence, sparse words and rasping cackles. Multiple TVs were being ignored by the punters – the barmaids giving them fleeting glances as they pulled beers. I ordered a chicken parmigiana and a Coke and found a table near a window that gave me a view of the street.

I'm not the only person to have a nostalgic response when going to a country pub. I knew Pop had been a part-owner in one such establishment in Kalgoorlie – a wild west town where beer was served by barmaids with bare breasts and G-strings. A feature about these alternative places of worship would poke whatever remained of his sentimentality. I pulled a notebook and pen out of my bag and tried to think of a catchy hook to begin an article.

Looking absentmindedly out the window, I saw Surfer Dude pull into the parking lot. It was my lucky day! He was in a rusty ute with the tray full of his surfer mates and their girlfriends. Sue was not among them. She was probably burning bacon back at the general store. Grabbing the number on my table, I moved to another one near a giant plastic fern. The group came in noisily and pulled together multiple tables. According to the natural law of gender equity and balance, the girls clustered down one end, while the guys took the end closest to the TV. Listening to their enthusiastic chatter, it was clear that a big footy game was due to start.

As in pubs the world over, the women took the food orders while a bloke was charged with getting the first round of drinks. Everyone put their cigarette packs on the table and lit up. As they exhaled, the smoke wound its way through the plastic foliage that was hiding me. It tickled my nose and burned my throat and I wanted to cough – a lot. I squeezed my lips together and gave an 'inside the head cough' that almost blew my inner ears to smithereens.

It didn't take long for the barmaid to drop my parmigiana on the table. It was a cardiologist's nightmare and exactly my idea of country pub haute cuisine: an EE breast and chips so deep-fried they created their own oil slick. I cut off a chunk of chicken and munched joyfully.

After the first swig of their drinks, the surfers started talking in tones that suggested a joint or three had been smoked before arriving. The conversation was dominated by football and the past performances of the teams before predictions were made about the winner and the efforts of individual players. Then they swapped to weather and wind and the state of the waves. There was spirited disagreement about the location of the best breaks and who'd be able to manage them once they had been found. I was almost rigid with boredom as they progressed through the minutiae of wind direction and the shape of waves and endless lists of breaks with names like Three Bears, Guillotine, Wildcats and The Quarries.

The TV in the corner switched to a shot of a screaming crowd pressed against a fence surrounding a football oval. In one movement, the surfer dudes turned their faces to the TV. The girlfriends lowered their voices in deference to their men watching football. Before long, the dudes were enveloped by smoke and I listened to their cheers coming out of a cancerous cloud.

My lips became slippery with oil as I chomped my way through brunch. I'd just finished when a siren coming from the TV designated quarter time. A guy took the opportunity to buy another round, while his mates did a quick summation of the game they'd watched so far. The girlfriends used the break to herd themselves in a pack to the bathroom where I imagined they'd whinge about their boyfriends, muse on the morals of an absent friend and wonder whether the new season black uggs were worth the hefty price tag.

'Right,' said Surfer Dude once they were gone. 'Who can't make it tonight?'

My ears pricked up and I leaned further into the plastic fern.

There was a general mumbling at the table before a bloke put up his hand. 'I can't cos my sister's birthday bash is on tonight and the fat mole has told everyone that they have to go. It's not even a special one.'

This was greeted with various attestations that his sister was indeed being selfish.

'Sorry you're gunna miss out, mate,' said Surfer Dude. 'The rest of you, be at Prevelly at eleven. The boat is due around half past but Matthew wants us there early to move some boxes.'

Another voice spoke out from the cigarette fog. 'So, everything is still goin' ahead?'

'The shipments come in no matter what.'

'It doesn't feel right.'

'The bloke's dead. It's one less arsehole we have to deal with.'

'That's a bit rough,' said another voice.

'Don't kid yourself, Blue. Mum says Rob at the cop shop told his wife, who told her, that Steve's head didn't snap off his neck accidently. I'm not makin' you come. But you won't get paid sittin' on your arse at home.'

'Okay. I'm only sayin'.'

'Matt's in control now and he wants it finished off tonight. Second last shipment means second last payday.'

This news didn't go down well.

'Maybe we should take a few packets to sell,' suggested someone.

'You want to rip off the Puhariches?' Surfer Dude was contemptuous.

'They're bringin' in so much, they wouldn't notice.'

'You're such a dumb shit. They know every last gram that comes in. They're probably killin' each other on that farm. How long do you think you'd last if you ripped them off?'

A siren sounded, the girls returned and all conversation ended. As for me, it looked like my evening's activities were set. There was no way that delivery was going to be made without me watching on. I felt both excitement and terror. If Matthew Puharich caught me, there was no doubt I was in the shit. I hoped he was enough of a gentleman not to punch a girl, but so far I hadn't seen much evidence of Puharich politeness. And I liked my head exactly where it was.

CHAPTER TWENTY-ONE

I wiped the grease from my face and gathered together my belongings. Then, approaching the bar, I caught the attention of a barmaid.

'Any good shoe shops in town?'

'Yeah, there's a couple. One across the road sells joggers. The one three doors up is where you can get hippie shoes.' She leaned over the bar to check for floral bell-bottoms. 'And then there's Jim's. Which sells proper shoes.'

'Thanks, I'll try there.'

I slunk through the pub, hoping Surfer Dude wouldn't see me. But he only had eyes for the telly. Stepping into the street, my breath caught at the back of my throat. The air felt arctic after the stuffy pub. I went quickly in the direction of Jim's and, once inside, was very thankful for its warmth. The smell of new shoes is one of life's great pleasures and Jim's Shoe Palace didn't disappoint. High shelves were along three walls and a large display box dominated the centre of the shop. Every inch was covered with shoes and boots and my eyes spun in all directions.

The shop assistant came to my aid. 'Hi, I'm Mandy, can I help you?'

'Yes, I'd like to buy some shoes.'

This was the illogical, yet necessary, exchange that signalled the beginning of the shopping ritual. And it had all the solemnity of the Eucharist.

Interrupted by the sporadic customer, we spent a couple of hours putting shoes on my feet, standing back and exclaiming on their gorgeousness and perfect fit. As I worked my way through boxes of beautiful leather and canvas, the young woman and I gossiped about people, places and events that were almost entirely foreign to me. It was while I was trying on a pair of red ankle boots that I finally got control of the conversation.

'Where are you staying?' Mandy handed me a shoehorn.

'At the Gracetown holiday park.'

She wrinkled her nose. 'Oh, that's The Pig and Valerie. Poor woman.'

'Do you know her son?'

'Yeah, we were at school together. He's nice enough, but a follower. You know what I mean?'

'Who does he follow?'

'There's a group of surfers. Always together, getting stoned and god knows what else. He tries to hang with them.'

'Are they the blokes who work for the Puhariches?'

She pursed her lips and nodded. 'The less said about that family, the better.'

'Why?'

Mandy dropped her voice and flicked her eyes around the store as if expecting a Puharich to leap out from behind the shoeboxes. 'There's lots of talk about their money. They are so much richer than any of the other cheesemakers. We all think those boys are total crooks, but no one has the guts to do anything.'

'Are they really that bad?'

'You bet. I s'pose you've met the brothers?'

'Yeah, the once. They seemed okay.'

'It's all a front. A friend of my cousin was on a date with one of them. She said he'd tried it on when he dropped her off. Apparently, he wasn't going to take no for an answer. She was so frightened he was going to rape her or something. She managed to get out. It totally scared the shit out of her.'

'Did you know that Stephen was found dead?'

'I heard!' She leaned forward: we were almost nose-to-nose. 'Everyone at the newsagency this morning reckons it wasn't an accident. It proves that when you lie down with dogs, you get up with fleas. Or, don't get up at all, in this case. Either one of those surfers have had enough or that gang of Croats they've got working for them knocked him off.'

'Really?' I was as breathless as the moment required.

'It's the way with foreigners. Who's to say they're not mafia? And those surfers. There are plenty of rumours around saying they do hard stuff. It's probably fried their brains.'

'Wow. I s'pose the mafia is everywhere.'

'Absolutely. The Puhariches are bullies and you can only push people so far.' With that insight, Mandy, who'd been kneeling near my stool, got to her feet and looked at the floor around me. 'Which ones have you settled on?'

Surveying my feet, I decided there was a further need to try on a wider range of leather goods. We resumed the task at hand, having a good time spending my money. When I left, there were five pairs to replace the three pairs I'd ruined. It was my kind of arithmetic.

I took the shoes back to the Jeep and returned to the main street to peruse the offerings in other shops. The following hours resulted in the purchase of a possum wool beanie, a pair of tongs in the shape of a crocodile for my mother and an implement whose sole purpose was to devein prawns. A worthy present for Ben.

At two o'clock that Saturday afternoon, the shops shut their doors. There was still several hours left to fill. I didn't want to go back to the holiday park where time dragged and where I might atrophy in front of bad TV. I did some window shopping before returning to the Jeep to sit and wonder what to do with all those dead hours then solved the problem by falling asleep.

~

I was woken in the late afternoon by a knocking on the car window. Dribble had run down my cheek and my face had made an oily smudge on the window. Why do naps, so often with the purpose of rejuvenation, end up making a woman look like a cross between a dugong and a salivating cocker spaniel? Through bleary eyes I saw one of the women from behind the pub bar. I wound the window down.

'You okay, love?'

'Yeah, yeah. Fell asleep.'

'Pete's been watching you from the bus stop. He was worried you might have died cos you haven't moved. Came to get me from the bar to check.'

'Sorry. Big lunch, stuffy car. You know how it is.'

'As long as you're all right.'

'I'm fine.'

She walked away. I looked towards the bus stop and gave Pete the thumbs up. Without his interference I might have slept until morning and missed the big show.

It's an anatomical fact that naps lead to hunger. My body was highly sensitive to this mandate. I'd go back to the pub: my previous meal had been great and I liked that the barmaid was brave enough to check out my corpse.

This time I opted for Indian – chicken curry made with the finesse of an Australian cook who'd never thought much of sub-continental food, but who followed a women's magazine recipe because curry was popular with the clientele. It was bits of chicken with potato and peas mixed in with a greenish-yellow sauce which had all the curry punch of a rice cracker. Amidst the jaundice colour, currants stuck to pieces of chicken like flies on a carcass. It was bearable washed down with a delightful chardonnay from a local winery.

Sipping my second glass, I pulled out my notebook to try and order my thoughts. There were three points to a triangle: the immediate Puharich family, now down by one, the steel-boot crew, Surfer Dude and his mob. All connected via the drugs – with the dead body of Stephen in the middle like the Eye of Providence. I had no idea where all of the Puhariches fitted. Although I hoped, for old times sake, Marie was what she seemed: a doting mum and not a murdering, drug-smuggling matriarch.

Looking back over my notes, I knew I had the makings of a juicy story for Pop. All it needed was a suitable denouement from Prevelly Beach.

By eight o'clock I'd finished eating and managed to drink another two glasses of wine. Wandering back to the Jeep via the petrol station, I bought caramel chocolates, a packet of Mentos and a large bottle of Coke – enough caffeine and sugar to keep me awake for days.

Although it was ridiculously early, I decided to drive to Prevelly. It seemed a better idea than sitting in a smoky pub watching the locals get drunk and frisky.

The Jeep quickly became a sauna on wheels with the heater on 'burning hot' and the fan on 'blow your eyeballs dry'. It was only twenty minutes from Margaret River to the beach, but I dawdled to stretch out the time. Arriving at the little hamlet of Prevelly, I drove straight to the sea and pulled to a stop in a gravel carpark. I grabbed Jess's torch and opened the door. Getting out of a car hot enough to stew your innards, I stepped into a southerly bracing enough to make a woman swallow her tonsils. There were a few minutes of gasping before I trekked down to the beach.

Prevelly is a beautiful and mystical place particularly when the moon is a tiny slice suspended among millions of stars. At one end a rocky promontory sheltered the sand from the southern currents. To the north the beach formed a gentle arc and I could just pick out the waves pushing swirls of seaweed onto the sand. Here and there flat brown rocks stretched out like fingers testing the temperature of the water. I stood perfectly still, savouring the quiet splendour.

A small jetty jutted out into the night almost directly in front of me. When my eyes had adjusted to the dark, I saw pylons covered in barnacles and little crabs, with their jerky gait, scrambling upwards out of the sea foam. The jetty wasn't very long, and there were heavy steel rings drilled into the wood where boats tied up. The boards of the walkway were in excellent condition, despite its obvious age. Someone had replaced the originals with sturdy planks of jarrah.

South of the jetty, built into the protection of a high sand dune, were two squat boathouses. I scuttled across the sand and up the beach to the one closest to the jetty. There were two salt-smeared windows on the seaward side. I crept up to the nearest one.

Although there was no sign of another human being, I felt the occasion called for stealth. Sliding up the wall, I used the sleeve of my coat to rub a bit of salt away, and peered inside. It took a few moments for me to register that I was looking through an internal security grill at the cardboard sides of boxes pushed up against the glass, blocking all view into the room. This was an unexpected affront to my spying skills. I kept my back against the wall and moved towards the other shed. Splinters of wood caught on my coat – I'd resemble a porcupine by night's end.

The windows in the second building were likewise covered in salt and had the same grille. A smaller one further along had been better protected from the wind by the shed next to it and was almost clear of white crust. Jess's torch beam revealed the same cardboard boxes, these stamped with the Puharich logo, filling most of the room. A small corridor separating the boxes gave me a view through to the other side. Apart from an old telephone, partially hanging from the wall, there was nothing else to see.

Looking around to make sure there was no one but me on the beach, I moved to the front of the building. The doorframe and door itself were relatively new and made of thick planks of jarrah. Down one side, four locks of various types secured the door to the frame.

I made my way back to the beach feeling unreasonable resentment at the Puharich security arrangements. With a few hours to kill before the surfers were due to arrive, I decided to wander among the dunes to check their suitability as a hiding place. There were plenty of choices as the humps, covered in spiky grasses, were pitted with little indentations perfect for surreptitious observing.

Back at the Jeep I emptied my new paisley loafers of sand and realised how exposed the car was. I started the engine and drove out of the carpark and turned south. Surfer Dude would be coming from the north, so I needed a hidey-hole further down the beach.

A curved break in a dune appeared a few hundred metres from the carpark. Pulling in tight against the dune meant the Jeep was completely off the road, hidden from the lights of cars coming from the north. I stopped the engine and waited. It took a few minutes of sitting still and I was ready to slash my throat. Now being outside in the freezing air seemed more bearable than staying in.

Rummaging around the detritus of my mother's car I unearthed a man's large raincoat she wore for night-time raids on chicken farms, and a pair of powerful binoculars: putting on both, I suddenly looked like a birdwatching flasher.

All my senses were on hyper-alert as I walked along the road. Before getting back to the beach, I heard the sound of cars and had to hunch into the sand before lights swept along the dune. They turned into the carpark and the drivers cut the engines. I had to risk getting across the open space before crawling to my hiding spot. Doing my fastest possible sprint across the gravel, I threw myself onto the spiny grass on the other side: it was like I'd fallen into the clutches of an enthusiastic acupuncturist.

Near the top of the dunes there was a large shallow dip from where I could watch the action. I sucked my stomach in to lie as flat as possible. My bum was poking above the bunker, but hopefully the surfer dudes wouldn't notice, or if they did, they'd dismiss it as another part of the undulating landscape.

Someone had opened the shack closest to the beach and turned on a light attached to the top of the roof line and pointing out to sea. Two utes were stopped at the edge of the carpark's gravel surface so that their bumpers hung over the sand. Both trays contained the supine bodies of the surfers. Through the binoculars I saw them clutching puffy flannel coats for warmth with woollen beanies pulled low over their ears. Despite what the Missus had said, they looked miserably cold. Like a bunch of arthritic pensioners, they climbed down from the utes and trudged across the sand to the jetty. I watched the flare of matches as they lit cigarettes, which they puffed and handed around as though playing pass-the-parcel.

At the same time the surfers and I heard the sound of a truck engine. One of the trucks that had been at the warehouse turned in and stopped beside the utes. Matthew jumped down and walked towards them. He had his back to me, so I couldn't hear what he was saying but his words made them drop their cigarettes. Like sulky schoolchildren, they followed him in single file to the first boatshed where he watched them pass in front of him before he turned and entered. Although Matthew had left the door open there was nothing to see other than boxes and the occasional surfer passing by.

It was probably half an hour before things started to happen. What sounded like a gun going off came from across the water. Turning the binoculars towards the water, there was nothing to see. But Matthew responded to the sound immediately, emerging from the shed and running to the beach, the surfers following him in single file. At the water's edge, he held a powerful torch which he flashed into the darkness. After a few seconds, similar flashes came from a boat that must have been at least a kilometre offshore. It wasn't long before I heard the sound of an engine coming in from the ocean. This was the signal for the surfer dudes to move down to the beach and cluster behind Matthew.

'It'll be here in five so get your arses into gear.' His voice was clear in the night air.

With a practised motion, the surfers climbed up onto the pier and arranged themselves in a line that went from partway along the jetty back to a couple who remained on the beach. Matthew disappeared into the shed, returning with a cart which had high sides and all-terrain wheels. He easily pulled it across the sand and stopped at the end of the queue.

It wasn't long before a strange-looking boat appeared at the feet of the surfers standing on the jetty. The vessel was a cross between an oversized inflatable dinghy and a runabout cabin cruiser. A marine canvas base was topped by a wooden cabin that housed a steering wheel and a couple of tall chairs that now held the bums of two enormous men in flannelette shirts and balaclavas. They looked like farmers ready to rob a bank. Tethering the boat to the pier, they took turns hoisting up hessian objects that I guessed might be rounds of cheese. The surfers formed a chain, passing the cheese down the line until it stopped at Matthew, who then piled them into the cart.

It wasn't long before the fancy dinghy was empty, untied and pushed back out into the water. The men on the beach helped Matthew pull the cart to the back of the truck, where they loaded the cheese into the tray. As they were tucking away the last of the packages, another of the dinghies pulled alongside the pier, and the process was repeated.

The two boats travelled in and out for well over an hour until the truck was full of cheese and Matthew had stored the surplus in one of the sheds.

With a rough authority I hadn't thought him capable of, Matthew yelled orders.

'Balance out the cheese and get back to the farm. Don't go to the warehouse. We want you to put it all in the creamery. I've made room along the back wall.'

'Is there a problem?' Surfer Dude sounded a lot less sure of himself around Matthew.

'The warehouse is off limits for now. Put it where I've told you and piss off. There'll be no hangin' around tonight and no extras.' This last bit created mumbles of discontent.

'What the fuck, man?' It was Surfer Dude. 'You don't pay us enough to go without our bonus.'

Matthew strode towards him. 'Pack it and leave. There'll be one more shipment tomorrow night and then no more for a while. When there is, I'll let you know.'

'We might not be around for next time.'

Matthew sniggered. 'I think you will.'

'Yeah?' I had to admire Surfer Dude for his bravado. 'Without our bonus I might find it hard to keep my gob shut.'

'Really?' Matthew was an arm's-length away from the surfer. 'You think you'll get away with biting the hand that puts food into your useless mouth? That's not the Puharich way.'

Surfer Dude moved back. 'I'm just sayin'. We don't have to hang around just for you.'

'We both know that you do. You're cheap and easy to replace if anything happens.'

I don't know if it was the guttural accent that gave these words an extra sense of threat, but they scared me. And, looking at the faces of the surfers, I wasn't the only one to feel a violent undercurrent. Rather than being dumb, it was easy to believe that Matthew was capable of anything.

CHAPTER TWENTY-TWO

Fear made me scurry back to the Jeep as quickly as my frozen legs could manage. That same sense of doom had turned my accelerator foot to lead and the old engine roared along at a hundred kilometres an hour until it came to an exhausted stop outside my door. I got into bed, fully clothed yet again, ready for a quick getaway in case Matthew turned up to slaughter me in my sleep.

Of course, in the tepid light of Sunday morning, even I recognised hysteria. Yet the level of threat I'd witnessed in Matthew made me re-evaluate him. Jess would have described his aura as a ruthless emanation and given it a colour and cosmic sobriquet.

My clothes were so rigid with salt and sand I felt like a tightly bandaged mummy. With difficulty, I swung my legs over the side of the bed. My feet, still in damp socks, touched the floor and almost froze on contact. I hobbled to the bathroom, turned on the bar heater attached to the wall, and shed my clothes. I was soon sitting at the kitchen table with a coffee, a thick slice of toast dripping with honey and a huge chunk of Puharich cheese. Only after enough coffee to cause a slight tremor in my hands did I consider the happenings of the previous night.

Matthew was in the smuggling operation up to his neck. He oversaw the receival operations with a hardcore single-mindedness, and it appeared to be a well-established process. The whole thing had a clockwork efficiency. Were it not for the fact it was illegal, Charles – a preternaturally ordered person – would have considered the slick operation a thing of beauty.

But Matthew wasn't running such a sophisticated operation on his own. It required a network of people stretching from the creamery in Croatia to the Albany port and, finally, to the warehouse in Margaret River. Then there was the distribution of the drugs. Brian had bragged about the efficiency of the import–export business that saw Puharich cheese spread across Australia and into lucrative Asian markets. How easy for Stephen and Matthew to use these pathways to circulate the Kat. And it was a simple matter for the grandfather to direct activities from his mansion in Croatia, where he lived completely out of reach of authorities.

I wondered if something had happened between the brothers. The exchange in the warehouse suggested their relationship was not as benign as the lunch had implied. Around the table they had seemed like men whose number one ambition was to eat their way through a herd of cows and a potato crop. Even in the most functional of families, things may go awry. The Puhariches operated more as a fiefdom and history has shown how quickly they can go belly up. If Stephen and Matthew had fought down in the vault, how simple for Matthew, after pretending to leave, to turn back, loosen the screws and send the cheese flying. It may have been a matter of which brother got in first.

As I sipped the dregs of my coffee, there was a knock on the door. Opening it revealed the Missus, wrapped up in an enormous army surplus coat, standing on the verandah.

'Hi.' I could see the tip of her nose and her mouth, everything else was covered by a bulky hood.

'We got a call at the office. You have to ring Brian Puharich. He said it's urgent.'

Before I replied, she'd turned and walked away, leaving me to fight the urge to get in the Jeep and bolt. Had Brian found the bug? I felt ill. There was nothing on the thing to suggest it was mine, but he'd remember my interest in the plant and put two and two together.

Urgent to Brian might be related to their current situation. Maybe he'd been contacted by so much media he wanted me to run interference. This was a happier thought as well as being a perfect opportunity to get the bloody bug back.

It took seconds for me to pull on my coat and beanie, pausing briefly to consider platforms or pumps. Opting for the former, I ran to the Jeep and spun the wheels racing to the manager's office.

Valerie had left the door open. I stepped into the room from where the manager ran his accommodation empire. I found myself in the kind of bombsite Surfer Dude would covert. A kitchen table, its formica top unglued and lifting off at the corners, was in the centre of the room. Pushed under it was a filthy canvas garden chair, a style once beloved by posh people at their St Tropez holiday homes.

Among household debris I saw the phone, sitting on top of a filing cabinet whose drawers were on the floor as a cluster of bins, now overflowing with chocolate wrappers and empty Coke bottles. I pulled the sleeve of my shirt over my hand and picked up the handset, dialling the number Brian had given me the day before.

'Good morning!' Brian's voice blasted into my ear.

I did a whole-body sigh. 'Hi. This is an early call.'

'It's after ten.'

I resentfully looked at a clock hanging by string from the curtain rail. Its placid face confirmed half my morning had disappeared. 'I didn't realise. You told the manager's wife it was urgent.'

'I thought it might have been the only way to get her to deliver my message. I tried ringing your mobile, but there was no connection.'

'So, nothing is urgent?' My fingers twitched to reach down the phone and smack him.

'Don't sound so annoyed. Did you have a late night?'

'I stayed up watching movies.'

'If you'd given me a call I'd have come over to keep you company.'

I'd rather watch the test pattern while eating broken glass than invite Brian into my cabin.

'I wanted to be alone. The whole Stephen dying thing was a bit overwhelming.'

'Speaking of which, I was ringing for a purpose.'

'Oh yes?'

'Marie's not coping very well. I was thinking you might like to come back down. Maybe you could distract her. Get her focused on contributing with some media management. It's Sunday and Baba Tete always puts on a special meal. An amazing spread.'

'Sounds delicious.'

'It is. Interested?'

So, it was a magnificent lunch with one or more murderers, or stay in a cold cabin eating reconstituted noodles? What were the risks? It was broad daylight, Marie was there and surely even the Puhariches didn't murder guests, at least not on an empty stomach. Besides, there was Jess's rabbit's foot and I'd tuck her crystals in my bra for extra protection. It was risky and worth it.

'Ok, I accept.'

'Great. Shall I come and pick you up?'

'Why on earth would you want to come up here and then have to drive me back?'

'The drive means some "we" time.'

A loud snort escaped my nose; I tried to cover it up by a fit of dramatic coughing.

'Are you all right?'

'Yep. Yep, fine. I'll drive down myself. What time?'

'We eat at one, but you can come whenever you want.'

'One sounds good to me. Gives me time to get organised.'

'I'm glad you're joining us. It'll be fun.'

Fun was not something I equated with Brian.

'See you soon,' I said and hung up before he replied.

Apart from my pathetic weakness for fabulous food, I saw lunch as an opportunity to watch the surviving cousins interact, particularly Matthew, my firm POI. Would he revert to acting dumb?

The other attraction was Marco. Yes, he was arrogant. Yes, he had a mean streak. But he was a superb kisser and his aesthetic appeal outweighed the downsides.

I took extra care getting ready. I'd packed a rather fetching pencil skirt, fashionably tight and flexible enough to allow me to tread like a normal woman, not a seventeenth-century Chinese concubine. My rust-coloured crushed velvet pumps gave my outfit a degree of *je ne sais quoi*. An extra thick coat of my favourite coffee-coloured lippy was the final flourish. I looked pretty good: fabulous shoes and a shimmery pout.

~

It was just before one when I parked the Jeep outside the creamery. My feet had barely touched the gravel before I was enveloped in Marie's plump arms.

'Welcome to our sad little home.'

This sounded like PR spin. There hadn't been much evidence of sadness when I'd been around.

'How are you?'

'It's very difficult, Alex. But the show must go on. Brian is counting on me. A shipment is due to go out on Thursday and I have a lot of work reassuring our customers everything is running as normal.'

The Puhariches had the weirdest sense of normal I'd ever come across.

'How long will you be down here? And what about your daughter?'

'My husband and mother-in-law are sharing those duties.' She put her hand on my arm and lowered her voice. 'Out of disaster comes opportunity. With Stephen dead and my father and uncle in Croatia, there's a big hole in the business that I can fill. I've got more smarts than any of my cousins combined.'

'Brian and Marco seem to know what they're doing.'

Marie shook her head. 'They're too busy butting heads. While they focus on being alpha males, I'll get on with things. Show Dida my worth.'

'What about Matthew?'

'You've met him. He manages to function with a scant brain stem.'

Like everyone else, she was underestimating him. The man I watched at the beach last night wasn't dumb and he was nasty. He'd certainly rattled Surfer Dude's briny buddies.

'I might be able to get him sent back to Croatia. Then we can really make changes.'

'Who's "we"?'

'Brian and me.'

'What about Marco?'

Marie looked at me slyly. 'Don't get your hopes up. He'll be out of here soon. My cousin is not in my plans.'

So, the patriarchy was to be brought to its knees. Replaced by a woman who suddenly seemed to be a baba in the making.

My face must have registered my ambivalence about her plans for world domination because she changed her tone back to one of sweet passivity.

'Your support has been brilliant. Thank you, Alex.'

'Oh. Okay. I haven't done much.'

'Brian thinks you have a calming presence.'

Brian was clutching at straws if that's what he thought. I mumbled something non-committal.

'Come on in. The midday meal on a Sunday is always special. Mass puts Baba in a good mood.'

She linked our arms and we walked in silence to the house. Out of the gloomy interior, Brian emerged to push open the door.

'Well, hello, Alex. I'm glad you accepted my offer.'

'Thank you for inviting me, especially at this difficult time.'

For the briefest moment a look of confusion passed over his face. 'Oh, of course. Yes. Stephen's death has been a shock to us all. But we are a tight family unit and that will get us through.'

Oh please! The Puhariches made my family look like *The Brady Bunch*.

Marie and I moved through the door and into the living space. Despite its enormousness, the room was cosy-warm. A huge fire burned in the giant stone fireplace and Brian now ushered us towards the blaze where Marco was already leaning against the mantel. He was at his handsome best. His 'resting face' was something of beauty; the bone structure and the body would've made Michelangelo reach for his hammer and chisel.

He flashed a divine smile. 'Welcome back. You don't seem to be able to stay away.'

'Brian keeps inviting me and I don't like to refuse.'

'I'm pleased about that.' He came forward and pressed his lips on each cheek. My insides went gooey.

Brian's hand was in the middle of my back as he steered me away from Marco and proffered a spot on the couch. Before her cousin could sit his saucy self next to me, Marie dropped into the seat.

'Can I get you a drink?' Brian was at his most solicitous.

'A white wine. Thank you.'

'Coming up.'

Crossing the room, he began to fuss around at the sideboard. The three of us sat in a silence: Marco leaning back looking at me with casual composure and Marie, head bent, fingers fiddling in her lap.

Brian returned and passed filled glasses to me and Marie. Marco was obviously going to have to get his own.

'*Zivjeli*.' Brian clinked his glass against mine.

'*Zivjeli*.' Marie did the same.

I took a long sip. As usual, the chardonnay was crisp and fruity on my tongue. 'Oh, lovely.'

'Cullens, nineteen eighty-four. A very special year for grapes.'

In my view, wine was the very best way to eat that particular fruit. In their natural form, grapes were bits of flesh hiding bitter seeds. As kids, my brother, Ben and I had spitting competitions to see how high up the pool room wall we might make them stick. As an adult I considered the pips to be a danger to my teeth, therefore, on dental grounds, it was best to consume them as wine.

I gave a little gasp when Baba Tete appeared without warning at the side of the couch, an enormous platter obscuring her face.

Marco moved towards her and said something in Croatian. She gave him her special smile and replied in a soft voice. He rewarded her with an indulgent laugh and took the platter. The old woman gave me the stink-eye as she stepped back into her kitchen.

Marco placed the platter on the table. It was covered in ham and salted meats, a range of Puharich cheeses, dried fruit and chunks of bread.

'Please, help yourself.' He looked towards me. 'Guests first.'

I tried to make my cheese cutting as quick as possible, staying decorous while juggling brie, a cracker and quince paste. Marie and then the men filled their plates in turn, and we all munched through the platter in a way that was almost companionable.

Eventually, Brian spoke. 'How much longer do you think you'll be down here?'

'Not sure. Apart from your food and the two vineyards whose wine you've served, I haven't done much research. You have to remember I'm down here to write about the whole area, not just the Puhariches.'

'When will you start? I'm eager to see what you have to say about us.'

Was Brian going to try and censure me?

'My first piece has to be filed on Wednesday. You won't have long to wait.'

'At least you've done the best first.' Marie spoke with a mouthful of bread and dried muscatels. 'There are two other creameries worth visiting and about half a dozen decent wineries.'

Marco leaned forward and gave me his full attention. 'I leave this Wednesday. I hope your time won't be fully taken up with writing.'

'Weren't you here for the long-term?' I tried to look as if this was news to me.

'It was a consideration given the restructure. But things are better than Dida expected so I can go back to Croatia and take care of things from that end. Will you miss me?'

'Of course not, Marco.' I smiled coquettishly, hoping cheese wasn't filling the gaps in my teeth.

'Shame.' His smile, dripping with flirtatious sensuality, made me quiver. The climactic sound of a gong brought me to my senses.

'Lunch is on.' Brian stood, offering me his hand, and escorted me to the table.

The three Puhariches took their seats according to a silent family understanding of who sat where. Stephen's chair looked very empty.

'Where's Matthew?' asked Marco.

'I haven't seen him since last night.' Brian was unconcerned.

'He knows we start at one sharp on a Sunday.'

Baba came through the door with a tureen and began serving tomato soup that had thin noodles swirling through it. She stopped at Matthew's chair. '*Mate gdje?*'

'We have no idea,' Marco spoke in English. 'Let's get on without him.'

Baba shrugged and continued to put ladles of the scalding soup into bowls. She spoke in Croatian again.

'What do you mean he didn't come home?' Marco asked. 'Not again.'

The split conversation continued as she served: questions from Marco in English, replies in Croatian. After a couple of minutes, it became clear that Matthew hadn't slept in his bed or bothered to eat the breakfast she'd left out. Baba had reached the conclusion he had slept at the home of his *Engleski kurva*.

'Not all Australian women are whores,' Brian observed.

Baba looked sceptical.

'Don't worry, Alex. The old people have very strange ideas about non-Croatian women. It's their way.'

I didn't care what the old witch had to say. She cooked fabulous food. As far as I was concerned, she might be accusing me of being the sluttiest whore of Babylon, but while I was tasting the delectable tomatoes of her soup and the crusty goodness of her bread, I was completely unruffled.

'I'm fine, Brian. I'm enjoying your hospitality.'

Baba disappeared, to emerge five minutes later with the trolley laden with the kind of food that puts an inch on my waistline just by looking at it. There was lamb and chicken and a whole baked fish smelling of garlic, lemon and something sharper I couldn't identify. Great bowls of hot vegetables and a green salad rounded out the offerings. She left more bread on the trolley, which she placed next to Marco. She had designated him responsible for its cutting and serving. Having completed her task, she retreated to her lair.

As knives and forks clattered, Brian resumed the conversation. 'I wonder who Matthew is seeing now?'

'It doesn't matter. What concerns me is his disrespect for Baba. He should let her know what he's doing and whether or not he'll be here for meals.' Marco didn't bother to conceal his dislike of Matthew.

'He's your brother. You need to pull him into line before you go. What we should be focused on is Stephen.'

'Why? We can't do anything until the police and coroner have finished.'

'There's the funeral to organise.' Now Marie spoke. 'Margaret River presents a few problems. Like the availability of an appropriate funeral home, and the issue of a burial site. And then, what about a will?'

It was clear her brother and cousin had not concerned themselves with such banalities.

'If we haven't got a date, we can't organise a funeral.' Marco was dismissive.

'That doesn't matter. We can still approach someone and get the process moving.'

Marco shrugged. 'Do what you want.'

'I think you should show my sister some respect.'

'Look, Brian, I don't care about a funeral. I won't be here when it happens, and Stephen is too dead to care.'

'Does anyone know when the police are likely to be finished?' Marie asked.

There was a knock on the window and a face peered in.

'There you go Marie. You can ask them yourself.'

CHAPTER TWENTY-THREE

The face of the sergeant I'd seen the previous day was pressed against the window. For a moment we were all too astonished to move. Then the kitchen door swung open and Baba moved quickly across the room. Pushing the door open, she positioned herself directly in front of the policeman with a wide-legged stance suggesting combat.

'Yes.' In her heavily accented English, it was a demand not a question.

'I've come to speak to Marco, Matthew and Brian Puharich.'

'Why?'

'It's a matter for them.'

Marco pushed back his chair and went to the door. He spoke to the old woman in Croatian and she retreated. After watching her go, Marco turned to the policeman. 'We're having lunch. Would you like to wait in the creamery while we finish?'

'No.'

Marco looked surprised that a person existed who didn't follow his commands. 'Can you tell me what this is about?'

'I want to speak to all of you.'

'We don't seem to have a choice. Come in.'

The sergeant followed Marco to the table.

The policeman looked at me. 'I don't know you. In the business too?'

'She's a family friend. Her father is a QC, so I think it is in our interests that she remains as a witness to whatever you have to say.'

As illogical as that was, it had the required effect. The sergeant paused. He wasn't to know Brian was speaking out of his bum and that I was completely witless when it came to the law. I imagined Charles' horror at knowing his name was being used to intimidate a country copper. But being able to stay and watch the drama would be great for my story.

The policeman gathered his thoughts. 'I'm Sergeant Cooper. Is this all of you?' He looked around the table.

'No.' Brian was bullish. 'My cousin Matthew isn't here.'

'Can you get him, please?'

'No.'

'I can't have you impeding our enquiries.'

'He's not here.'

'Where is he?'

'We don't know where my brother is. He spent the night somewhere and hasn't come home yet.' Marco pulled out a chair. 'Please sit down. Let's keep this short.'

Sergeant Cooper sat.

'Can I get you a coffee or something to eat?'

'A coffee please.'

Marco went to the kitchen door, pushed it open and called out to the old woman. Returning to his chair, he sat down and coolly looked at the policeman. 'Do you have anything new to tell us?'

Cooper pulled a notebook and pen out of his top pocket and, with slow deliberation, he opened it and flicked the pages. Baba crashed the door against the wall and stomped to the policeman's chair. She slammed the coffee cup onto the table, grabbed the food trolley and started to clear the remnants of the meal.

'We've spent most of the last twenty-four hours going over the crime scene photos and there are a few anomalies.'

I saw Brian and Marco glance at one another.

'The photographs suggest Mr Puharich's death requires further investigation.'

'Don't you think you should wait for the professionals from Perth?' Brian didn't bother to hide his disdain for the country copper.

'Senior Detective Murchison-Burrows has asked me to speak to you ahead of his arrival tomorrow.'

A sudden intake of breath made me cough like a cat trying to dislodge a hairball. They all turned towards me. 'Pepper,' I spluttered. Ben! Just my luck.

'You should remember that we are a family in mourning,' Marco said.

Sergeant Cooper looked as though he didn't believe this any more than I did.

'My apologies, Mr Puharich, if you think I am being insensitive. We need to work quickly.'

'What can we do to help you?' Marie's voice broke through the thick air of male one-upmanship that had settled around us.

'We want you to stay here and make yourselves available for questioning over the next few days.'

'I won't be here. I'm due to fly out from Perth to Croatia early Wednesday morning.'

'That won't be possible.' Cooper's tone was firm.

'It's a statement, not a question.' Marco was no longer polite. He sounded menacing to me. Even Baba had stopped packing food away. I was astonished to see the policeman so calmly sitting in his seat.

'I think it's in the best interests of the family that everyone is guided by the police.' Marie's suggestion sounded sensible to me.

'Then you have no idea what constitutes the best interests of the family.'

If Marco had looked at me like he was looking at his cousin, I would have spontaneously combusted.

Marie didn't flinch. 'One of you has to ring Dida and tell him what's happening. Our fathers also need to be updated. Everyone seems to have forgotten about them.'

The fact that there were mums and dads responsible for these angry people had certainly escaped my mind.

'Ring who you need to. Make sure you are available to my people.'

'I won't be here,' Marco repeated.

A loud crash came from the direction of Baba. We all turned. She stood there, still gripping the silver platter she had slammed down on the table.

'Marco does as wants.' The old woman took a deep breath before she continued in her broken English. 'Who cares 'bout Stepe? He was *idiotski*. Shame to his Dida. Shame to his family. Zorka made them stupid. Them brothers were *blesav*.' She was on a roll. 'Thanks god he dead.'

Before she got any further, Marco went swiftly to her side, put his arm around her shoulders and leaned down to put a tender kiss on the top of her head.

'You are only good one. My boy. *Moj dragi*,' she said, while he led her away.

At the table sat four people who had no idea how to proceed. Sergeant Cooper got a frog in his throat and started to cough; Marie stood and gathered plates, or rather, she mindlessly rearranged them; and Brian fixed his eyes on his knife as he sawed it back and forth across the tablecloth, cutting a gash in the fabric. My body was completely still while my mind was a muddle thinking about the witch, her darling boy, and what the police might make of her unhinged tirade.

Clearly I'd completely underestimated Baba Tete's antipathy towards Marco's brothers. Hopefully Matthew stayed wherever he was for the rest of the day. I imagined the old woman flying at his throat if he put his head round the door. Every atom of Baba's withered body was focused on Marco. Her love was so fierce I could easily imagine her climbing the ladder and tipping the shelf to kill Stephen.

When he'd stopped coughing, Sergeant Cooper spoke, 'Well, that's an interesting take on events. Anyone care to clarify her comments?' Silence. 'None of you have anything to say?'

'She's a bit odd,' I suggested.

'She's old,' Brian corrected me.

'My grandmother is old,' Sergeant Cooper's voice suggested his distaste, 'but she doesn't go around telling everyone how happy she is that a person is dead.'

'The current situation with Stephen has stressed her, and she can't be held responsible for what she's saying.' Marie was scrambling to create some calm.

'I want to talk to everyone. Even the old woman. Were any of the workforce here yesterday?'

'I don't know. Matthew would be able to tell you.' Brian answered.

'When do you expect Matthew to return?'

'No idea. It seems he's had a sleepover at someone else's house. It will be a woman he's met around town.'

'You don't have any idea who she might be?'

'No.'

A door at the back of the room opened and Marco returned to the table. 'I've settled her in her room.'

'He wants to talk to everyone who was on the property yesterday, including the casuals.' Brian looked straight at Marco when he spoke. It suggested an implied agreement that this was not going to happen.

'There were no casuals around yesterday. They don't work on a Saturday.' I wondered why the cousins were lying. 'You'll have to ask Matthew.'

The copper shook his head. 'But he's not here.'

'No.' Marco and Brian spoke in rare unison.

'All right, I'll start with you.' He pointed at the men. 'One at a time and then I'll talk to your sister and her friend. I don't want anyone to leave the property.'

'Although I was here yesterday, I'm not part of the family or the business.' Maybe pleading ignorance was the safest route to take. I knew people in the family were involved in drugs, there were Croats and surfers helping, and Stephen had been murdered. And I couldn't tell the sergeant any of it. I'd done a few things that weren't strictly legal. And there was the issue of Ben's listening device. I wasn't about to get him in the shit.

'I'll decide who to speak to, and you are on my list.'

I didn't want to be on any list that included the Puhariches. I sighed dramatically. 'Well, if I must.'

'Yes, you must.'

Marie took my hand and pulled me towards the door. 'We'll be in the creamery, if that's okay?'

Sergeant Cooper nodded. 'I'll find you.'

~

We took the path leading to the creamery. The bare canes of the grape vines twisted around the beams forming the colonnade that linked the two buildings. It had seemed so romantic when I'd first seen it. Now the grey, gnarled wood reminded me of the old witch Baba and the cracked bark looked forbidding. We didn't say anything until we'd settled on one of the chesterfields in the creamery.

'This is such a mess.' Marie was flat. 'Someone has to phone Croatia and let them all know what has happened.'

'I have a feeling Marco has already made that call to your grandfather.'

'If he has,' said Marie, 'he hasn't told me. Brian wants me to sort the PR on this disaster and Marco doesn't think we need it and that I'm surplus to requirements. I know you're a bit infatuated with him. Most women are and none of you are suitable.'

I felt like giving her a list of all the reasons why I was astonishingly suitable, but I knew it wasn't true. I felt sorry for Marie, stuck in the house with a bunch of alpha males and one crazy old witch with an unhealthy devotion to one and a spiteful vendetta against the others.

'Why don't we go for a drive into Margs tomorrow?' I suggested. 'You could get away from here for a little while.'

Marie brightened. 'If you came in the morning, we might go and do some shopping. Then get an ice cream at Simmo's.'

I smiled back at her. 'Only if you agree to come with me to Jim's Shoe Emporium again.'

'Great – about ten?'

'I'll be here.'

After that, there was little to say. We were both relieved when Brian arrived to take Marie back to the house for questioning. Left on my own, I took my shoes off and lay along the chesterfield, rearranging cushions under my head so my hair wouldn't go flat. It took about three minutes for me to fall asleep.

My twenty-minute power nap was interrupted by Marie shaking my shoulders.

'I'm finished. He wants to speak to you.'

'That was quick.'

'What might I tell him that he didn't already know?'

We went back to the house. Sergeant Cooper pointed at the seat in front of him.

'Please sit.' He looked at Marie. 'I won't need you anymore today.'

She turned to me. 'I'll see you at ten tomorrow.'

I watched her walk across the room and disappear through a door halfway along the back wall.

'Marie told me you were at school together and that you and Brian were an item.'

God help me! 'Yes, about school and, no, Brian and I were never together.'

'Can you describe your relationship with the Puhariches?'

'Don't really have one. I met up with them fortuitously in Croatia a few weeks ago and they invited me to come down here. I'm a freelance journalist, writing food reviews as well as some longer, more investigative pieces. So, the local food and wine is the reason I'm here.'

'When was the last time you saw them?'

'Six years ago, for Marie's daughter's christening. I hadn't seen them for ages before that.'

'What about Marco and his brothers?'

'I've never met Stephen and Matthew before and I met Marco for the first time in Croatia.'

'And what do you think about them?'

What did I think? Definitely handsome. Definitely drug runners. Possibly murderers.

'I suppose you could say they're passionate about their business. In fact, I think their business sums them up. The entire family is focused on cheese – how good it is, and how great they are.'

'As a journalist, you must notice things. Have you seen anything troubling or out of the ordinary?'

I crossed my fingers, knowing I was going to tell a very big lie. 'Nothing comes to mind. They only seem to think about cheese.'

The sergeant wrote something down then shut his notebook. 'I spoke to the senior detective about you. He said he didn't think you should be considered a suspect. A "bit of an airhead" were his exact words.'

I gave an appropriately vacuous giggle. Ben would suffer later.

'I'm happy to let you go, although don't drive back to Perth yet.'

'Fine.' I got up. 'Nice to meet you.' I bared my teeth in a pretend smile and left the room.

There were no Puhariches in sight as I made my way back to the carpark. Getting into the Jeep, I felt uneasy. Turning on the ignition, the rabbit's foot bobbled about and a wave of comfort enveloped me when I touched its silky fur. It was with relief that I turned onto Caves Road and headed north. If I'd had a premonition about the next day, I would've kept driving all the way to Perth.

CHAPTER TWENTY-FOUR

I woke to the sound of rain and a window-rattling wind. It took an hour of silent self-cajoling to get me out of bed, taking the top quilt as a defence against the frigid air. Racing to switch on the kettle, I didn't do the usual morning detour to the loo because even my wee had frozen – I'd be passing ice cubes for hours.

While waiting for the water to boil, I dressed quickly. My toes had turned purple and the rest of me was bluish-grey before I pulled on jeans, my favourite crushed velvet skivvy and the woollen coat bought in Japan while on assignment reviewing a sushi festival. I sat cooking in front of the radiator until my face looked like corned beef. Then I sprinted to the car and began the forty-minute drive to the creamery.

My watch read exactly ten o'clock when I turned off the ignition. A solitary police car was parked nearby – presumably following up from the day before.

Of course, Marie wasn't ready. I'd strolled to the house and come face-to-face with Baba Tete, who had looked at me through narrowed black eyes.

'Is Marie around?'

'No.'

'She's expecting me. We're going shopping.'

The old woman turned up her nose. Clearly shopping was a smelly business.

'Can you go and tell her I'm here?'

'No.'

'Righto.'

We stood looking at each other. It felt like being stared down by the bunny-boiler from *Fatal Attraction*.

'I go to Marco.'

I didn't care where she went. 'Fine.'

She turned and flew in the direction of the kitchen.

I felt like an unwelcome interloper in the house, so I trotted back to the Jeep. I was bored within minutes. I wondered if it was possible to retrain my brain so that it was able to spend more than thirty seconds in its own company. I doubted it. The best antidote to boredom, or any other malaise, is food – and the creamery, with all its wonders, was sitting right at the front end of the Jeep.

I got out and wandered to the door of the building. I pushed and its smooth surface swung inwards. I stepped into the cool interior. Walking its length, I got to the bar and stepped behind to where the fridge hummed. Opening it, a delightful array of cheese greeted me, all ready and waiting for me to cut. I felt no guilt. It was my right to occupy myself if Marie insisted on being late. I put polite chunks of a triple-cream brie, some blue, and a bit of something crumbly onto a plate, then turned in the direction of the chesterfields. Strolling and chomping, I pressed my nose against the glass wall dividing the retail space from the manufacturing area. Benches, vats and long cheese baths were arranged to reflect the stages of the cheese-making process.

I moseyed down to the door leading into the inner workings. I opened it and was immediately overcome with the smell of curdling cream as I stepped inside. Oversized mixing bowls were arranged along the back wall and I heard the hum of the stirrers as they turned, separating the cream. Partway down the middle of the room were the long baths Brian had said were used for making strings of mozzarella and large squares of fetta before both were cut and moulded into their commercial sizes. I wondered what it'd be like to pick up a fresh ball of mozzarella and squeeze.

I sauntered to the nearest bath, biting off another piece of brie. Later on, I wasn't sure if I'd swallowed or spat it out. Either way, it wasn't in my mouth a few seconds later when I saw what was floating in the whey. Rather than bouncing balls of mozzarella, Matthew's face looked up at me, his eyes wide open, his skin a creamy-grey.

Stumbling away from the bath, my legs flew out from under me and I felt my coccyx crack as it hit the concrete floor. Although not a dead body aficionado, I was pretty confident Matthew had become a corpse. He certainly didn't have that skin tone or fixed stare the last time I'd seen him. Scrambling to my feet, I turned and staggered away on uncertain tippy toes, just in case I woke the dead.

~

'There you are!' Marie was leaning against a sofa.

I watched her face as if from a great distance, babbling on about something – hair, teeth, world peace – and all I could do was stretch my arm out behind me and point.

She followed the direction of my finger. 'I wondered where you were. Marco told me you'd arrived. But I lost all sense of time. Did you have a bit too much to drink last night? You're a horrible colour. That's okay, I have some blush you can use. It'll give you some glow and –'

I heard a scream. Then her body hurtled past me, her face contorted in a Munch scream.

Within minutes, people were running everywhere. First Sergeant Cooper, then Marco and Brian and, shortly after, several of the police I'd seen walking like tin soldiers the day before. I was mute as they passed, their urgent feet clacking on the flagstones. It was a few minutes before I regained some composure. Then Pop's voice roared in my brain: 'Get back there and get me a fucking story.'

It was the only motivation I needed. My knees felt like they were folding backward as I returned to the window separating the two parts of the creamery. With my nose almost touching the glass I watched the drama happening around the bath of mozzarella. Marco and Brian were standing to one side. Brian looked about to vomit, while Marco seemed to be cut from stone. The sergeant's mouth was moving in ways suggesting commands but most of his constables were following Brian's lead. This might get messy very soon. Somewhere in the distance Marie was crying in operatic tones.

Brian moved out of my line of sight. The next thing, he was taking my hand.

'I'll have that.' It was then I realised there was still a piece of brie in my hand. I'd squeezed it so tightly, its soft creaminess had pushed through my fingers, gluing them into a sticky fist.

Brian uncurled them and peeled off the biggest pieces of the cheese. 'Let's go to the bar and get this off. Then I'll put the kettle on and make us some tea.'

The moment of throwing up had passed and now he was being so gentle, I thought I'd cry. He walked me down to the end of the room still holding my hand. When we got there, he ran warm water through my fingers, dislodging the gooey mess.

'Here we go, just this last bit. Then you sit down on the couch and I'll get the tea and some brandy.'

I managed a nod and did a Thunderbird wobble back to the chesterfield. I didn't register anything more until Brian put a tray on the coffee table and sat beside me. He reached forward and picked up two water glasses which were filled, almost to the brim, with brandy.

'Drink this as fast as you can manage.'

I tipped the glass, opened the back of my throat, and let the alcohol slide down. An old boyfriend had taught me how to skol – it was the only decent date we had. I emptied the entire glass before Brian had finished half of his.

'You obviously needed that.'

I nodded.

'I'm sorry about all this. I know you've come to pick up Marie. Why were you in here? Shame you didn't learn a lesson about trespassing when you were in Croatia.' Even through his kindness, Brian was still capable of telling me off.

The brandy hit my brain and unclenched the synapses.

'She wasn't outside and I didn't want to wait in the house because of the old woman.' Maybe because I was a bit defensive, my voice was crackly, as though I hadn't used it for decades. 'It was cold outside. So, I decided to come in here.'

'Baba Tete has that effect on people.' He took my glass and put both his and mine on the table. Then he picked up my teacup. 'Here you go. Your tea chaser.'

I took a sip of the milky liquid. It was syrupy and warm enough to drink easily. 'This is wonderful.'

'My mother always gave us sweet tea when we'd had a fright or were upset. She called it her comfort medicine.'

'It's a very English thing to do.'

'My mother is not your typical Croatian woman. She loves tea and she plays tennis.'

'Really?'

'Yep. She's crazy about it. They play during the week for fun, then compete on a Saturday. I've gone to watch her.' He shook his head. 'You'd think they were playing at Wimbledon. They're ferocious.'

This unexpected story about his mother made Brian more human. His voice was softer and reflective. I appreciated the way he was trying to distract me, until he added: 'First Stephen and now Matthew. This sort of thing can happen to that type of person.'

The reversal was astonishing. 'What do you mean?'

'It wouldn't surprise me if Marco was next.'

'What an extraordinary thing to say.'

'My cousin must be aware he's the only one left. Maybe he should leave before Wednesday. I'd be sleeping with my eyes open if I were him.' Brian took a long drink of tea, looking at me over the rim of his cup. 'Someone doesn't like those boys.'

'Not liking someone and drowning them in mozzarella are poles apart. I'm assuming no one thinks he hopped in and drowned himself.'

'Hardly. Those brothers live according to the laws set by my grandfather. It's old Croatia where reward and retribution are ingrained.'

'That can't apply here in Australia.'

He snorted. 'On Puharich land, wherever it is in the world, what my grandfather says and thinks is what we're all expected to follow. No exceptions.'

I must have turned a peculiar colour, because Brian took my hand. 'Are you all right? Do you need to throw up?'

'No, I'm okay.'

'You look awful.'

'I've just found your cousin floating in one of your cheese baths.'

'Well, I didn't put him there.' Brian dropped my hand.

'I didn't say that. Matthew was not looking his best.'

'Now you know how I felt when I found Jure and Zorka. At least Matthew was in one piece.'

I turned to look at him. 'Don't you find it odd that your family has had four violent deaths in three weeks?'

I could almost hear the cogs in Brian's head whirr. When he spoke, his tone was measured. 'I've told you before, my family has a lot of power and it can lead to envy and resentment. Jealousy can be a compelling incentive for violence.'

The door to the inner room clattered and we were joined by Marco and Sergeant Cooper. They sat opposite Brian and me, pushing their bodies tightly against the leather arms, leaving a large expanse between them.

'The police doctor will be here shortly. Senior Detective Murchison-Burrows and his team are on their way.' Cooper looked at me. 'I believe he's a friend?'

'The guy in charge is your mate?' Marco asked.

'Not a close friend,' I lied. 'He's more connected to my brother. They went to school together.'

'Did you know he was part of the team coming down?' Brian too was frowning at me.

'No.' Another lie tripped off my tongue. 'Of course I didn't.'

'You might've mentioned your connection when we were told the Major Crimes unit was coming down.'

'I didn't think of it at the time.'

Brian and Marco looked at each other, another one of those silent communications passed.

'I don't care who knows who,' Cooper said. 'There are two unexplained deaths, both on this property. Nobody leaves until everyone has been interviewed.'

Brian ignored him and spoke to Marco. 'I'll ring our lawyers while you deal with the police.'

Marco nodded. 'Put a call in to Dida. He can tell our parents what's best for them to hear.'

Brian stood and looked down at me. 'Tell the police the basic details. They don't need your thoughts or suspicions.'

I met his eyes and said nothing.

He walked out of the creamery, giving a faint acknowledgment to the policeman and a final glance at Marco.

Sergeant Cooper turned his head to contemplate Brian's cousin. 'Organise your staff for me. We'll speak to everyone on the property, including your housekeeper. You,' he pointed at Marco, 'will make yourself available to be her interpreter.'

I was sure Marco was going to translate what he wanted the police to know. It was a useless exercise.

'Where do you intend to start?' I asked.

'With the person who found the body.'

Marco looked at me with a chilling intensity, then he leaned forward as if to kiss my cheek and murmured in my ear, 'Only what you saw and nothing else.' Standing, he smiled in the direction of the sergeant. 'Here's your woman.'

The sergeant's eyes followed Marco as he left.

'They're very forceful personalities, aren't they?' Cooper said.

'You can say that again.'

'You've known them a long time. Have they always been like this?'

'Pretty much. They don't like outsiders.'

The sergeant nodded and flipped open his notebook. 'Start from the beginning and tell me every detail.'

'We were meant to go shopping.' I took him through every step of my visit, up to the point where Marie had charged past me, screaming her head off. 'She's a mess and I don't feel like shopping now.'

'I never feel like shopping.'

I looked at his shoes. They were scuffed and the heel was unevenly worn. These were the feet of a man who possessed one pair of 'good' shoes, a pair of thongs and runners smelling of toe jam.

I gave a little cough. 'Is there anything else you want to know?'

'I need you to think very clearly and tell me if you saw anyone around this building when you parked and went looking for Marie.'

I closed my eyes and pictured the scene. It felt like my brain was swelling, pushing against my skull.

'I didn't see anyone. I was looking towards the house not to here. I was annoyed that Marie wasn't waiting for me.'

'Where was she?'

'Still getting ready.'

Cooper narrowed his eyes and wrote in his notepad. Was he writing about Marie?

'You told me you hadn't met Stephen and Mathew before last Thursday.'

'That's right. I didn't mind them, but Marco and Brian thought they were too dumb for anything other than grunt work around the property.' Little white pills and boats in the night flashed into my head. I hoped the sergeant wasn't a mind reader.

'What do you think?'

'They didn't say much.' An urge to spill the beans was almost over-whelming. Maybe I'd give Cooper a hint. 'I wonder if Marco and Brian underestimated them.'

The sergeant raised an eyebrow. He scribbled in his notebook, giving me a moment to think. It was easy to imagine a whole phalanx of people wanting to bring down the Puhariches: to teach them a lesson and to make them retreat to the Dalmatian mountains to live in caves and forage for food.

'Do you have anything more to add?'

'Not really.' I shrugged my shoulders and put a slightly stunned expression on my face.

Cooper looked towards the cheese room. 'I don't think I'll eat mozzarella ever again.'

I understood why he wouldn't want to eat the cheese from that particular bath, but it was no reason to give up those plump squishy balls altogether. I felt the sergeant lacked courage.

'I'll be glad when the Perth team gets here.'

He wasn't the only one. 'Two murders in two days. That must be some kind of record.'

'It is down here. Raiding marijuana crops is the closest we get to serious crime.' He shut his notebook. 'It's been a bad day. Your whole visit seems to be a bit of a shambles.'

'I'm so tired. Can you let me go?'

'I've got your details. If it's urgent, I'll give you a call. Otherwise you can wait for more questions from your senior detective friend.'

'Thanks, much appreciated.'

There was something zombie about me as I shuffled back to the car. Climbing into the Jeep, I looked towards the house. Under the trellis, Brian and Marco were standing, heads almost touching, talking, their intense faces revealing the family likeness I'd noticed before.

~

The trip back was slow. It felt like there wasn't enough energy left in my foot to press the accelerator. I almost cried with relief when the cabin came into view. Once inside, I crept to my bedroom, wriggled deep down in the mattress and fell asleep.

Sleeping was never a problem for me: I am constitutionally recumbent. After a couple of hours tucked away, I woke up with a gluey mouth and an addled brain, happily snuggled into the quilt.

Then the bloated face of Matthew, looking up at me through a halo of cheese balls, burst into my mind. How long had he been there? It was possible he'd been bobbing about while Marie and I had sat yakking on the sofa the previous afternoon. The thought gave me the creeps. Maybe a shower would wash them away.

What is it about hot water? Under a steady stream of H_2O, I become an apple-red Socrates who can mull over conundrums with a clarity that disappears the minute the water is turned off.

Matthew had told the surfers to be back that night and he was now too dead to cancel. At eleven o'clock they'd arrive expecting to see Matthew. Would they wait in vain, or was someone ready to take his place?

The only way to find out was to be there.

Out of the shower and into the kitchen, I perused what was left of my food supplies. It was only five o'clock. To kill time, I flicked through *A Guide to Surfing the South West* left by a previous occupant, and ate my way through my last Cup Noodles, the remnants of the Puharich cheese, and all the porridge. Every so often, I stopped reading and eating long enough to wonder who might be taking up where Matthew had left off.

By nine thirty I'd eaten enough oats to keep me regular for a month. I put on extra layers of tops, jumpers and a puffy coat before pulling on my new ankle boots – a contrivance of shiny black leather, pointy toes and silver-studded heels. If I was going to witness bad people doing bad things, I wanted my feet to be at their best.

~

The Jeep could almost find its own way down Caves Road. I barely noticed the forest or the bright eyes of wildlife as the headlights flicked past their faces. I parked the Jeep in its hidey-hole a smidge after ten-thirty. I had time to scurry to my spot in the dunes as the first of the surfers turned his ute into the carpark. Unlike the Saturday night, a further two utes and a small flatbed truck lined up along the beachfront. The men mingled around at the back of one of the vehicles and talked in low voices while they smoked and drank from litre bottles of Coke.

Watching these young men made me think of the other young men I had seen on a similar beach on the other side of the world. Their bodies had been broken by bullets fuelled by territorial intransigence. And here I was watching their counterparts with their strong fit bodies trading in drugs that inflicted a different type of destruction. Yet both groups of young men on beaches were merely tools, manipulated by powerful men in distant rooms far away from the havoc.

I looked through Jess's binoculars to study each face in turn, hoping to give Ben the best information possible. Apart from Surfer Dude and Surly Man, there was no one else that I recognised: the Puhariches were not around. The men were split into two groups: one lot were bunched against the door of the first shed and the other group lined up along the jetty. The sound of an outboard came across the water. It wouldn't be long before the inflatable rubber boat pulled alongside and the first of the hessian-wrapped cheese wheels was passed along the row of surfers.

Engrossed as I was, I didn't hear the footsteps crushing the vegetation behind me until it was too late. I almost went into cardiac arrest when a voice said, 'It's amazing what you can find among the sand dunes on a dark night.'

CHAPTER TWENTY-FIVE

'Turn over.' Marco's voice was icy.

I wanted to sink into the sand rather than roll onto my back. But I did what I was told. Tucking my arms by my sides, I twisted my body around, the strap of the binoculars wound around my neck, pressing against my throat.

'Fancy seeing you here,' I said. His handsome face was all dark, flinty angles.

He leaned over me and I saw the gun he was holding in his right hand. 'Get up.'

With sand pouring from the crevices of my clothes, I got up to face him. He moved the gun level to my chest.

'This isn't quite how I imagined our first midnight stroll.' Marco's calm added to my sense of foreboding.

My attention was on the firearm. I wondered if he was a good shot.

He followed my eyes. 'I'm used to shooting vermin, so you're an easy target.'

The ability to speak had left me. Besides, I had no idea what would be appropriate under the current circumstances.

'Let's get you down to the beach.' He grabbed my shoulder and turned me seaward. With the gun pressed against the middle of my back, I had no choice other than to walk forward down the face of the dune.

Stepping onto the beach, I looked south towards the jetty where the guys were chucking the cheese from one to the other. Hopefully they'd turn around. But their focus was firmly on the movement of the hessian wheels, the little Kats tucked safely in their creamy innards.

'Go right.'

I did what I was told, and we moved north, away from the surfers and any chance of being rescued.

My boots were completely unsuitable for the beach. Every time I stumbled, Marco pressed the gun into my back and growled.

'For fuck's sake, can't you walk properly?'

'No.' A little surge of anger sparked behind my eyes. 'I've got my new boots on and they don't work in sand.'

'You're a superficial bitch, aren't you?'

I took this as a rhetorical question.

We continued along the beach, and I began to wonder if he had a plan. The way we were going, I'd be back at my cabin in a short while. A craggy collection of rocks came into view. They stretched from the dunes and out into the sea, forming a natural fence towards which Marco pushed me.

'Take it slow and climb over.'

'If you thought my boots were bad on sand, they'll be hopeless on rocks.'

'Take them off.'

'I'm not going to do that. I've already lost enough shoes down here.' My fear was making me dimwitted.

'Keep moving.'

Staying on my feet was impossible: I staggered and slipped, one foot after the other disappearing into crevices. It was the grab of Marco's hand under my armpit that stopped me from falling onto the jagged edges of the rocks. I managed to clamber to the other side of the outcrop and stood in soft sand. Turning, it was clear that Marco and I were now out of sight of the surfers. My heart sank.

'I don't understand what you're doing.'

'You're not that thick, Alex.'

On any other occasion I'd have taken this as a compliment, but accompanied by a gun, it wasn't a tonic to my self-esteem.

'You're referring to the drugs you import in your cheese?'

This seemed to amuse him. 'You've been spying.'

'Listen, I won't tell anyone. You can safely get on the plane Wednesday morning without a peep from me.'

'Are you saying you haven't already told someone? Not even your favourite copper?'

'No. I've spoken to no one. I've been researching stories on the food industry down here. I wasn't ready to share.'

'Your arrogant self-interest might save you.'

'You'll let me go?' I was astonished.

'No. Just playing. Go forward.'

By now terror meant I was beyond thinking about escape. Talking was all I had left. 'The pills are coming from Croatia?'

'Of course. You saw the lab where we manufacture. Going where you shouldn't.'

'How do you do it?'

'Through Albany. Most product comes here via road. The special shipments come by boat. All those pills and no one can find them. Smooth as silk.'

'All in your cheese.'

'Cheese is a beautiful thing.'

'I thought Matthew and Stephen were running everything.'

'They were not born with my entrepreneurial talent.' His voice was distorted with scorn. 'And they were stealing. Jure took pills from the lab, marked them with a sign my brothers would recognise, then, when they took delivery, the boys hid these in the boatshed to sell for themselves.'

'Well, clearly they were smarter than you gave them credit for.'

'Too stupid to realise my grandfather discovered Jure. It was easy to work out what was happening once he knew that.'

'Your grandfather got the old people killed!'

Marco grabbed my arm and turned me towards the sea. 'Walk.'

I walked. With every footstep I regretted not telling Sergeant Cooper what I knew. Now I crept slowly, needing time to think about an escape plan.

'Is Brian involved?' I said, over my shoulder. 'Did he kill Stephen and Matthew?'

'My cousin lives in a fantasy world where he thinks people get rich from hard work. He can't comprehend that behind every rich man there is a long line of accountants, lawyers and politicians who have bent over. My grandfather and I share an appreciation of the *flexibility* of our systems.'

'You murdered your brothers?'

'There's always collateral damage in business. Over there!'

I felt the gun nudge my shoulder blades.

'I'll get wet if I go too far forward.'

'That's the idea.'

It was then I understood his intentions.

'You should know I'm a very good swimmer.' My speciality was dog paddle at the shallow end of the toddler pool.

'Not good enough to escape the rip that starts about five metres out then.'

Another prod got me to the point where the sea hit the sand.

'In.'

In I went. The waves splashed up my legs. I kept going, past my knees, then up to my thighs. I stopped and called back to the shore. 'Are you sure you want to do this? Another murder on your conscience?'

'You are incorrectly assuming I have a conscience. You're about to drown after getting drunk and deciding to go for a midnight swim.'

'The people who know me won't believe that.'

'I don't care. By the time they find your body, I'll be back in Croatia – untouchable.'

He was right. My body wouldn't be found for days. He'd be sitting in front of a cheese platter drinking a dry red before I washed ashore.

'Alex won't be swimming anywhere!'

A thin beam of light flashed across the sand. Brian's voice was electric. At that moment, the water eddying around my crotch, I forgave him his nose, his soggy lips, and his deification of my father.

'What are you doing here?' Marco couldn't keep the surprise from his voice.

'I followed you.'

'Of course you did. Always thinking that I was going to hook up with your girlfriend.'

I felt the ridiculous urge to turn and yell that I was *not his girlfriend*.

'I've got the rifle, Marco.'

'And I've got a gun. Who's going to shoot first?'

'You chuck yours in the water. I won't put mine down and I will shoot you.'

Marco sniggered. 'We both know you haven't got the balls. I suggest you throw the rifle away and go back home. This isn't the place for a yellow-arsed jerk like you.'

'I'm not going anywhere.'

'Then you'll have to shoot me in the back because your girlfriend is going for a swim.'

A brief moment of silence, then a gunshot fired.

I dived under the water, risking a chat with a shark rather than dying in crossfire. Under the waves I heard screaming. Popping my head above the waterline, I turned towards the shore.

Marco was on the sand, clutching his knee and screeching. Brian was standing over him, the shotgun almost touching his cousin's face. I got to my feet, the waves threatening to push me down again. Brian didn't take his eyes off the body writhing in the sand at his feet.

He yelled in my direction. 'Come back in. He can't do anything to you.'

'You've shot him.' My voice was shrill. 'You actually shot your cousin.'

'He's got a bullet in his knee. I didn't want to kill him.'

I felt safer standing like a popsicle in the freezing water. 'Has he still got his gun?'

'Of course not!' Brian's voice was exasperated. 'It flew out of his hand. It's somewhere in the sand and he's not about to go looking.'

'Okay. I'll come in.'

That was easier said than done. I was buried to the knees in wet sand and my body was rigid with cold and fear.

'I can't move. It's like quicksand out here.'

A string of expletives came across the water.

'I'll come and get you.'

I watched as Brian pulled off his belt and knelt beside the howling Marco. Through the gloom I saw him use the belt to fastened Marco's hands behind his back. Then Brian walked down to the sea and strode into the water. It didn't take him long to reach my side.

He put his hands under my armpits. 'I'll pull and you try and jump at the same time.'

'Okay. After three.'

With a great sucking sound, the sand released my legs. Brian put his arm around my shoulders and we waded slowly back to shore.

Flopping onto the sand, I looked at Brian. 'There's a bunch of blokes hoisting cheese ashore down at the jetty.'

'I know.'

Shit! My mind was spinning. So, Brian was involved in the drug operation?

'What are you going to do with me?'

He shook his head. 'Nothing.'

'You're not going to shoot me next?'

'No. Why would you think that?'

'The men at the jetty! You know about them.'

'I walked through the carpark on the way here. I've got no idea what they're doing, but I'm guessing it's got something to do with this arsehole.' He kicked Marco's leg. His cousin's ear-splitting scream seemed to spread out in waves of sound over the water and up and down the coast.

Almost immediately we heard the sound of feet scrambling over the rocks. It was just moments before a group of startled surfers were standing metres away, their heads swivelling between Brian and I and the body on the sand.

'Stay there.' Brian yelled in their direction. 'None of you move.'

I didn't think any of them were capable. They were fixed, looking like a bunch of wax figures. Brian went towards them, the gun in plain sight.

'Does that old phone in the shack still work?'

'Dunno.' A voice came out from the huddle.

'Then go and try. Police first. Tell them someone's been shot.'

'What about an ambulance?' To me that seemed the obvious first choice.

'Do you think I give a fuck if he bleeds to death? The coppers can call the ambulance.'

Brian moved the gun in the air. 'Can any of you use a phone?'

'Okay, mate, okay, I know how to use a phone.' The same voice grumbled out of the pack.

'Then fuck off and make the call.'

The surfers turned and half ran, half stumbled, back to the carpark. Only Surfer Dude remained. He had a stillness at odds with the strange triptych a few feet away from him. I admired his calm in the face of one half-drowned woman, a man whose leg was spraying blood like a water hose and another bloke clutching a shotgun whose facial expression was a bit too much like Jack Torrance in *The Shining*. After barely a minute, he looked in my direction, gave a slight nod and turned to follow his mates. Shortly afterward, on the night air, we heard engines and the sound of squealing tyres as the surfers left the scene.

'I hope they've called the police. Cowardly bastards.'

'Well, if I were them, I wouldn't want to be caught with that particular pile of cheese.'

'What do you mean?'

'I'm tired and my brain is too addled to be coherent. To put it bluntly, your cousins are drug runners.'

I expected Brian to explode in loud protestations. All sorts of things defending them and accusing me of besmirching the Puharich name and its cheeses. But he said nothing.

The hand holding the gun dropped to his side and he spoke into the air. 'It doesn't surprise me. Maybe it should.' Brian turned towards me. 'They're family, right? We're all meant to support and care for each other. What a joke.'

'I'm really sorry.'

Brian shrugged. 'Not your family. Not your problem.'

He took my hand and we stumbled over to where Marco was lying. His body was curled up and blood had seeped onto the sand, forming a wide circle, jet black in the darkness.

Brian looked down at his cousin. 'You're an arrogant bastard. I followed you all the way here and you didn't even notice.'

His tone was sad. Now knowing that his cousin was a drug smuggler was bad enough – his attempt to murder someone was another thing altogether. His belief in the integrity and power of his family was irrevocably cracked. Something that would only become a bigger chasm when he found out about his grandfather and that the mess in the little Croatian kitchen was just the start of the bloody chain.

As we stood by his body, Marco was silent. In fact, I was never to hear him speak again. Even when the police eventually arrived, he had nothing to say.

Brian took off his coat and put it around my shoulders. Then he positioned his body on my left side to block the wind coming in from the sea. As Marco disappeared around the headland, Sergeant Cooper approached us.

'We've picked up a gun and a rifle. Can I assume one or both of them belong to you?' He looked at Brian.

'I've never seen the gun. The rifle belongs to the business. It's kept in a gun safe in the office.'

'Do you have a licence?'

'Yes.'

'You decided to take it tonight and use it to shoot your cousin?'

'I won't be saying anything more.' Brian pursed his lips. 'I'll be calling my lawyer and I'll take his direction before I speak with you again.'

'That's fine with me. It means you'll have to spend tonight in the lock-up until we can charge you tomorrow.'

I leaned forward. 'Is that necessary?'

'Yes, it is. We've had an unlawful shooting or an attempted murder, depending on the circumstances. So, your boyfriend is going to a holding cell in town.'

Brian looked at me and shrugged. 'It's hardly Alcatraz.'

Cooper gestured to a constable. 'Take care of him, Rob.'

Rob nodded and pointed towards the path back to the carpark. Brian moved away, not giving me a second look.

'I'll bring your coat back tomorrow,' I called after him. But he made no acknowledgment that he'd heard.

The sergeant looked at me. 'I wonder what grounds I can detain you on.'

'Detain me? I'm the victim. Marco tried to kill me and if it hadn't been for Brian, I'd be a cork bobbing somewhere out there.' I waved my arm towards the sea.

By now, even Cooper looked like he'd had enough. 'We'll need a detailed statement that includes a full description of your activities since I last saw you. Luckily for you, we don't have the staff, so it'll have to wait until the Perth crew get here. In the meantime, you can go.'

'Thanks. I've left my car a little bit down the road. I'd appreciate it if you or one of your blokes could walk me back.'

'We have police at the Puharich compound, so you'll go back there.'

'Why? I've got a cabin near Gracetown.'

'For tonight you will stay where we have men on the ground.' He couldn't keep exasperation out of his voice. 'I am required to keep you safe until we have time for an interview. There is no negotiation.'

I sagged. The adrenaline was leaving my body and I'd run out of fight. 'I'll get one of the constables to take you.'

Another copper was summoned, and I was escorted to a police car. Sitting in the back seat, I looked down at my boots. The creases in the leather were filled with dried salt, one toe had come away from the sole and the sparkly studs were either discoloured or missing entirely. My beautiful new boots hadn't lasted forty-eight hours.

~

When the car stopped at the end of the Puharich driveway, I saw Marie standing underneath the vines of the trellis. She opened my door as soon as the ignition was turned off.

'What's happened? Where's Brian? He ran out of here immediately after Marco left. Now we have police everywhere.'

'It's a long story, Marie.'

The constable put his hand on my arm. 'We ask you not to speak, Ms Grant.' Turning to Marie, he said, 'Ms Puharich, we have had a situation at Prevelly Beach which has made us temporarily detain your brother. Your cousin has been taken to hospital with a gunshot wound to his leg.'

'I don't understand. Has Brian been shot?'

'No. Just your cousin.'

'Marco? How did it happen?'

'I can't give out details, I'm afraid. An officer will take you and Ms Grant into the house and stay with you overnight.' His look challenged Marie to protest.

She bit back anything she was going to say and took my hand. 'Come on, let's get you into a shower. I'll give you one of my nighties.'

Marie took me along the path and into the house. We were followed by a sulky young constable, who perhaps had taken umbrage at being pulled away from the excitement at the beach to guard two women.

Taking me to her bedroom, Marie chose a white cotton monstrosity for me to wear. Putting a pair of granny knickers into my hand, she escorted me to an enormous red-tiled bathroom and turned on a steaming jet of water.

'Get under that and clean yourself up. I'll get Baba to fix a sandwich and a hot drink for when you get out.'

I waited for her to leave before I peeled off my ruined clothes, kicked aside the sad remnants of my boots, and stepped under the shower. I let the scalding water wend its way into all my nooks and crannies. There was no residual energy left for soaping, so I leaned against the wall and let the heat penetrate my skin and defrost my bones.

Right before the point of scalding, I turned off the water and got out to dry myself on the biggest towel I'd ever seen. While I was struggling with the enormous sheet of fluffy cotton, there was a knock on the door and Marie's voice sounded from the other side.

'I've put a tray on your bedside table.'

'In what room?'

'It's the third door on your right. Look for the policeman.'

'Thanks, Marie.'

'Well,' she hesitated, 'goodnight then. Come out to the dining room when you wake up. You won't be disturbed before then.'

'Okay. See you at breakfast.' I heard her footsteps go down the hallway.

I finished drying and put on the knickers, whose elastic waist stopped just short of my nipples. The nightie was like a giant pillowcase tied at the neck with a pink silk ribbon. I looked like a doll whose skirt hid the toilet roll in the lavender-scented privies of old ladies.

By the time I emerged, the copper had set himself up on a wooden chair opposite my room. I gave him a cursory acknowledgment before shutting the door.

The bed was a high platform covered in plump lacy cushions, an enormous duvet and a mattress that threatened to swallow me whole. On the bedside table was a doorstop of fresh bread and ham, and the hot chocolate was served in a bucket. I ate it all with relish, grateful that I was dry, warm and alive.

CHAPTER TWENTY-SIX

It was a dreamless sleep. When I opened my eyes, the sun coming through the window suggested it was late morning. Every particle of my body ached and I didn't fancy poking around inside my head. It was a hot mess of confusion and mortification. Why didn't I see what Marco was really like? Ben was always telling me I was a dreadful judge of character, and this escapade had proven him correct on several fronts. Thankfully, my self-examination was cut short by a knock on my door.

'Who's there?'

'It's me. Marie.'

I didn't want to see her. 'I'm still in bed.'

'That's okay. I don't mind.'

But I did. 'Alright. Come in then.'

The young cop, looking worse for wear, opened the door wide enough for her to slip through. She plopped herself on the end of the bed making the duvet puff up like a flowery explosion before it settled back down. Her skin was a shade of jaundice and the bags under her eyes were like bruises.

'I've been up since six.'

'What time is it now?'

'Close to eleven. The team from Perth has just arrived.'

'Ben's here?' There was a mix of relief and apprehension in the question. I hoped for a hug and expected a bollocking.

'They've been here since seven. They're in the warehouse and creamery and another lot are down at Prevelly going through the boathouses. What happened? No one's telling me anything. Brian came home, had a shower and disappeared into the office. I haven't seen him since.'

'I'm glad they let Brian come home. He was very brave.' For the first time I was actually sincere about her brother.

'He told us not to wake you. Said you'd been through a lot and needed to sleep. Brian's a decent person, no matter what you think.'

My cheeks blushed with shame. 'I know he is.'

'Baba washed and dried your clothes.' Marie pointed across the room. 'She's left them on the chair. If you get up now, we can have some brunch before you have to speak with the police.'

I shuddered at the thought of the old witch touching my smalls. I wouldn't put it past her to sprinkle them with chilli powder.

'That's great. I'll have to thank her.' Not that she'd care to be thanked by me.

'See you at brunch.' Marie gave me a weak smile before disappearing into the hallway.

A sudden rumbling in my stomach gave me the impetus to climb out of bed and dress. I had to admit Baba had done a wonderful job with my clothes. They were starched so that every strand of cotton formed an exact weave. She'd even done my undies – the crutch so stiff I'd be walking like John Wayne for at least an hour. My hair was matted like a Rastafarian's and I couldn't be arsed untangling it, so I twisted my trusty scrunchie around the mess.

The young copper escorted me to the end of the hall and opened the door before positioning himself near the dining table. I saw Marie and Baba standing outside the kitchen door having a less-than-friendly exchange of words. They both looked in my direction. The old crone addressed me in Croatian.

Marie cut her short. 'Stop it. We'll have coffee and exactly what you made for Brian.'

The flat brown face gave me a look of contempt before it disappeared back from whence it came.

'Can I assume Baba Tete isn't going to nominate me for woman of the year?'

'She's angry. She thinks Marco should be let out so that she can look after him while he waits to go to trial.'

'He killed people.' I was incredulous.

'I know. But that doesn't matter to her. Come and sit down. Her pride will make sure we have something good to eat.'

We sat opposite each other at the end of the table closest to the large windows overlooking the walkway. The constable stood with his back against the glass, watching us as we ate. Between Marie and I there was a silence that lengthened as we avoided looking at one another. I wasn't sure what I was allowed to say.

'I'm really sorry about your brother,' I said. 'If he hadn't been following Marco, a shark would now be using my bones as a toothpick.'

'Did Brian really shoot Marco?'

'Yep. In the dark. In the knee. It was an excellent shot.'

'Dida always made sure his grandsons could shoot. Jure took them out to kill birds.'

'Your brother saved my life.'

The kitchen door clattered open and the crone emerged with her trolley piled with Danish pastries, pancakes and covered platters: the smells of bacon and sausages floated in our direction making my stomach lurch in anticipation. She was muttering furiously as she pushed the trolley.

'Don't be rude, Baba. It won't help Marco.'

The old woman stopped mid-sentence and started to sob. '*Moj dragi. Moj dragi.*' I was worried she might crash the cart before I filled my plate.

'You don't have to worry about him. Dida will have the best lawyers.'

This didn't seem to console the woman. She continued crying while she put the dishes onto the table. Sniffing loudly, she returned to her domain from where we heard the first of the great wails that assailed our ears on and off for the next hour.

'Will she be okay?'

'The doctor came last night and gave her a pill. She spat it out and refuses to take any more.'

I glanced at the police officer. 'Does she understand that Marco will go to jail for a very long time?'

Marie started to put food on her plate. Then she poured coffee from the percolator and passed me a cup. I followed her example and filled my plate with a mixture of bacon, fried eggs and an apple Danish.

'Marie?'

She looked squarely at me. 'Don't underestimate my family. They'll find some way to spin it. They always do.'

Marie pursed her lips, ending the conversation. I was relieved when Ben pushed open the dining room door.

'Good morning, Ms Puharich.' He nodded at Marie. 'Hello, Alex.' His tone had an exasperated edge.

'Can I pour you a coffee, detective?'

'No, thank you. We're hoping to finish up here as soon as we can. Maybe by tomorrow evening. Then we can leave you in peace.'

'Do you need anything more from me?' Marie put the coffee down and turned an exhausted face towards the policeman.

'I believe you've spoken with a constable and we have your statement. Your whereabouts have been confirmed by your housekeeper and brother, so we won't be bothering you any further.' Ben turned to me. 'However, you, Ms Grant, will need to come with me to the creamery and give an account of your involvement in the activities of last night.'

He sounded formal and detached. I was in deep, deep trouble.

'Shall I come now, or after I've finished my coffee?'

'Now.' It was a command. He turned towards the door.

I got up and pushed my chair back under the table. 'I'll see you later, Marie.'

'I'm not sure where I'll be,' she said stiffly. 'I'll say goodbye now. I've got to get busy helping Brian.'

Moving around the table, she gave me a perfunctory kiss on the cheek.

'Maybe we'll see each other in Perth sometime?'

Her smile was sad. 'Maybe. At least you got a good story.' Marie walked to the hallway, closing the door softly behind her. I watched her go, knowing our reacquaintance would probably not survive my attempted murder.

In borrowed slip-ons, I glumly flip-flopped after Ben as he led me to the creamery.

I sat down on the chesterfield once more. My right side was facing the glassed-in room where Matthew had been floating. That side of my body felt hot and twitchy as though residual emanations of death were settling on my skin. I wished Jess was here, swishing around bundles of incense and reciting incantations with a sing-song voice punctuated by deep sighs. But now, it was just Ben and I in that vast room. And Ben wasn't happy.

'First you steal and lick a Class A drug, then you don't ring me when you promised, and then I hear you almost got killed. You're a catastrophe. How many times do I have to tell you to mind your own business? I'll get a constable to take your official statement later. The last thing we need is the department to find out about the not-so-legal bits of your story. You need to tell me exactly what happened. Leave nothing out.'

It took me two hours to go through everything. Ben asked questions when I lost track and brought me water when I'd talked myself to a standstill.

'Where's the equipment I gave you?'

'In a pot plant in Brian's office.'

'Seriously?' He shook his head. 'You left my bug in a pot plant?'

'With a leaf over it. Do you want me to go and get it back?'

'You can't. Brian's in there with my team. I'll get it later. You'd better hope no one finds it in the meantime.'

'Thanks.' I was weary. The shock from the previous night was beginning to spread through my body again. 'I want to go home.'

Ben put an arm around my shoulders. 'I'll get that young bloke to take a formal statement. It won't take long, then you can go. I think you've done enough down here. Margaret River will be safer with you back in Perth.'

'My car's not here.'

'Don't worry. Jess keeps a key stuck to the inside rim of the spare tyre. I had one of the local lads drive it back last night.'

My lips parted in a sad imitation of a smile.

'I have to go.' Ben was all business. 'I'll see you back in Perth.'

He left me, a disconsolate figure in over-starched underpants and someone else's shoes.

~

When I got back to the cabin, I couldn't pack fast enough. Jeans, shirts and jumpers were thrown into the plastic crates. I didn't bother clearing out the fridge. The Missus needed all the food she could eat. I hoped she got to it before her hubby. I stuffed everything into the Jeep, took a quick final look around the cabin and left. The last thing to do was drop the key into the 'Return' box attached to the office wall.

It took two minutes to leave the key and set off. Looking through the rear-view mirror, I saw the fat face of the manager looking around the corner of the dunny. I flipped him the bird, turned onto the Gracetown road and put my foot to the floor.

It had been a rugged few weeks. Laying on a sunbed by the shimmery blue of the Adriatic felt like decades ago. Dead bodies, bad people and a near-death experience had robbed me of all residual holiday self-satisfaction. Fifty-cent coffee wasn't enough to entice me back to Croatia. At least, not until I was old enough to join the kind of cruise where the women wore crimplene trousers with elasticised waists and the men wore socks with sandals.

Heading off, I wondered if it was time I got the type of job and life my father considered appropriate for a woman in her mid-thirties. It was some kind of irony that, as a daughter, Marie was more to my father's liking: a good education, a degree, marriage, motherhood and a career squeezed in around her other responsibilities. Her life was structured in a way that he understood. Other than an education, I had none of these things. Yet Marie's life, as I had learned, was not all that it seemed.

Getting back onto the Bussell Highway, I chucked Johnny Cash into the cassette player and sang about a Ring of Fire stuck in Fulsome Prison all the way home.

When it came down to it, I loved my life, even though it lacked structure, and I loved the freedom to sticky-beak afforded by journalism. I knew Pop would salivate over the Puharich saga, giving me the front page and a couple of weeks of leading follow-ups. He'd be glad I pushed the envelope.

'You have sniffed out a great story, Alex,' is what he'd say. 'And you didn't actually get killed, because you kept your head.'

It wasn't exactly true, but Pop was canny in telling the story in exactly the right way to make me go back for more.

ACKNOWLEDGEMENTS

Many years ago, my year nine English teacher, Vicki Masters, read my stories and listened to my ideas with care and great kindness. So, much of this is her fault.

My unfailing gratitude goes to the enthusiastic and gracious editor Georgia Richter, and Fremantle Press, who have shown faith in me by waiting for Alex while I did the cancer 'thing'. I really hope your belief will be rewarded.

To my first reader and friend, Christine Nagel of Nagel Literary Services, thank you for your amazing patience and the thoughtful critical feedback that gave me the confidence to keep going.

To the South Perth library and librarians, you have provided me with a 'desk with a view' and an environment which encouraged the words to flow.

Thanks to my mum for letting me read by torchlight under my blankets and for enabling my extended education.

Thanks to my wonderful women friends who have nurtured me unconditionally: Julia Clark, my reading rival and loyal friend since grade three; Olga Ward, one of the smartest and kindest people I know; the fabulous bubbles women who make me feel so loved with their generosity and *joie de vivre*; and to my 'big sister', Tineke Schoonens, who I love like only a 'little sister' can.

For always including me and bringing me so much joy, I thank my adopted families: the magnificently funny and chaotic Dessauvagie clan; the Englishes at 38; and the Schoonens of BrisVegas.

Croatia is a very special place and my extended family-in-law on the Dalmatian Coast are exceptional people, particularly Ivan and Senka Bebek who welcomed me with openness and warmth. On my visits, there has always been so much truly wonderful food, wine, a vibrant culture and absolutely no criminal activity.

Enormous and deeply heartfelt thanks to the people who looked after me through my cancer treatment. Corinne Jones and Daphne Tsoi are truly brilliant women who made a formidable team. To the nurses in the Ivy Suite at SJOG Subiaco, including the glamorous Joan, I cannot express how much I am indebted to you for your magnificent care and compassion. You are extraordinary people.

Many, many thanks to Linley Ford who has, at all times, shown patience and unequivocal support.

At the end of this list is my husband George Nuich. His love, ridiculous sense of humour and belief in me has been sustaining beyond words. To my Cro-man goes immeasurable gratitude. *Volim te dragi.*

I acknowledge the Wardandi and the Whadjuk peoples on whose lands this novel is set.